Nicholas Luard was born in London but spent his childhood in the Kashgai tribal territory of Iran. He was educated in Britain and at eighteen enlisted in the Coldstream Guards. Detached from regular duties, he trained as a long-range night patrol commander with NATO forces in a special sabotage unit and took part in unspecified border activities during the Hungarian revolution of 1956.

On leaving the army, he studied first at the Sorbonne in Paris and later obtained master's degrees from both Cambridge University and the University of Pennsylvania. A fluent linguist and avid traveller, he currently lives in a remote valley in the southern Spanish region of Andalucia. He is married to the wildlife painter Elisabeth Baron Luard, and has four children. Among his earlier novels are *The Robespierre Serial, Travelling Horseman* and, most recently *The Orion Line,* which was called 'sensitive, exciting and brilliant' by the *Daily Telegraph,* and 'enthralling and superbly written' by the *Financial Times.*

D0711404

Other Futura Books by the same author:

THE ORION LINE

Nicholas Luard

The Dirty Area

Futura Publications Limited

A Futura Book

First published in Great Britain by
Hamish Hamilton Limited in 1979

First Futura Publications Edition 1980

ISBN 0 7088 1758 0

Reproduced, printed and bound in Great Britain
by Hazell Watson & Viney Ltd
Aylesbury, Bucks

Futura Publications Limited
110 Warner Road
Camberwell, London SE5

1

The small fat one who smelt of Pernod noticed it first.

He flicked through the pages, slid the passport across to his assistant for the entry stamp, then suddenly snatched it back and looked at the name again.

'Monsieur Callum?'

'Yes.'

'Monsieur Ross Callum?'

'That's what it says.'

'Ah—'

He studied the photograph, glanced up, plucked nervously at the frayed wing of his grubby white collar, and finally hunched himself back over the table. The other one, younger but wearing the same cheap blue uniform, chewed impassively at the nail of his little finger.

Steele waited. There were only three of them left in the forward saloon, the two Moroccan immigration officials seated side by side behind the table and Steele himself standing in front of it. He'd deliberately hung back to the end, letting the other passengers check through first, because he guessed it would start, everything would start, as soon as the older one saw the name.

He was right and now there was no point in delaying any longer.

'It's the same Ross Callum,' Steele said, 'I've come back.'

The small man said nothing. Uncertainty had made him sweat. He wiped his forehead with his sleeve and prodded the passport gingerly like a letterbomb which might explode in his hand. Then he made up his mind.

'You will please stay here.'

He spoke quickly in Arabic to his assistant and marched across to the telephone which had been linked to the shore when the

1

ship docked.

Steele walked between the empty chairs to the curved glass screen above the bows. It was a hot star-filled night and a steward had opened the sliding panels. Below on the quayside a group of official guides in brown jellabahs were arguing by the gangplank, their shadows printed black on the pale dust that layered the stones. Above them the lights of Tangier glittered in the darkness. The scent of coriander laced with charcoal smoke drifted upwards on the still air, and in the distance he could hear the sound of bells.

Steele propped himself against the glass and rummaged in the pocket of his canvas jacket for a pack of Camels. Sharp cold contractions tugged at his stomach but his wrist was steady when he lit the cigarette. He inhaled, coughed at the coarse tobacco, then he smelt a wave of Pernod again.

'The Inspector will come straight up.'

Steele turned round. 'Which Inspector and why?'

'The Inspector of the harbour police. In the circumstances I consider it correct.'

'What bloody circumstances?'

The small man opened his mouth, closed it again, reddened and strutted back to the table.

'You will please just wait, m'sieu.'

He sat down and ostentatiously occupied himself with a dogeared file. His assistant had stopped biting his nail and was watching Steele with slackjawed astonishment.

The harbour police station must have been on the same quay, because it was less than five minutes later when the swing doors opened and the Inspector came in.

'Mr Callum?'

The Inspector held out his hand. He was gaunt and olive skinned with grizzled hair and moist weary eyes.

'In spite of everything I believe we never met before,' he said, 'I trust it will be a mutual pleasure we do so now.'

He pointed at a chair. The small man had spoken in French. The Inspector talked in pedantic but fluent English. He beckoned for the junior immigration official to bring over the passport, thumbed through the blank visa pages, checked the issue date and looked up.

'So it is new this month?'

2

Steele nodded. 'The last one expired.'

'I see—'

The table was between them. The Inspector paused, gazed at Steele in silence for a moment, then he leant back shaking his head apologetically.

'I fear I was staring, Mr Callum. I am sorry. I can only say it is not often one comes face to face with – how shall I call it? A legend, maybe.'

Steele laughed. 'I'm hardly that.'

'Here in Tangier of course you are. You know it, I know it, these men behind us know it, so does everyone else in the city—'

He waved towards the ribbons of light outside. Then he sat upright again with his elbows on the table.

'Why have you come back now, Mr Callum?'

'Just to tidy up. The boat, some questions about the insurance, a few odds and ends,' Steele shrugged, 'nothing else.'

'To tidy up? After five years?'

'I've been busy, I haven't had time until now. And there's no reason I shouldn't return, is there?'

The Inspector frowned, adjusted his shirtcuffs, spun the passport with his finger on the waxed mahogany, but didn't answer.

'If you're thinking about the accident to the boat,' Steele added, 'That was cleared up long ago—'

He pulled out the pack of Camels again, offered a cigarette to the Inspector who refused it, and lit another for himself.

'The launch was taken without my consent, the consulate lodged by sworn deposition, the coast guard and the criminal police accepted it. I wasn't even in Morocco at the time – and it all happened outside your territorial waters anyway.'

'If even one of the stories is true,' the Inspector said, 'it wasn't the only thing that happened outside our territorial waters then.'

He was looking at the large gold Cartier lighter lying by the cigarettes.

Steele laughed again. 'People exaggerate. Anyway that was five years ago too. This time I'm just a tourist.'

'With perhaps a few old friends to visit?'

The tired smile was an attempt at a leer. Steele chuckled.

'Maybe, but that's all.'

'No one in Tangier is going to believe it.'

'They can believe what they like. It's true.'

3

The Inspector hesitated. Somewhere below a wandering kebab seller was wheeling his brazier along the quay. A circle of smouldering coals glowed in reflection on the glass and the man's call echoed across the water.

'I will consult Casablanca,' he said finally.

The Inspector went over to the telephone. Steele pushed back his chair and walked to the window again.

The ship had swung with the making tide and the lights of Tangier were on his right now. To his left, across the Atlantic mouth of the straits, another smaller cluster sparkled below the steady pulse of a lighthouse beam – Tarifa on the Spanish mainland, the southernmost point of Europe. And then far in front of him at the entrance to the Mediterranean three dim bowls of incandescence glowed on the rim of the night sky. Ceuta on one side, Gibraltar and Algeciras on the other, their lights hidden by the rocky curve of the African coast.

Five ports like a constellation studding the narrow sea lane between the two continents. 'The dirty area' as the elegant Mathieson had described it with distaste. Not for its squalor, the summer heat and dust, the tawdry flaking buildings and the swarming flies, nor for the vicious winter winds and rain that lashed the channel. But because of what had happened there century after century. War, piracy, smuggling, ambush, intrigue, slaughter.

The dirty area had been ideally suited to the activities of the man called Ross Callum.

Steele flicked the butt of his cigarette into the darkness and wiped his palms against his jacket. Then he turned. The Inspector was coming back across the saloon.

'You will be staying at the Minzah, Mr Callum?'

Steele nodded.

'You may go ashore but they wish me to keep this for tonight,' he held up the passport. 'In the morning one of my colleagues from the *Brigade Criminelle* will return it. I am sure there will be no problem but as you know I only represent the harbour police.'

He spread out his hands deprecatingly.

'I understand, Inspector.'

'Thank you.'

The Inspector moved away, spoke to the two immigration officials and all three went out.

4

Steele glanced down through the window. The guides had vanished and so had the last of the taxis which had been waiting there earlier. The Minzah hotel was only fifteen minutes on foot up the hill from the harbour, but Steele wasn't going to walk anywhere in the city until it became absolutely essential – and least of all at night.

He pushed open the swing doors and crossed the deck to the purser's desk.

'Call me a cab,' he said.

'Yes, sir.'

The news must already have spread through the ship because the man stared at him with the same wide-eyed curiosity as the immigration officials before he reached for the telephone.

'It will be here in a few minutes, sir.'

'Get someone to fetch my baggage from the cabin. I'll wait on the quay.'

Steele stepped through the hatch and climbed down the gangplank.

Apart from the kebab seller, pushing his brazier along a concrete loading ramp to Steele's right, the quay was deserted. Steele stood for a moment gazing round, sniffing the air, searching the wells of shadow behind the waterfront bollards, listening to the distant bells and the rumble of traffic in the high hidden streets.

There couldn't be any reaction yet. It was too soon, barely an hour since the ship had docked. The crew knew, the harbour police and Casablanca knew, inevitably others were being told at that moment. But not the little man with the mild haunted face waiting somewhere out there in the darkness. Like the rest of the dirty area it would be morning at the earliest before he learned Callum had finally come back.

Steele frowned. That had been the analysis in London. In reality Steele knew that from the instant he stepped ashore he couldn't assume anything, that nothing was safe any longer. And already, even in these first few minutes, he'd begun to sense something was wrong, something was out of place in the stillness of the waterfront. He hesitated. Then he walked forward to the ramp.

Opposite the ship's bows the concrete wall angled sharply back towards the harbour entrance. From the corner he could watch

5

the approach road to the docks where the taxi would appear and both sections of the quay. He stepped into the cover of the seaward flank of the angle and stood utterly still listening.

The brazier's wheels clattered towards him, the Arab's call wailed out, the glow of the approaching fire wavered over the dusty stones, then Steele tensed. He'd suddenly realized what was wrong – and it had nothing to do with the approach road or the silent docks or the menacing spaces of night-black shadow.

The man on the ramp above his head was still selling his wares although there was no one left on the quay to buy them.

Steele whirled away from the wall. As he moved the clatter stopped abruptly. Then he heard a new sound, a metallic grinding as the brazier was swung round. He checked in midstride, glanced upwards and caught a glimpse of a silhouette above the fire. An instant later the brazier started to tilt.

Steele ducked and wrapped his arms round his face as a cascade of flame and burning ash rained across his head and body. Sparks bit into the exposed skin on his hands and he flailed wildly while a stench of scorching hair and cloth enveloped him. Then there was another clatter and the brazier cannoned down into his back.

The impact of the massive iron drum hurled him to the edge of the quay. For a moment he staggered blindly above the water. Then he turned and plunged down.

The sea was milky and lukewarm, searing his skin where the sparks had burned it. He swam below the surface, guiding himself by the line of the quay's piles, until he saw the ship's bow shimmering to his left through clouds of phosphorescence. Then he floated gently upwards.

His head broke the surface in a cone of dense shadow between the ship and the quay. The smell of the harbour filth was overpowering and clots of floating refuse nudged his shoulders. Steele gripped a line trailing from the forward mooring rope and listened. There was no sound apart from an occasional hiss as a coal dropped into the water behind him. He waited for two minutes. Then he pulled himself to the quay and climbed a rusting service ladder.

Embers were still glowing on the stones and the iron drum was lying on its side by a stanchion, but the ramp above was empty – a bare flat line against the stars. Steele waited again, crouching by

6

the ladder supports. Then he stood up and ran to the gangplank.

'M'sieu Callum!'

He was on deck now and there was light and the purser was staring at him bewildered.

'What happened, sir?'

Steele steadied himself against the desk-rail. He was panting, his clothes were sodden and reeked of sewage, and he could feel water slopping round in his shoes.

'I took a swim,' he said. 'Isn't that what the sea's for?'

The purser went on gaping at him. Then a car's engine sounded below, headlamp beams swept over the hatch and the man peered down.

'The taxi, sir.'

'I've changed my mind—'

Not the eighteen hours London had promised but five minutes ashore, that was all, and it had started.

'I'll be staying on board tonight.'

Steele headed for the stairs. Then he forced himself to stop. He rummaged in the jacket, found the pack of Camels and casually shook out a cigarette. He'd forgotten Callum's pockets were waterproof – but then three days ago he'd never heard of Callum.

He snapped a lance of flame from the lighter and walked down towards his cabin.

2

'So there really isn't anyone, then?'

It was a measure of his anxiety that Mathieson, silver-haired, debonair, normally imperturbable, had asked the question at all. After combing through the possibilities all night he knew the answer as well as Wintour. There was no one.

Wintour, perched on the radiator opposite Mathieson's desk, hadn't even bothered to reply. He'd just cleared his throat huskily and shaken his head.

'I dislike it intensely, James,' Mathieson reached for the telephone, 'but I believe you're right — for the first time I can remember I don't think we've any option.'

That had been at 9.30. Now at midday Wintour was shuffling quickly down St James's Street with his head lowered and his collar turned up in spite of the bright October sunlight. The furtive hunched scuttle, his invariable gait on his rare forays outside Baker Street, gave him the appearance of a derelict travelling though a dawn hailstorm from one doss-house to another. Inside the linked Georgian houses he'd left half an hour before the effect of his presence was very different. There, as Mathieson's deputy and operations co-ordinator, he was recognized as the second most powerful man in the entire department.

'Yes?'

He'd turned off the pavement, climbed the steps of the club and was standing by the reception desk, small and stooped in a worn gabardine suit, his fingers stained with nicotine and his sparse untidy hair flecked with scurf. There'd been no 'sir' tacked on to the porter's blunt query. In places like that there never was until Wintour stated his business. Even if it came then, it was only given grudgingly.

'I'm looking for Brigadier Jardine.'

The endless cigarettes, which always trickled ash from one end and leaked tobacco from the other, had long since made his voice hoarse.

The porter inspected him expressionlessly.

'He's expecting me,' Wintour added.

'Upstairs,' the porter pointed across the hall at a marble staircase.

'I'm afraid I don't know the Brigadier. Can you tell me what he looks like?'

'A tall upstanding gentleman with a moustache.'

'Thank you.'

Wintour turned away.

Jardine was waiting from him at the top of the stairs. Tall, tweed-suited, imposing. Exactly as the porter had described him with a port-and-grouse stomach and a moustache that curled down like a grey Atlantic breaker. Both the stomach and the moustache vibrated as she shook Wintour's hand.

'You must be Dickie's friend. Splendid!'

His voice boomed out jovially but there was a certain embarrassed awkwardness in the speed with which he escorted Wintour across the landing and through an open doorway.

'Thought we'd be quieter in one of the gaming-rooms. Bar downstairs gets a bit crowded round about now. Easier to talk up here.'

The room was shadowy, high-ceilinged, carpeted with old wine-red Wilton and hung with eighteenth-century portraits that glowed against the walls. Two hundred years earlier Charles James Fox was reputed to have lost three fortunes in the club on successive nights. Judging by the silver punch bowls and the baize faded almost to whiteness on the small square tables by the bow window, nothing had been changed since.

'What are you going to have?' Jardine closed the door firmly behind them, 'Had the steward send up a tray. I'm a martini man myself but we do our own sherry, first class it is too, if you prefer that.'

The tray was on a Chippendale cabinet in the corner. Wintour chose the sherry. Then he watched Jardine fill his own glass from a leather covered flask.

'What do you think of it?'

Wintour lifted his glass and tasted. 'Very pleasant,' he said.

9

'Capital! We have it shipped direct, you know, makes all the difference—'

Jardine's voice rumbled heartily on but there was something forced and uneasy in the bluff small talk. He drained his glass and immediately filled it again. Wintour waited patiently. It was obviously going to be as difficult as Mathieson had warned him.

'Well, I gather from Dickie you've got a bit of a problem on your hands.'

The second martini seemed to have finally given him the courage to bring up the subject.

Wintour nodded. 'A rather serious one.'

'Not of course that Dickie told me anything about it,' Jardine added hurriedly, 'just something urgent had cropped up and I might be able to help.'

'We very much hope so.'

'Yes—'

Jardine paused, frowned unhappily and revolved the glass between his fingers.

Then he asked abruptly, 'How much do you fellows know about the Special Reserve Register?'

'Very little, Brigadier.'

It was true. Until that morning not even Mathieson had been able to establish more than the Register's existence in the War Office archives. But he and Jardine, who headed the military records bureau, had been brother officers at the Anzio beachhead, and in the ten-minute telephone conversation Mathieson had exploited the past, the bonds and memories and uncalled debts, as coldbloodedly as Wintour had ever heard him plan to manipulate the present.

The result was this appointment at noon. As Mathieson had said after their nightlong consideration of the alternatives, they had no other option.

'I'll be quite frank with you,' Jardine went on, 'it's not something we like to talk about even internally. The legal issues alone are a nightmare. All it needs is for some bloody fool to start asking questions in Parliament and there could be hell to pay – and that's just from our point of view. If there was the slightest chance of involving the War House in something outside our control—'

He broke off, closed his eyes briefly and shook his head.

10

'We quite appreciate that,' Wintour said soothingly, 'there'd be no question of any link. It would all be handled entirely at arm's length.'

Jardine hesitated again. Then he finished the second glass and said, 'Well, I suppose you'd better know how it works—'

He started pacing the floor, occasional shafts of sun glittering on the gold watch-chain across his stomach. He was still wary and reluctant but Wintour knew he'd committed himself now.

'Started towards the end of the war. Eisenhower's people asked us to raid a German observation post in Jersey to see if they'd keyed into the *Overlord* naval buildup. Five Commando were all set to go when we got another signal. Seemed Jerry kept all his records locked up in a damn great safe. Know what happened? We had to postpone the raid a whole bloody week before we found someone who could open the safe in the time!'

Jardine barked out a laugh.

'Sounds funny now, wasn't then. Caused one hell of a panic all round. Eventually someone had a bright idea. Went to Scotland Yard, asked for a list of top-flight safebreakers from Criminal Records and checked their names against conscripted personnel. Turned out half of them had already been called up and there was even one who'd been assigned to commando training. Shifty little shit he was by all accounts, but brilliant with his hands—'

He circled the card-tables and reached for the leather covered flask. Wintour, his glass still almost untouched, waited in silence.

'He solved that one,' Jardine was in the centre of the carpet again, 'but it set our people thinking. Even on a peacetime basis at any one moment we're dealing with the population equivalent of a medium sized town. And in any medium sized town there are going to be a number of people with—'

He snapped his fingers, searching for the appropriate phrase.

'Unusual skills?' Wintour suggested.

'Got it in one,' Jardine nodded, 'some of them you wouldn't normally touch with a barge-pole, but they can be damn useful, not to say essential, in an emergency. We'd been overlooking them before, not any longer. In fact today we go much further. Someone crops up now with something special, we don't just put him on file, we actively encourage him. Take mountaineering—'

He waved towards the bow-window as if not St James's Street but the snow-covered flanks of the Himalayas lay outside.

11

'Fellow signs up who's keen on climbing hills, odds are we'll find an expedition to send him on. That sort of thing, see what I mean?'

'Certainly, Brigadier.'

A pool of individuals whose special attributes were developed during their service, and then recorded so the men could be instantly traced and put to use in an emergency. As contingency planning it made sense, total unexceptionable sense. And that was the puzzle. It was all too logical and straightforward to explain the evasions and denials which questions about the register invariably evoked. There had to be something else.

Wintour tapped out another cigarette from the crumpled pack, lit it from the butt of his last one, and went on waiting.

'Of course that's simplifying it a bit—'

There was something else. For the last few minutes Jardine had sounded frank and unconstrained. Now, striding away from the cabinet, his voice was edgy and reluctant again.

'Problem is there's damn all point in creating a reserve unless you've got access to it when you need. Easy enough in war but bloody difficult in peace. I've had fellows through my hands I'd give my eye-teeth for now for the SAS units in Northern Ireland. But once they've served their term, do you think I can get them back on emergency recall? Not a bloody prayer because it's just a 'civil disturbance'. Civil disturbance! Try explaining that to the family of some lad who's caught an Armalite bullet in the spine—'

Jardine emptied his glass again and shook his head quickly, violently. Wintour coughed and hunched himself forward on his chair. Somewhere behind Jardine's brief flare of rage there had to lie the explanation for the SR Register.

'So the odds are just when we want these men most, we've lost them. Unless, well, bluntly unless there's another way of getting hold of them again—'

He'd walked over to the rear window and was standing there, stiff and remote, almost as if in distancing himself from Wintour he'd also distanced himself from what he was going to say next.

'There is another way. Unattractive but unavoidable. Comes down to this. The sort of fellow we list tends to be a trouble-maker. Don't ask me why, it just seems to be a characteristic of these people. Inside the service we've got our own sanctions for

12

dealing with troublemakers. Bloody tough they are too. I can tell you, compared to an army prison any civilian gaol's like a children's picnic. So faced with twelve months at our place in Colchester, your average soldier's going to jump at any damn alternative—'

Jardine swung round as a taxi hooted on the street below, awkward and blustering but still defiant.

'Most of the ones we pick get themselves into bother of their own accord. If they don't and we want them badly enough, then we bloody well manufacture it for them. Either way they get a simple choice. Co-operate and we waive charges, or stay pigheaded – and it's a court martial.'

'Co-operate?' Wintour asked.

'Sign a voluntary transfer to the SR Register. It comes under Article 49 of Queen's Regulations. Under that we can recall them any time over the next fifteen years, whether they like it or not. And if they try to skip we can send for the civil police to pull them in. Simple as that.'

'I understand now, Brigadier.'

Wintour understood very clearly indeed. It explained all the obfuscation surrounding the register. What Jardine had been describing could have been equally well expressed in a couple of words. Institutional blackmail.

'Well, there you are—'

Jardine's voice was almost jovial again in his relief at having finished. He came forward and picked up a large manila envelope which Wintour had noticed on one of the card-tables.

'I checked the possibilities against the profile Dickie gave me. This one seems the best bet.'

Wintour took the envelope, pulled out a file and began to read through the typewritten pages inside. There was silence for several minutes. Then he looked up.

'He sounds very interesting, Brigadier,' Wintour said, 'in fact he could be exactly the man we want.'

'He's a bloody tough customer, I can tell you that. Damn lucky it wasn't a murder charge. That wouldn't have been something we could have tucked under the carpet—'

Jardine hesitated and fiddled with his watch-chain.

'It really is important, isn't it?'

For an instant his expression was almost anguished as he

13

watched Wintour put the file back in the envelope and tuck it under his arm.

Wintour nodded. 'It could hardly be more so, I'm afraid.'

Jardine shook his head, 'Well, give my regards to Dickie.'

He turned reluctantly and opened the door. Wintour crossed the room. Then on the landing he paused and glanced back.

'There's just one thing I don't quite understand, Brigadier. You said everyone selected for the Register possesses certain unusual skills or qualities. This man's obviously got several, but I don't see what particular category he fits into.'

Jardine was still holding the doorhandle. When he answered his voice was flat and hard.

'He qualifies under an all-round category called bastard. In every other context they're poison, but in war, in the field, they're the people you want more than anyone else because they win. After what he did I'd put him high on the list of the biggest ones we've got.'

'Yes, of course. Thank you.'

Wintour went down the marble staircase.

Thirty minutes later he was back in Mathieson's cramped office on the top floor of the Baker Street houses. He handed Mathieson the envelope and shuffled over to the window.

'He's even got red hair,' Wintour said.

He heaved himself onto his perch on the radiator and settled down to wait for Mathieson to read the file.

3

'Told him you was out, but he said he'd wait anyhow. Down in the hall he is now—'

Mrs Martin, heaving, wheezing from the climb upstairs, her voice a throaty whisper, jerked her thumb over her shoulder.

'Said for me to give you this if I happened to see you. Did all I could, Mr Steele, but he's got the look of a stayer, that one.'

Steele took the envelope, studied the black coat-of-arms franking the right-hand corner and frowned.

'Never mind, Mrs Martin.'

Mrs Martin watched him rip the envelope open.

Normally she wouldn't have dreamed of climbing the stairs for one of her lodgers – a bellow up the five draughty flights in the peeling terraced house at the northern end of Camden Town was the usual announcement of a visitor's arrival. But Steele was an exception.

Not that at first sight he'd been any different from the others. The same frayed suit, the same shabby case baring damp card-board through the broken seams, the same gruff introduction that he'd been 'recommended' – Mrs Martin never really knew how her lodgers found her, but like Steele they kept on coming. And a few days later, as with the rest of them, the same men hanging around on the street outside waiting to slap court orders on his arm.

Yet something about him had appealed to her almost from the day he moved in. He was good with the rent for instance. Most of the others she had to chase, waiting up in the hall to all hours at the week's end. Not Steele. Every Friday morning, soon as he came back from the employment, he'd knock at her parlour door regular as clockwork. Other little things too. After he discovered she liked seeing the evening paper, he'd leave his copy neatly

15

folded on the stairs every night. Then once he found a bunch of daffs in the street, fallen off a barrow they must have done. He brought them back and gave them to her. None of the others would have done that, they'd just have left the flowers in the road.

A funny one, Mr Steele, with his big burly shoulders, his fierce red hair and his silences. She often wondered what had happened to him. The rest of them were only too anxious to tell her, long maudlin stories after the pubs shut about bad luck and injustice and spiteful bank managers who'd foreclosed the week before everything would have come right. But from Steele nothing, not a word of explanation ever.

'Thanks, Mrs Martin,' Steele put the envelope in his pocket, 'I'll come down.'

'You sure, dear?' Mrs Martin peered at him solicitously. 'If I tell him he can wait in the parlour, maybe you could nip out the back.'

Steele shook his head. 'He's not one of those. This time it's different.'

Mrs Martin shrugged and Steele followed her down to the hall. The man was standing by the table. Different or not in Steele's view, Mrs Martin's opinion of him hadn't altered. She gave a contemptuous stare, gathered her housecoat round her and swept into the parlour, slamming the door loudly.

'Mr Steele?'

As the man stepped forward a ripple of sunlight, falling through the stained glass fanlight, touched a rough tweed jacket, cavalry twill trousers, a regimental tie and a military moustache in a square florid face.

Steele nodded. 'That's right.'

'Crawley,' the man said, 'Major Crawley. I'm with records. The good lady gave you the notification?'

Steele nodded again but didn't say anything. Crawley glanced round the hall and up the uneven flights of stairs where the tarnished brass doorhandles glowed dimly on the landings.

'Perhaps it would be easier to talk outside—'

'We can talk here,' Steele said.

Crawley hesitated briefly but didn't argue. Instead he reached for his wallet and pulled out a sheet of paper.

'I'm here under Article 49. First of all I'm bound to remind you of the provisions—'

'You can save your breath,' Steele cut him off, 'I can remember every bloody one of them.'

Crawley swallowed and paused again. Then he put the paper away and held out a card.

'It's a notice of recall,' he said. 'The instructions are all there.'

Steele took the card. He read through it quickly and looked up frowning.

'What the hell is this? Recall for *secondment*?'

Crawley nodded. 'Correct.'

'Secondment to what?'

'I'm afraid I don't know. I'm merely here to remind you of the provisions and see that you sign the notice.'

'Now listen,' Steele shook his head, 'when I agreed to sign under Article 49 it was on a straightforward basis, not with any mumbo-jumbo about secondment. And, Jesus Christ, what's this—?'

He'd glanced at the card again.

'"Report to Flat 14, Abercorn Mansions, Prince of Wales Drive". What in the name of fortune is that supposed to be?'

'The re-registration and briefing address.'

'Come on!' Steele thrust the card back at him, 'I told you I could remember every line of the Article. On notification report to a specified military barracks, depot, transit post or training camp, that's what it said. Are you trying to tell me some flat in Battersea is one of those – with the brigade of guards out on manoeuvres in the bedroom no doubt? Grow up!'

Crawley stiffened and the colour of his face deepened.

'If you can remember as well as all that, you'll obviously remember the final paragraph—'

Either he was naturally meticulous or he'd been warned to expect trouble, because he quoted the lines now without needing to refer back to the paper.

'"The conditions of recall for service may be varied at any time and in any way by the appropriate department of the War Office on instruction from the Army Council".'

Steele listened in silence. Afterwards he said nothing for a few moments. Then he swore out loud so violently that Crawley involuntarily stepped back.

'The small bloody print that covers everything, doesn't it?

17

Give me a pen!'

Crawley reached into his jacket, Steele snatched the pen and signed the card against the wall. One of Mrs Martin's cats, the big marmalade tom, appeared from the darkness of the passage, urinated into the sandbox at Crawley's feet and settled down on the floor. Outside two children ran along the pavement, shouting and rattling sticks against the rusty iron railings.

'All right,' Steele handed the card back, 'so when am I due to report?'

Crawley twitched his moustache. 'They're waiting for you now.'

'Now?' Steele gazed at him incredulously. 'What the Christ is going on?'

'I'm sorry if the urgency inconveniences you,' Crawley ignored the question and turned towards the door, 'however I wouldn't have thought you had many prior engagements at the moment.'

He stepped over the tom and went out, momentarily a stiff black silhouette against the oblong of sunlight. Then the door closed and Steele was alone in the hall.

'Everything all right, dear?'

Mrs Martin had appeared at the entrance to the parlour, apprehensively clutching another of her cats.

Steele turned. 'Not really, Mrs Martin. I'm afraid I'll have to be leaving.'

'Oh, I am sorry, Mr Steele,' her face was blank with shock, 'it's serious, is it then?'

'Well,' Steele paused, 'it's like I said – different, very different.'

He climbed the stairs, picked up his jacket and stood for a moment by the small high window looking round the little bedroom.

It was shabby, cramped and untidy, on the surface no different from dozens of other rooms he remembered, just another brief staging-post. Yet somehow after all these months comfortable and familiar too, almost protective like the rest of the house was with its lingering atmosphere of wartime London fortified against the blitz – the gasmask still hanging behind the parlour door, the sandbags in the back yard, the basement windows' ancient tapes against the blast of falling bombs.

A safe place. That's what it had been. No longer – and the

18

coldness he'd felt when he saw the envelope gripped his stomach again. He'd lived with the possibility for eleven years and five months – if he took the trouble he could even remember the precise number of days too. Now it had happened, now reaching back across all that time a debt had been called in that he'd long since despised himself for ever acknowledging.

Steele clenched his hands until the tendons of his wrists throbbed. Then he swung round and went down to the hall again.

'I suppose you'll be back to collect your things a bit later, dear?'

Mrs Martin was scrubbing the doorstep. There was the laundry to be settled and even with someone as reliable as Mr Steele she liked to be sure.

'Of course, Mrs Martin.'

She swabbed out the last pool of water on the worn stone, squeezed out the mop and stood aside to let him out.

'Right bastards, aren't they, Mr Steele?'

Steele smiled. 'We'll get them one day.'

He stepped through the door and headed towards the bus-stop. Mrs Martin leant on the mop and watched him. A real funny one, he was. Sometimes she thought he almost might have been a gentleman, although what a real gent could have been doing in her establishment defeated even Mrs Martin's imagination to work out.

He disappeared round the corner, she scolded the marmalade tom who was leaving paw-prints on the clean stone, then she went muttering inside.

Abercorn Mansions was the last building at the Battersea end of Prince of Wales Drive.

Not one of the tall houses, full of expensive scrubbed pine furniture and deep scatter cushions, that looked out across the park over late flannelled cricketers and bronze leaved trees in the evening sun. But smaller, tacked onto the end of them as an afterthought, smoke-bleared from the fumes of the power station and facing the wrong way – towards the grey concrete towers of Wandsworth.

Steele arrived there a few minutes before six. He inspected the building from the other side of the street. Then he crossed the road and climbed the steps. There were no names, just numbers

19

on the row of bells by the door. He pressed the button marked 14 and waited.

'Good evening.'

Instead of a voice through the loudspeaker grille a woman had appeared. Neat, plump, blacksuited and smiling.

'I'm looking for Flat 14,' Steele said. 'I'm expected.'

'It's on the top floor. The lift's in the corner.'

She let Steele in, closed the door behind him, smiled again and walked away. Steele crossed the floor and opened the metal gates.

For an instant he felt he recognized the hall as if he'd been there before. Then he realized why. It belonged to another boarding house although this one was several rungs up the social and income ladder from those he knew so well like Mrs Martin's. The same neutral carpet but thick piled instead of threadbare, the same cream paint but applied that year not three decades ago, the same veneered furniture but new and waxed and substantial.

Yet overall even more anonymous and soulless than the others. A building for transients, assignations, overnight stops, private abortions – the neat smiling woman could easily have been a doctor's receptionist. No one lived in a place like that. They used it. Air hostesses, car salesmen and furtive lovers passing briefly through, then discarding and forgetting it.

Steele watched the vases of plastic roses on the successive landings and shuddered. At least in Mrs Martin's house the rare bunches of flowers, like the daffodils he'd given her once, were fresh. Then the lift stopped. He got out and pressed another bell. He didn't know if his arrival had been observed from a window but the door opened instantly.

'Come in, please.'

He was a small lopsided man with a persistent hacking cough that echoed off the walls as he led Steele down a passage to the living-room – warm and comfortable but as barren as the hall without even a newspaper to interrupt the tidiness.

'Mr Steele? Thank you so much for coming—'

There were two other men in the room. The one who'd spoken was standing, a tall elegant figure with silver hair and a fastidious drawling voice. Behind him the second one was getting to his feet. He was short and stout and had a bright cherry pink face.

20

'My name's Mathieson, Colonel Mathieson,' the tall man held out his hand, 'the gentleman who showed you in is Mr Wintour. And this is Major Greville—'

He pointed at the man with the high coloured face.

Steele shook hands and sat down on a cord covered chair, bland and soft and beige to match the curtains. The other three sat down too, ranging themselves in front of him like the board of a small provincial company at its annual general meeting.

'I regret this has happened at such short notice,' Mathieson was opposite him with a file open on his knee, 'But from our point of view time is absolutely critical. So I'll summarize the situation as shortly as I can, starting with yourself. I understand you're a former regular army officer, Mr Steele—?'

Steele didn't answer, and Mathieson went on.

'In 1968, after five years service, you were promoted to the rank of full captain. You had an excellent military record, you were a first class linguist and also a distinguished athlete – you boxed in the Rhine Army championships and twice captained your unit's team in the NATO sailing regatta. In fact you had an extremely promising career ahead of you—'

Mathieson paused.

'And then you were chosen to lead a special long-range night patrol group in a major NATO exercise. On the last night of the exercise I believe there was an unfortunate "accident" involving one of the umpires—?'

Mathieson broke off.

Steele gazed at him for a moment. Then he turned to stare through the window over Battersea Park. The cricketers had gone now and the light had wasted to a chill gunmetal dusk. It had also been dusk eleven years before when he'd been escorted from the barracks, still under open arrest, to an upstairs room in the small hotel of the local town.

He clenched his hands again as suddenly all the memories, the images, even the smells of that week welled up. There was no holding them back any longer. The frosted scent of the wintry landscape, the silent tracking in the darkness, the fast ruthless assault, the unconscious figure on the ground afterwards with blood streaming from his mouth, the bleak recital of the medical evidence at the court of inquiry, – a broken nose and jaw, five fractured ribs, a ruptured spleen, multiple bruises and abrasions.

The man from the War Office waiting for him in the hotel room five days later had been friendly, patient, sympathetic – and explicit. Twenty minutes after he arrived Steele had signed the paper voluntarily transferring himself to the Special Reserve Register.

He glanced back at Mathieson.

'There was an incident involving another officer,' he said curtly, 'after that I left the army.'

It was the first time he'd spoken and Mathieson nodded benignly.

'I quite understand. You voluntarily discharged yourself and you took up a new career in business which didn't prove, shall we say, altogether successful—?'

Mathieson was consulting the file again.

'A boatbuilding firm that was put into liquidation. A marina scheme that went the same way. A plan to sell marine insurance that finished in a Department of Trade investigation. And quite recently yet another venture, chartering yachts this time, wasn't it? Only I gather that ended too.'

In bankruptcy. Mathieson didn't say so but it was something else he knew, the rawest and most humiliating episode in the long catalogue of disaster since his discharge.

There was a short silence. Then Steele swung his head up.

'Who the hell are you?' he said.

To his left Wintour coughed huskily and ran his hand through his hair, sending flakes of dandruff spiralling down. The chubby, pink cheeked Greville uncrossed his legs and frowned. Even Mathieson hesitated before answering.

'Who the bloody hell are you?' Steele repeated in the silence, 'And what do you want from me?'

His palms were sweating and he could feel a vein pulsing beneath his ear. Yet there was more than anger now. There was dizzying bewilderment.

The woodenfaced Crawley at least had been a soldier, a recognizable figure from a world that, however much he'd come to hate, Steele knew and understood. But these men in their dark suits sitting in this bare rented apartment had nothing to do with that world. They used military ranks and they wore regimental ties, even the grubby little Wintour, yet they came from somewhere else, somewhere alien and furtive and ignoble, and as he

22

watched them, his eyes switching from one to the other as Mathieson remained silent, Steele knew that any moment he would erupt in open baffled rage.

Finally Mathieson spoke again.

'Mr Steele, perhaps I can put it in a nutshell like this. We represent an arm of the intelligence services. We work very closely with the War Office. That's why you're here, on loan if you like from them—'

Mathieson leant forward. Wintour had stopped coughing and Greville was sitting erect, puffy hands motionless on his spread knees.

'Six years ago circumstances arose in an area of particular importance that required us to "invent" a man. By "invent" I mean we had to project his identity so vividly that his existence would be taken for granted without anyone ever actually seeing him. The area was the mouth of the Mediterranean, we named our creation Ross Callum and the operation, under Major Greville's direction, was successful. After eighteen months we were able to withdraw Callum. Unfortunately—'

Mathieson glanced at Greville who was gazing studiedly at the wall.

'It's just emerged we were in a sense too successful. You see, if one creates an individual as magnetic and flamboyant as we felt Callum had to be, people are going to fantasize about him. There are those in the area who still boast that they knew him. Others came to see him very differently. To them he was a competitor, a thief of good business, a scapegoat for God knows what misfortunes. One such is a man called Velatti—'

He reached into his pocket, pulled out a corncob pipe and filled the bowl.

'Until forty-eight hours ago Velatti worked for us. Then he disappeared. He left behind a letter. It's an emotional tortured rambling document full of imagined but obsessive grievances against Callum. Somehow Velatti's convinced himself that Callum destroyed his career. Now he's determined on vengeance – bluntly he wants to see Callum dead. He says he's gone into hiding. He's given us ten days to return Callum to the area. If we don't he threatens to expose all our activities there for the past twelve years. Names, identities, networks, payments, everything—'

Flame leapt up from a battered lighter as Mathieson hunched himself over the bowl and smoke drifted across the floor.

'Clearly he's had a sudden and acute mental breakdown, but we've no doubt he intends to do exactly what he says. We simply cannot afford that. Not least it would put some two dozen lives in jeopardy—'

Mathieson took the pipe from his mouth and paused.

'We want you to assume Callum's role, Mr Steele. We want you to go back there, convince Velatti you're who you claim to be and draw him into the open before his deadline runs out.'

Steele looked at him blankly, disbelieving for a moment.

Then he said, 'You mean you want to peg me out there like some bloody goat so this figure you've lost, this Velatti, can walk up behind me and stick a knife in my ribs?'

'Oh, we'll have you covered on every side, Mr Steele, don't worry about that. But it's essential we get our hands on him again – and in his case I'm afraid there's no Article 49 we can invoke.'

He smiled. Steele sat quite still in his chair. Before he could say anything else, Mathieson turned to Greville.

'In view of the urgency, Miles, I think you should start right away. You've got just two days to have Callum fitting Mr Steele like a second skin. After that he'll be on his own.'

4

There was a balcony at the end of the hall, a little concrete box with an iron railing above the street.

Steele stood there in the darkness with the night air icy on his skin. Each time a bus rumbled by below its lights flickered over the living room window and he could see his reflection in the glass. Broad hunched shoulders, a seamed and truculent face, slate-grey eyes narrowed against the cold, red hair rumpled by the wind.

By chance red hair had been one of the features Greville had given Ross Callum.

Steele gripped the metal bar until his knuckles whitened. Behind him through the wall he could hear voices talking. The two days were over and they were all inside now waiting to see him off. Then he leant back and laughed.

He was there because he'd had no choice. He'd known that from the moment Mrs Martin came wheezing up the stairs with the War Office envelope. Until then he'd thought there were no more indignities, no more humiliations he could go through. Mrs Martin's lodging house was the end of the line. He'd lost, he'd moved in and he was finally safe. Solitary, private, taciturn, he could survive there indefinitely – anonymous and untroubled.

He'd been wrong. There was one last sanction against him, the unspoken threat from the past, from the incident that had triggered everything else.

Mathieson had called him an excellent officer. Mathieson was right. It was all Steele had ever wanted to be. Yet the others, his fellow officers in the lancer squadron where the War Office had posted him when he was commissioned, had never accepted him. He didn't have their interests, their attitudes, their friends or their money. They treated him first with condescension, then with indifference, in the end with contempt.

For five years, as all his bright hopes soured and tarnished, Steele endured it. Then that February night his stored-up bitterness and frustration boiled over. In a mindless flare of rage and exhaustion he took his patrol back onto the plain, hunted down the umpire they'd passed earlier and attacked him. The man, stumbling ineptly across the heath, was a major in Steele's own unit. Over the past few months he'd come to symbolize everything Steele loathed, from the casual arrogance of inherited wealth to the trivial discourtesies of his companions.

The man had almost died and Steele, with a vast and corroding sense of betrayal, had left the army. Afterwards in resentful defiance he'd set out to make something on his own. He'd failed, everything he'd tried had failed. When the final venture collapsed and the bankruptcy notice was served he'd given up.

Now, victim of the ancient blackmail, he was being returned to the point where it had all started. Steele laughed again. The irony in what they'd claimed him back for was so appalling he could only laugh. They'd pulled him out of the gutter, a loser, a bankrupt, the ultimate failure, a man who was even forbidden by law to write cheques – and they wanted him to be Ross Callum.

'Glamour, that was the essence of it all—'

Greville on the first evening after the other two had gone, his plump thighs splayed and his fingers drumming restlessly on his knees.

'Impossible to define, really. Easier to list the people who've got it. Garbo, of course, Lawrence of Arabia before the war, the Kennedys as a family, that big black fellow today – what's he call himself now? – Mohammed Ali. They all have something that sets them apart, makes them unforgettable—'

Greville paused. Then he asked suddenly, 'Ever see a film called *Casablanca*?'

Startled, Steele had nodded.

'On television this year, ninth time I watched it,' Greville beamed, 'Now he had more of it than anyone else. What a wonderful man! Keep him in mind throughout. For Callum to be convincing he had to be unforgettable too. I knew from the beginning if we could give him what Bogart had we couldn't lose.

26

Girlfriends, champagne, money, but most of all style. Bogart's style—'

Greville shook his head wistfully. Then with reluctance he returned to the file he'd taken over from Mathieson.

Steele watched him.

At the start, listening to his highpitched effeminate voice punctuated constantly with bubbles of laughter, Steele had thought he was a buffoon. Very quickly he realized he was totally wrong. In reality Greville was ruthless, meticulous and possessed of an imagination so rare and extraordinary that it would have been more understandable in a poet.

Mathieson had spoken of Callum as a joint creation. It wasn't so. Callum was Greville's creature – a poet's invention.

Ostensibly, to the local population of the straits, he'd been the owner of a twin-diesel Swedish Härfagel launch, fast and rugged and shallow draughted. The launch, crewed and looked after by a mate, had been berthed in Tangier while Callum, based across the water in Gibraltar, directed its operations – running men and weapons to the Sahel rebels and contraband to anyone who would buy it.

That was the public story. In fact the Callum legend had been an elaborate cover for an intelligence source. A Soviet Jew, a cryptographer assigned to a communications post in Ceuta, one of the five ports, had volunteered to pass on information about Medecon, the creation of a massive Russian naval presence in the Mediterranean.

Medecon represented the largest and most threatening move the Russians had ever made into western Europe. Intelligence about the Soviet fleet was critically important. Callum had been devised as a smokescreen to conceal the origin of the crypto-grapher's reports.

Within weeks of Medecon's start the Russians knew their signals were being intercepted. There were only two explana-tions. A traitor in their communications network or a mobile surface monitoring station. Very shortly, as intended, they began to suspect the latter – and Callum's launch.

For eighteen months they shadowed the boat on its mysterious and unpredictable voyages round the straits – voyages when everyone else believed Callum was running illicit cargoes be-tween the ports. Finally they moved in. A Russian escort vessel 'accidentally' rammed the launch. The mate, alone on board, was killed in the collision. When the Soviet crew searched the damaged boat they found what they'd been expecting – a battery of sophisticated radio reception equipment.

The 'accident' was reported to the Moroccan coastguards, the launch was towed back into Tangier, and the matter ended – as did Callum. By then the Medecon picture was virtually complete. The Russians had positive confirmation of their suspicions, the cryptographer, his usefulness exhausted, was safe, and Callum was discreetly withdrawn from the dirty area.

His function too was over.

Until now. Now, to Greville's delight, he was about to be resurrected. For Greville, as Steele had learned, Callum had been far more than a device in an intelligence operation – he was the projection of a private fantasy. Reckless, cavalier, virile and laconic, a gambler, an adventurer, an incisive man of action, Callum was the rotund little Major, deskbound and cautious, playing Bogart in his mind.

Steele looked at the stars, hazy through the October mist above the Thames, and shuddered. Then he pushed himself away from the rail and walked inside.

'No final questions?'

Mathieson, who'd spoken, was standing in the hall. Greville was at his side and Wintour coughing hoarsely, persistently behind.

Steele shook his head.

'Though I say it myself,' Greville put in, 'given the time factor I really think what we've managed to achieve is remarkable. As far as I'm concerned Mr Steele *is* Callum now.'

Greville linked his fingers across his stomach and smiled proudly.

Steele glanced round the three faces. Two days, that was all he'd been given. Two blurred exhausting days filled by members of the Callum team from dawn until after midnight.

They'd given him a passport in Callum's name. A new wardrobe, the shirts with labels from a Jermyn Street haberdasher, the shoes handcrafted by Lobbs, the canvas sailing jackets from a gunsmith by royal appointment on Piccadilly. A collection of personal belongings, a pigskin wallet, a Rolex chronometer, a gold lighter engraved with the initials RC, every item chosen with

28

scrupulous care to fit the imaginary personality.

Then they'd primed and briefed him. Grave pedantic men like elderly schoolmasters, brisk middle-aged figures with maps and phrasebooks and film projectors, casual young ones in jeans and sweaters. All of them instructing him in everything from the autumn tidal patterns in the straits to the best patissier in the French quarter of Tangier, from the alley names of the Gibraltar dock area to the muzzle velocities of the new Belgian automatics on the weapons black market.

Steele swore under his breath. They'd wrapped Callum round him like a tightfitting coat. Once maybe he could have worn it, believed in himself as the legendary success Callum was supposed to be. Not now because whatever else they knew about him from their files, there was something they couldn't know. Steele didn't believe in anything any longer.

'Well, I must congratulate you, Mr – Callum,' Mathieson smiled, then he turned to Wintour, 'Has the car arrived yet?'

Wintour nodded. 'The driver's waiting downstairs.'

'Perhaps you'd better be on your way,' Mathieson held out his hand. 'We all wish you the very best of luck.'

Steele ignored the outstretched hand and gazed briefly at Mathieson's face.

'For the sake of Article 49 and my own skin I'll do the best I can,' he said, 'but I'll tell you something now before I go. The War Office sent you the wrong man.'

He picked up his cases, went out onto the landing and kicked the door shut behind him.

The road to the airport was crusted with the first frost of the year and the street lamps were haloed with mist. Steele sat beside the driver, tense and upright. In his pocket there was a photograph of a small man with a melancholy oval face, olive skin and dark impassive eyes. It could easily have been the face of a bank clerk. According to Greville it belonged to a tormented and obsessed killer.

Steele gazed through the windscreen. There'd be no ice or mist in the dirty area. Instead dry arid heat and the clear brilliant light of autumn. Turning into the terminal forecourt he suddenly remembered a maxim of his firearms instructor at the officer cadet academy. 'After his rifle, good light's the sniper's best friend'.

According to the profile on Velatti he had a marksman's rating with both rifle and handgun.

The car stopped and Steele got out. Moments later he was crossing the departure lounge with a group of laughing late season tourists.

5

'Where you want to go, sir?'

The taxidriver glanced back over the seat, his teeth black in a wrinkled walnut coloured face.

'Take me up to the Grand Socco first,' Steele got in and slammed the rear door, 'I'll tell you where to go from there.'

'You want to see all the sights of Tangier? I make you very good, very special price—'

'I know all the sights and I don't want any bloody special price. We'll do it by the meter.'

'Okay, sir.'

The driver shrugged, started the engine and pushed down a button above the farecounter.

'When I say meter, I mean the official meter—'

Steele leant forward, reached under the small metal box by the wheel and flipped over a switch. Then he punched the button twice. The original figure in the window, nine dirhams, vanished and a new one appeared – four. At the same time the ticking of the meter slowed.

'Okay?' Steele said. 'Or shall we go and discuss it at the *Bureau de Circulation* on Rue Lafayette?'

The driver didn't answer. He thought for a moment. Then he shrugged again, crashed the old Peugeot into gear, pulled out from the quayside rank, and set off through the harbour towards the town.

Steele wiped the sweat from his forehead and loosened his tie. It wasn't yet ten o'clock but the morning heat was already as he'd imagined it in London, harsh and dusty with the sun glaring off the dirty white walls along the wharf.

He'd been up since seven when he telephoned the hotel to say he was still on the ship. Two hours later a plain clothes officer

31

from the *Brigade Criminelle* came aboard. This time the interview was much longer. Steele retold his story, answered questions about the launch, denied again and again that he knew anything about the accident, and emphasized throughout that his account had been accepted long since.

Finally the new Inspector, wary and intrigued like the other, gave him back his passport and escorted him down to the quay. The man hadn't said anything specific – he was as polite as the first one – but Steele was certain he'd be under observation from then on.

Steele had carefully avoided any reference to the night before. Someone had been waiting for him, he had no doubt about that, but the motives for the attack were baffling. It was almost as if he'd been given a warning except that Velatti wasn't interested in warning him – he wanted Callum dead. Whatever the explanation it wasn't something for the police. It was for Greville's team when he locked onto them and for the moment Steele had deliberately pushed the incident to the back of his mind.

Now, as the driver slowed to check out with the policeman at the harbour entrance, there was something much more important – Tangier itself. Callum's town. The town that during the past two days, 1800 miles away in a rented London apartment, Steele had learned so much about he even knew where to find the tripswitch on a rigged taxi-meter.

Steele pushed himself forward and looked through the open window for his first view of it.

The harbour front, flat and grey and almost deserted with half a dozen cargo boats berthed against the quay. Then a sharp swing right and the Rue du Portugal. Narrow, winding, climbing steeply away from the sea towards the town's centre. And suddenly crowds, clamour, bustle, smells. Ragged scampering urchins with cupped hands begging. Peasant women from the hill tribes trudging upwards in scarlet and white striped skirts, huge bundles on their backs. Old men squatting at street corners over piles of jade green mint, shopkeepers shouting from open doorways, mules heaving and lurching, sunlight flickering on stalls of spice and herb, car horns raucous and insistent, jellabahed Moroccans arguing, haggling, gesticulating.

'You want to stop here, sir?'

The street had opened out abruptly into the Grand Socco, a

32

circular space with a broad island in the middle.

'Pull into the side for a moment,' Steele said.

The driver parked, Steele got out and stood by the car gazing round, taking his bearings, matching what he'd memorized from photographs, plans and maps with the reality in front of him.

He was at the heart of Tangier. Immediately ahead was the entrance to the souk, a warren of twisting streets and alleyways that ran back down to the old port. Towering above it on a hill to the left the sultan's palace. Then, further to the left still, the sweep of the French quarter with its villas, shops, banks and offices. Finally behind him the cramped food market – scents of bread, olives, cheese and fruit lying heavy in the hot still air – and beyond the main residential district sloping round the curve of the bay towards the sea.

A compact filthy vibrant town set like a medieval watchtower in the bowl of hills that dominated the western entrance to the straits. At first sight it was everything Greville's team had portrayed.

'Right,' Steele swung himself back into the cab, 'now up past the Minzah Hotel, then down the Boulevard de Paris.'

Fifteen minutes later they'd circled the town and were back on the seafront, with the coastal road swinging to the right round the bay.

'Keep going until I tell you to stop,' Steele said.

He spotted it two kilometres further on. A stone jetty running out into the sea, a ramshackle clapboard building, a sign hanging lopsidedly from the roof. *Donovan & Cie, Chandlers, Moorings and Charters* – with the same legend repeated below in French.

'Pull in here.'

The driver drew up by the building and turned off the metre. Steele glanced at the figure in the fare window. Twenty-seven dirhams. He reached for his wallet and handed a hundred-dirham note across the seat.

'You got smaller, sir? I can't change this—'

'You keep the change,' Steele said. 'Just remember next time not to trip that cogwheel you've fitted. Not with me as a passenger anyway. It might get to be even more painful than the *Bureau de Circulation*. My name's Ross Callum.'

The driver's head jerked up and he stared at Steele.

'You the same Mr Callum?'

'Right. Now get my bags out.'

'Yes, sir.'

He opened his door, scuttled round to the trunk and put Steele's baggage on the ground in the shadow of the roof. As Steele walked past the building towards the jetty he was still staring after him, the hundred-dirham note fluttering in his hand.

Steele stopped on a wooden platform linking the jetty with the shore. A girl was sitting a few yards away on a bollard above the water. Young, maybe seventeen or eighteen, with long fair hair falling across a denim jacket that had faded almost to whiteness.

'Where can I find Captain Donovan?' Steele called out.

The girl swivelled round, her face indistinct against the glare of the sun behind.

'Inside,' she pointed at a shed beside the main building, 'in the office at back.'

'Thanks.'

Steele crossed the platform. The girl's voice had been slow and clear, the accent American. Donovan's daughter, he guessed. He reached an open doorway and stepped through.

Instantly there was a dusky greyness after the brilliance of the bay. Windows furred with salt and cobwebs, splinters of light reflected off chains and brass, coils of rope, a tattered calendar, a rusting anchor, a tangle of smells sharpened by the heat. Not the clean strong scents of the market but rancid and bitter. Caulk, hemp, dry varnish, lead paint, turpentine and, lifting above them all, stale beer and gin.

Steele blinked in the half-darkness and swallowed. Then he saw a second door – glass-panelled with two of the panes shattered and someone slouched over a desk beyond. He picked his way through the litter on the floor and went in.

'Captain Donovan?'

The figure propped himself up. 'That's me.'

'Callum,' Steele tossed his passport onto the desk, 'Ross Callum.'

Donovan looked at the passport, gazed disbelievingly at Steele, checked the photograph, then slammed his fist down on the desktop.

'Jesus Christ Almighty! It's really you?'

'If it's not and someone's impersonating me, I'll break his neck myself.'

34

Steele smiled briefly as Donovan shook his hand in bewilderment.

'And all these years I've been saying for sure you'd be back—'

Donovan broke off speechless. Then he heaved himself unsteadily to his feet, roared with delighted laughter and held out his hand.

Donovan. The owner of the boatyard where Callum's launch had been berthed. A former American naval officer in his sixties now. Huge and paunchy and grizzled with wet patches staining the armpits of his T-shirt, a strong pumping handshake and a booming voice. And something else.

The aging debris in the store. The dust and yellowing papers on the desk. The stench of beer and gin almost overpowering now at close quarters. The fluttering tendons in his wrist as he half stumbled and steadied himself against the chair.

Steele recognized the signs instantly. It was a condition that had needed all his own resources and willpower to fight against when the marina scheme went under. Donovan hadn't even tried to resist. Whatever he and the boatyard had been like five years ago, the business was a failure now and Donovan, under the bluster, a pathetic drunken husk of a man.

'Hell, if anything ever deserved a celebration, this is it.'

Donovan produced a bottle of gin, poured measures into a couple of glasses, topped them up with water and gave one to Steele.

'Welcome home, Mr Callum.'

He finished his drink in a single swallow and poured another. Steele took a light sip. The glass was filthy and the gin tasted of gasolene.

'So how long is it? Five years, right?' Donovan gulped again. 'And you handled everything all through that time without ever making it over here?'

He gazed at Steele, eyes red veined, watery, admiring. Steele said nothing. He took another sip. Then he put the glass down and winked slowly.

'Hell!' Donovan laughed again. 'At my age I should know better. Well, I didn't ask any damnfool questions then and I won't now. Except – what can I do for you?'

'How's the boat?'

Donovan shrugged. 'I patched up the damage to the cabin

to keep the rain out, and I've greased the engines every six months like you said in your letter. That's all. Otherwise she's much the same as when the coastguards brought her in.'

'Let's take a look.'

'Sure.'

Donovan took a bundle of keys from a hook on the wall and led the way out into the dazzling sunlight on the platform.

'There she is—'

Steele peered in the direction of his outstretched arm. They were further to the right than when he'd stopped to call out to the girl and he hadn't seen it then. An iron cradle angled down to the sea with the launch winched up out of the water at its centre.

'Christ, when you picked that lady, Mr Callum, you picked yourself a princess.'

There was awe in Donovan's voice and even in a single glimpse through the heat haze Steele understood why.

He'd studied photographs of the boat but they hadn't conveyed the reality. Power, that was the immediate dominating impression, power and speed and grace. Power in the massive twin screws set deep at the stern. Speed in the raked bow with the foredecks flaring in wings on either side. Grace in the whole silhouette, long and low and dark against the sun like an immense hunting seabird poised to dive.

Steele whistled involuntarily. Even six years old, beached, damaged, dilapidated, paint flaking and hawsers rusting, the *Lara* – as Greville had christened Callum's launch – was still extraordinary.

'Maybe they make them bigger now, faster, rigged out with all manner of fancy gadgets like goddam whores. But for class, real class, I never saw nothing to touch her—'

Donovan broke off as another shadow fell across the planks. Then he added, 'Hey, meet one of your greatest fans, Mr Callum.'

Steele turned. It was the girl who'd been sitting on the bollard. He held out his hand.

'Good to see you,' he said.

Mary-Beth Donovan. Eighteen years and four months, Steele remembered now, Donovan's only child by his dead wife. She'd been living with him during the Callum era. There had even been a photograph of her in the files, a solemn little girl peering nervously from behind steel-rimmed glasses.

Except that was six years ago and in the interval the child had become a woman. Tall and slim with long fair hair framing an oval face, suntanned and freckled. The glasses had gone and her eyes, narrowed against the light, were flecked with green. She was wearing a loose white shirt under the denim jacket and a pair of frayed jeans. Above her bare feet her ankles were ringed with dried sea salt.

For an instant Steele smelled the sharp clear scent of the salt over the fumes that enveloped Donovan. Then Donovan draped an arm round her shoulders, pulled her clumsily against him and rocked forward, bringing back the stench of gin.

'Know what she used to do?' Donovan chuckled. 'Each time I got word the boat was coming back after a run, she'd park herself out here on the jetty and wait – in case you were on board. Jesus, she'd have sat up all night if I'd let her, right, Mary-Beth?'

The girl was blushing slightly. Steele said, 'Listen, Captain Donovan, maybe we can go into the past some other time. Right now I want to see the boat.'

'Sure, sure,' Donovan disengaged himself hurriedly, 'I'll show you on board—'

He turned towards a gangplank running up from the jetty to the boat's stern, but Steele stopped him.

'I'll take a look round on my own first.'

Steele took the keys and climbed the swaying gangplank. As he dropped into the cockpit he glimpsed the two figures watching him from below, one burly and shambling, the other supple and erect, both gazing intently upwards. Then he ducked under the swept back canopy of the cabin roof, unlocked the hatch, slid it aside and walked down some wooden steps.

Inside it was dark and musty. He pulled back a porthole cover, letting a funnel of light fall across the floor, and dropped onto a bench seat that ran along the cabin wall below. For the moment he wasn't interested in exploring the boat. All he wanted to do was relax in the silence and think.

An hour ashore and he could feel the strain already. The Inspector from the *Brigade Criminelle*, the wide-eyed stewards on the quay, the taxidriver with his rigged meter, now the gin-sodden Donovan with his rundown yard and the daughter who'd waited up night after night as a child in the hope of seeing her hero. Every one of them in different ways probing, demanding, curious, awed, enthralled because Callum had returned.

Against all habit and inclination – he'd never smoked before but Callum had got through two packs daily – Steele reached for a cigarette. Even those first few had been difficult enough and it hadn't even started yet. There'd be more, hundreds more, as word of his arrival spread out across the city and then the straits like ripples across a lake. And somewhere hidden among them all, waiting, watching, listening, Velatti.

'*By birth he's Maltese,*' Greville had said. '*We recruited him as a youth during the war and he's worked for us ever since. Never had the makings of a highflyer but he was excellent second echelon material. Dedicated, conscientious, reliable. Until now of course—*'

The Callum operation had been so secret that even in the department only those directly involved knew its nature. Velatti wasn't one of them. Like everyone else he'd believed in Callum's existence.

Then, soon after the operation ended, stories began to circulate. A major intelligence coup had been pulled off in the area and Callum had been its architect. Velatti felt bitter that he hadn't been involved. By chance at the same time a routine change of personnel took place. The Tangier station head was moved. Velatti thought he'd be promoted to take his place. Instead he was passed over and a new man was brought in from Ankara.

In Velatti's mind the two events became connected. His bitterness increased with Callum now as its target. Finally, after five years of brooding resentment, his mind snapped altogether. He wrote the letter, issued the threats and disappeared.

'*That at least is our analysis,*' Greville finished, '*exactly what he's planned we obviously don't know. He'll learn you're back within hours of course, but he's never seen you. So before he makes a move he'll want to be absolutely certain you are Callum. That means you've one task above all – be the man Velatti thinks you are. Act in character. Do the things Callum would have done. Convince Velatti before his week runs out and he'll surface – and then we'll grab him.*'

One week. One week of being trawled like bait through the straits while, unseen, Velatti tracked and examined and assessed him.

Steele leant forward to stub out his cigarette. As he touched the boards he saw his hand was shaking. He stared at it for a moment hypnotized. Then he swore angrily and stood up.

Act in character – Callum's character. The launch had been Callum's symbol and the cornerstone of his operations. Steele began to explore it.

On one side of the cockpit steps a galley, on the other a washbasin and WC. In the main cabin two bench seats, a table, a row of brass lamps on wall hooks, shelves piled with dusty charts, lockers full of mildewed oilskins, rotting boots and sodden coils of rope. Everything dank, tarnished or corroding.

Then at the forward end a bolted door. Steele wrenched it open. Inside the darkness was complete. He flicked on his lighter and peered round. The cargo area, a long hold narrowing towards the bows. It was empty now but in the shadows he could see a tangle of cables and the brackets that had supported the battery of planted radio equipment – the receivers stripped by the Russians after the ramming.

He turned, climbed back into the cockpit and went up into the wheelhouse. Once it had been the *Lara*'s nerve centre, bright and functional and pulsing with energy. Now, like everything else on the launch, it was patinaed with neglect and decay. The controls rusting, the instrument counters bleared, the wheel spokes crusted with grime, the mahogany console scarred by rain and seasalt.

Steele gazed over the bows. If Callum was no more than an image in Greville's mind, the *Lara* at least had been a tangible expression of his dream – swift, fierce and beautiful. The collision and the five years' abandonment had reduced it to a virtual wreck. Yet beneath the rotting surface the structure was still lean and strong. Somehow, like the bones beneath a proud old face, the beauty still showed through.

He tapped the wheel gently, almost affectionately. Part bird and part courtesan. That was how boats had always seemed to him, even the little dinghies he'd sailed. Suddenly this one was no different.

'Mr Callum.'

It was Mary-Beth's voice. He swung round, saw her standing in the shadow of the cradle's strut and climbed down onto the jetty.

39

'I'm sorry,' she shouted hesitant and uneasy, 'it would be easier if my father didn't see us talking.'

Steele glanced at the light glittering off the office windows and stepped into the shadow beside her, where the cradle hid them from the shore.

'I guess you'll be wanting things done to the *Lara*,' she said.

He nodded. 'Sure.'

That at least had been one of the few positive instructions Greville had given him. The first thing Callum would have done on his return would have been to see the launch was seaworthy again.

'Then you'd better shift her to another yard.'

Steele looked at her startled. 'Why?'

'Hell, you must have seen for yourself,' her voice was still strained and embarrassed, 'the office, the mess, what it's like all round. Don doesn't do much except drink any more. He forgets things and what he doesn't forget, he rips off. I hate saying it but it's true. The charter side packed up a while back, so did the moorings. Now the whole place is shot.'

'Why are you telling me?'

She shrugged. 'I guess I don't like the idea of the *Lara* getting screwed up.'

Steele smiled. 'So it wasn't me you used to wait up for – it was the launch?'

'A combination, maybe—'

Mary-Beth smiled back. She paused and then added suddenly, 'There's one way it could work. Get him to make out three copies of everything you want done. Give me one of them. I'll check out the job step by step when he's not around. I fixed that once before and it went fine then. This time for the *Lara* I'd pull out everything—'

She raised her head. 'Don was pretty good once and I've learned a lot. Believe me, I had to.'

She was gazing at him intently, green flecked eyes steady in the shadow, forehead slightly puckered, her face resolute.

Steele stared back at her. It would be time consuming and complicated to move the *Lara* to another yard. Yet far better that than risk Donovan making a fiasco of the repairs – a risk he couldn't take because Callum would never have taken it.

Except there was something different about this girl. Different not just from the others in that first hour, with their greed, seediness and sycophancy, nor simply because she was so much younger. Mary-Beth had grown up way beyond her eighteen years. The fact the yard was still functioning at all, Steele guessed, was due entirely to her. She was candid, competent, professional and tough – and he decided that instant to trust her.

'Okay,' he nodded, 'we'll give it a try.'

'Thanks—'

A quick smile of warmth and gratitude that made her briefly a teenager again, and not the embattled protector of an alcoholic, holding together what was left of his business with her wits and her bare hands.

'I won't kid you. We need the bread to see us through the winter. But the *Lara*'s going to come out great, I promise you.'

Steele nodded and began to move out of the shadow onto the jetty. Then he checked and turned back.

'How well do you know Tangier?' He asked.

'Enough, I guess,' she looked surprised, 'I've lived here ten years now. I speak French and some Arabic, at least what they use on the front. I know the people and most of the city. Why?'

'I want you to do a couple of things for me—'

This time Steele didn't hesitate. He'd gambled, committed himself, over the launch. Now he was going to gamble again.

'I don't know how long I'll be here, at most a week. As far as anyone knows I'll be staying at the Minzah. But I want somewhere else, an apartment, even a couple of rooms. But somewhere so private that no one – and I mean no one – knows anything at all about it.'

Mary-Beth frowned. 'Where were you thinking of?'

'Somewhere not too far from here. Maybe in the Ligiers quarter. What's that like now?'

The pretence, the constant pretence, that would go on and on until it was finished.

She wrinkled her nose. 'I guess much like it used to be before – dirty as hell.'

'Before' to Steele was some slides on a portable screen, the commentary of one of Greville's assistants and a name he'd filed away. Not for the reason he'd been given, as part of his knowledge of the city, but for something else – an idea that even then in the bland beige living-room was taking shape in his mind.

41

'Take a look round,' Steele said, 'if you find something that fits, rent it for a week under your own name. That's the first. Next, as soon as I check into the Minzah I'm going to rent a car. I want someone to drive it.'

'A Moroccan?'

'Listen, providing he's discreet, reliable and he'll do any goddam thing I want, I'd settle for a Martian.'

'How soon do you want them both?'

'By this evening.'

Mary-Beth's eyes widened. Then she shrugged and smiled. 'Give me until six. I'll see what I can do.'

Steele grinned and walked back along the jetty.

He reached the office and looked through one of the windows. Donovan was sprawled in the chair behind the desk. As Steele watched he picked up a ginbottle, drained it from the neck and pitched it into a crate in the corner. He sat there for a moment belching. The he heaved his feet onto the desktop, rocked back and closed his eyes.

Steele glanced at his watch and turned away.

I think we can assume you have an absolute safety period of four hours the first morning,' it was Greville's voice again, '*But from then on, from midday, don't count on anything. Just make sure you're in the hands of—*'

Greville had paused then and given one of his rapid falsetto chuckles.

'*Your guardian angels, perhaps. I think that's an appropriate description. Certainly your lifeline, your oxygen supply, your bulletproof shield. So make contact with them and keep contact. If you lose it, you'll be walking naked in a jungle – a very dirty jungle.*'

Steele headed for the coastal road.

Greville was wrong. There'd been no safety period at all. For the moment Donovan and the repairs to the *Lara* would have to wait. More important, far more important, was a telephone number and a voice at the end of a line. The voice of a guardian angel.

6

'*Bonjour*—'

The automatic interceptor cut the line and Steele heard a series of rapid highpitched pips. He juggled the one-dirham coin into the slot, hammered it down with the palm of his hand and the line cleared again.

'*Voyages Africaines à votre service*.'

'I'm checking on my trip to Safi,' Steele said. 'Have you confirmed my reservation on the midday coach?'

'I'll put you straight through, sir.'

In English the voice was flat and adenoidal. The home of this particular guardian angel, Steele guessed, was somewhere north of Birmingham. It sounded all the more incongruous against the noise of mules' hoofs and Arabic cries outside the telephone booth.

He wiped the sweat from his face and waited.

'The protective surveillance screen', as Greville had referred to it more formally, should have wrapped itself round him as soon as he landed. Four armed operatives, backed up by others at fixed observation points covering the boatyard and the hotel, shadowing him constantly wherever he went by day or night – ready to close in the instant there was any move by Velatti.

They were in contact with each other and the operation's centre by shortwave radio. Steele had no radio. Alone, in the open, the set would have been too bulky and conspicuous. Instead he had just a telephone number for a Moroccan travel agency – and instructions to use it only from public callboxes.

'About your visit to Safi—'

A click and another voice on the line, brisk, quiet and business-like.

'You'll have to change coaches at Chamoun. But you'd still

43

like to leave at midday, right?'

'Yes,' Steele answered.

Safi and Chamoun were coastal towns to the south. He'd been given Safi as his own identification. Chamoun had been assigned to the surveillance network controller. 'Midday' meant that Steele was able to talk freely. If he was under constraint for any reason, he was to start the conversation by naming another time.

'Good,' the voice went on crisply, 'so you're quite clear on procedures. How did it go at the Minzah?'

The Minzah was the best hotel in Tangier. Steele had checked in there fifteen minutes earlier after leaving the yard. The clerks at the reception desk had been impassive when he gave his name and signed the register, but he'd seen the staring faces behind him in the mirror as he walked towards the stairs and all four bellboys had escorted him up.

'They were civil,' he said.

Steele hadn't specified which room he wanted. He was Callum and Callum would have expected the best without asking. As soon as he was shown in he knew it was what he'd got. Large and cool and luxurious with a mosaic floor, rich tapestry hangings, a carved oak bed and an immense window overlooking the bay.

He thought of it now, standing cramped and sweating in the stifling booth. The hotel room wasn't only cool – it was high, private and walled with stone. The callbox was on a public square and made of glass.

'You seem to have made a good start. We've been behind you all the way of course—'

Unconsciously Steele had been scanning the crowds on the sidewalks. Suddenly he realized the man was speaking again. He shook his head and tried to concentrate.

'Two on scooters, one in a 2CV van and the fourth in reserve in a Citroën – he'll be alternating between that and an old Simca.'

Steele stared through the glass again. There were endless scooters and vans and cars circling the square.

He thought for a moment. Then he asked abruptly, 'Where am I speaking from?'

'Suspicious?' There was a chuckle in the earpiece, 'All right, you're at the southern corner of the Place de la France. You got there by walking up the Rue de la Liberté from the hotel. If you like I can take you through the whole morning—'

44

'That's enough,' Steele cut him off, 'I'm satisfied.'

'Don't worry. You're wrapped up tight as a nut.'

Another chuckle and Steele tried to visualize him. Trim, spruce, tweed-jacketed, another officer like Mathieson with the same edge of casual arrogance in his voice.

Normally he'd have been another representative of the world Steele despised. Not now. Now and in the days ahead he was going to be one of Steele's few links with sanity and normality. He hunched himself over the telephone.

'Listen,' Steele said, 'someone was waiting on the docks to welcome me last night—'

He described what had happened after he walked down the gangplank in the darkness. There was silence for a moment when he finished.

Then the man said, 'You were due to go up the hill at seven. Cancel that. You're wanted there now anyway. Meanwhile I'll relay this back and you can find out at the same time if we know anything.'

'What the hell else has happened?'

'You'll be briefed. Go back to the hotel and pick up a cab. Check with me again at six.'

The line went dead.

On the street the air was somehow even more hot and humid than inside the booth. Steele searched briefly for the scooters and the 2CV again. It was impossible to pick them out in the noisy concourse of flyhaloed mules, clattering hand-drawn carts, horn-blaring cars and scurrying Arabs, the women veiled and furtive, that was eddying round the square. He stepped off the pavement and headed across it.

Standing in the callbox, with the buildings at his back and the barrier of traffic in front, he'd been at least partially hidden. Now it was different. For the first time he was utterly exposed on the open expanse of gravel. As he reached the far side he suddenly realized he was running.

Steele swore, checked deliberately and forced himself to walk.

High walls on either side, a towering brass-studded door, the gutter swept and clean, the silence of the street broken only by the occasional hum of an expensive car, a Mercedes or a large American limousine.

45

This was another world again from the squalor of the docks, the raucous clamour of the souk, the beggars and half-blind whimpering children and the mounds of rotting fruit. On the way up from the centre there'd been broad avenues and shaded gardens and guards at wrought-iron gates, with glimpses of great villas, pink or white or yellow stucco, behind the elegant French grilles. 'Up the hill' was where the Tangier rich lived – hermetic, isolated and protected.

Steele rang the bell and waited.

'M'sieu?'

The door opened and a Moroccan houseboy appeared. Steele registered a fez, a white jacket with shining brass buttons, white culottes, and liquid black eyes.

'My name's Callum,' he said. 'I think Mr Wedderburn's expecting me.'

The houseboy stood aside to let Steele through, closed the door and set off down a path.

They were in a narrow garden, framed by the same high walls that faced the street, with great banks of white flowers and silver leaves on either side – the white and silver mingling, interweaving, shading from ivory to cream, from pale plate to dark chain-mail grey, so that together they formed two rippling curtains against the brick. Someone had just watered the beds. Moisture gleamed on the flagstones and scents coiled slowly in the air.

'Through here, please, m'sieu.'

The houseboy opened another door at the end of the path and Steele stepped forward.

It was the hall, cool and dusky after the heat outside, with a marble floor, whitewashed walls, a scattering of embroidered cushions, soft and opulent on the veined stone, and a low table – at its centre, floating in a jade bowl, a single blossom. Light filtered through intricate Moorish arches and on a patio beyond water was falling from a fountain onto turquoise tiles.

'Mr Wedderburn comes now, m'sieu.'

The Moroccan, young and graceful, padded away through one of the arches.

'Callum? I'm delighted to meet you. Wedderburn—'

He came in quickly, carpet slippers brushing on the marble, both hands outstretched in greeting.

'Quite excellent you're here. Vodka, I think, at this time of

46

day, don't you? Vodka, some fresh peach juice and lots of ice. Fouad—!'

He clapped his hands, the houseboy reappeared and Wedderburn spoke to him in Arabic.

'Right,' he turned back to Steele, 'and as there's usually a little breeze up here, why not out on the terrace?'

Steele followed him towards the fountain.

'From my hands you'll pass into his,' Greville again at the final briefing. *'We've dressed you as Callum, we've taught you the straits, we've given you an invisible shield. What we can't do is direct you once you arrive. He can. He knows more about the area than anyone alive. Trust him, consult him, do exactly what he says. He'll be your brain—'*

Greville had paused then, smiled vaguely and shaken his head.

'As our director down there he was actually Velatti's brain too.'

Steele watched him as he pulled two cane chairs into the shade of a magnolia tree.

Wedderburn. A big man with a fleshy choleric face, small eyes that almost disappeared in the sunlight, flared nostrils and thinning black hair without a trace of grey although he must have been over sixty. Rolls of fat bulged through a silk shirt at his stomach, but there was still massive strength in his neck muscles, in his sloping shoulders and heavy wrists.

Aging, powerful, handsome in a coarse masculine way – and something else, something Steele recognized instantly.

The subtle and delicate blend of the white flowers and silver leaves. The marbled hall with the cushions and the blossom in the jade bowl. The exquisitely-uniformed young Moroccan. Above all in something indefinable that came off him, in the feel of his hands when he greeted Steele, in an inflexion in his voice, in the set of his head as he gazed across the terrace.

Wedderburn was a homosexual. Not one of the effusive mincing variety but a different callous breed. The cultured English gentleman who might marry briefly to procreate but who took his pleasures greedily and sadistically in young boys – boys that in Tangier could be bought, used and discarded as cheaply and easily as the local cigarettes.

Looking at him Steele felt a quick instinctive dislike. Then a sudden sense of unease. Wedderburn, the man he was to trust above everyone else, wasn't only decadent. He was also, Steele guessed, unpredictable and dangerous.

'So there was a little trouble last night?'

Wedderburn leant forward. The houseboy had left the drinks on a table between them and Steele, dehydrated by the heat, was gulping thirstily from a tall icecold tumbler.

He stopped drinking as Wedderburn spoke.

'I got a load of blazing coals tipped over my head and an iron drum in my kidneys,' he said slowly, 'if that's a "little trouble", yes.'

Wedderburn waved his hand dismissively. 'All we're concerned with is Velatti and whatever else that episode doesn't fit the pattern of Velatti's behaviour. But I suggest you take it as a valuable lesson. Velatti isn't the only one with a grievance from the past. There must be a number of others equally anxious to see Callum dead.'

Steele hurled the rest of the drink into the bushes and put the glass down.

'I find that extremely comforting,' he said.

'And then this morning you started at the boatyard,' Wedderburn continued, ignoring him. 'What did you make of it?'

Steele didn't answer for a moment. Then he told him. The pervasive air of decay, Donovan with his gin bottle and his bluster, the launch tarnished, battered and crumbling.

Wedderburn nodded. 'Afterwards you went to the Minzah. You told surveillance control they were "civil" when you checked in. What exactly did you mean?'

Steele glanced up. He realized what was happening now. He was being tested just as Greville had tested him in London. Only the emphasis behind the questions had changed, changed totally.

Greville's interrogations had been obsessively concerned with the fantasy he'd created. For the little Major the idea of Callum was almost more important than the operation itself. Not out here. Steele had been handed on like a parcel. He was Wedderburn's property now and to Wedderburn Callum was utterly uninteresting – a device, a puppet. All Wedderburn cared about was how convincingly Steele would pirouette when he manipulated the strings.

Steele stared at him. He could feel the returning clench of anger at his chest. He wasn't even left with the dignity of impersonating a man. He'd been reduced to a strutting dummy carrying a target flag.

'I told them I was Callum and they gave me the best bloody room in the joint,' he snapped, 'that was all I meant.'

'Please—'

Wedderburn raised his hand. Then he brushed it across his head. His hair glistened with some dressing whose scent mingled with the smells from the garden.

'Remember you were briefed in London. But what London made of you may be rather different from the way people see you here in the straits. I know what they believed before and what they think now. You need all the protection and help I can give you. That means you're going to have to tell me everything – beginning with the reactions to your return.'

He paused.

Steele hesitated. Then he said curtly, 'Donovan accepted me without question. I guess it was the same at the hotel.'

'Excellent—'

Wedderburn rocked back, his hands bunched in the pockets of his shirt.

'And those are the only initiatives you've made so far?'

Steele frowned. 'Apart from agreeing to the repairs to the launch, yes.'

'What repairs?'

'Just the basic ones to get it seaworthy. I've still got to make out a schedule, but the girl looked competent,' Steele shrugged, 'I figured it was simpler than finding another yard.'

'Did you clear it with surveillance first?'

'No, it just seemed sensible.'

'Sensible—?'

Wedderburn heaved himself upright again, his voice suddenly harsh.

'What's sensible out here is what surveillance or I say. Nothing else. Something that seems a bright idea to you may not only lose us Velatti for good – it could cost you your life too. From now on you don't take a single decision without our sanction. Do you understand?'

He gazed at Steele across the table, small white patches flaring on his cheeks. Steele gripped the arms of his chair and dug his fingernails into the underside of the cane. Then he managed to control himself.

49

'Yes,' he said flatly.

Strangely for an instant he sensed there'd been more than anger in Wedderburn's outburst – there was something close to solicitude as well. He might be indifferent to Callum the invention, but it was almost as if he felt concern for Steele the man. Steele though of the liquid-eyed young houseboy and shivered involuntarily.

'An hour ago I had a call from the North Front—'

The tension had passed and Wedderburn was leaning back in the shadow.

North Front. Steele frowned. Then the name came back to him from the briefings. It was the headquarters of the British military base in Gibraltar.

'That was why I sent for you immediately.' Wedderburn went on, 'in addition to the main armoury they've got an auxiliary one attached to the ranges. Our people have access to it to practice for the annual classifications. This morning the weekly weapons inventory was carried out. They're missing a Browning 9mm automatic. The records sheets show it was issued to Velatti five days ago. That's only twenty-four hours before he disappeared. Somehow he must have smuggled it out with him when he left the armoury—'

Wedderburn pushed his glass away.

'No one knows of course exactly what he intends to do. But frankly we hadn't considered a handgun, let alone a 9mm. Its effective range is only a few yards. All the other options are still open to him but if he's planning on using the Browning, he'll virtually need you in the same room. It means the danger's no longer just in the open spaces, but in closed ones too—'

He stopped. Steele said nothing. Then Wedderburn stood up.

'Five days ago Velatti was in Gibraltar. For all we know he's still there. The whole of the straits is supposed to be your territory, but the Rock most of all. Take the early ferry over tomorrow. Visit the woman, show yourself, make your presence felt—'

He turned and Steele walked back with him across the terrace.

The noon sun was tracing rainbows in the water as it soared from the fountain, and carp were moving slowly in the turquoise bowl below – golden bodies shadowed by the leaves of floating lilies.

'Velatti has to be sure. Even the sight of you won't be enough.

50

Sooner or later he's going to drop a fly on the stream, a fly Callum would have risen to without hesitation. If you take it, he'll be convinced. Watch out for that fly, be ready for it any time, anywhere. Alert us as soon as it drops and we'll tell you how to pretend to swallow it. Afterwards we'll reel in the line from the other end – your end.'

Not only were Wedderburn's eyes very small, so was his mouth. A thin tight line in the florid face that barely moved when he smiled as he did then.

They were in the hall and Steele stared at him again.

Gibraltar in the morning. Not just because it was the first logical trip for Callum to make after his return – to his base, his mistress, his source of money. But because the little Maltese might be waiting there in the complex of narrow streets and alleyways, as warrenlike as the Tangier souk, with the Browning automatic he'd stolen from the North Front armoury.

Steele turned without speaking and walked through the garden to the street. As he opened the courtyard door he saw Wedderburn bend over the table behind him, remove the flower from the bowl and float a fresh blossom on the water.

The taxi was parked a few yards up the road. Steele got in and sat slumped low in the back, limp, sweating, his head barely showing above the window as they drove down to the harbour.

Fear. He'd held it back in Wedderburn's presence. Now it came in waves, total paralysing fear that numbed his brain and made even his limbs weak. He knew it and he let it wash over him unashamed. Not just the rifle, the long gun tracking him in the sunlight, but a revolver too, the short weapon waiting for him round every corner, levelled at him in every crowded street, from every shadowed doorway, even in the sanctuary of his room.

He reached for a cigarette, lit it, arms leaden on his chest and hands shaking, inhaled – and suddenly the fear had dissolved and his mind was functioning again.

Steele sat up very slowly.

Evening on the second night in the Battersea apartment, a flurry of cold rain against the windows, the lift clattering on the landing below, Greville's face prim with shock at a question from Steele – would he be given a gun before he left?

'Good heavens, no! In these days of international terrorism you'd be picked out by a metal detector before you even left

Heathrow. Besides, there isn't any need. I never saw guns as being Callum's style, but we left a pair on the launch as a general precaution. Even if we hadn't, it wouldn't have mattered. In Tangier, in any of the five ports, weapons are as much a normal commodity as bread or potatoes. You can buy them on any street corner.'

Steele drew on his cigarette.

Velatti had spent twelve years in the dirty area. He wouldn't have needed to risk stealing a weapon from the North Front armoury. If he wanted a handgun he'd have acquired it in the way Greville had described – on the nearest street corner.

Wedderburn had never had a call from Gibraltar. The whole story was a lie. Yet against all logic he'd deliberately set out to heighten Steele's fear of the little Maltese.

They reached the docks and swung right onto the coastal road. Steele gazed steadily through the windscreen. Every last trace of fear had gone now. Instead his mind was churning with bewilderment.

7

Six o'clock. The heat was still strong and humid but the air was already beginning to cool, and the light was translucent now as the sun lowered towards the Spanish shore – a distant mistline on the horizon.

Steele paid off the taxi and stood for a moment on the coastal road. Gulls were screaming and tumbling above the water, foam from the last hovercraft to Algeciras trailed in a screen of oyster-grey and rose across the bay, and the *Lara*'s silhouette hung crippled and tethered against the early evening sky.

Then he walked down towards the office. It was his third visit to the yard that day. The morning reconnaissance first. Another two hours in the afternoon with Donovan, when they'd compiled the schedule of repairs for the launch. Now, after a hurried shower at the Minzah and the call to surveillance control, who had no new instructions, he was back again to keep his appointment with Mary-Beth.

He pushed open the door of the inner cubicle. Donovan was behind the desk with a fresh bottle, already one third empty, in front of him.

'Can you do it?' Steele said.

He'd given Donovan three days to have all the repairs completed and the *Lara* in the water again.

'Sure we can do it. This time tomorrow and we'll have the yard humming like a top—'

Donovan waved expansively. Then he tipped back his head and gulped from the bottle.

When Steele had left him earlier he'd been in the trough of a hangover from the morning's celebration. Now he was on an alcoholic uplift again, his voice slurred and the liquor fumes thicker and ranker than ever. Yet there was something underpinning his confidence now, something that wasn't gin or even the prospect of money. Donovan's lucky charm had come back and he'd started to believe in the magic again.

'Here,' he pushed forward a pile of papers, 'three copies like you said. With the instrument replacements it comes to sixty thousand dirhams – in bucks say fifteen grand. Either way to the lady it's a whole new outfit and to you a goddam bargain.'

He chuckled.

Steele leant over the desk, checked through the estimates, signed them and put two copies in his pocket.

'Right,' Steele straightened up, 'just make sure you bring it in good and tight and clean like before. Where's Mary-Beth?'

'Down by the *Lara*. Listen—'

He struggled to his feet as Steele turned.

'She's a good kid, one hell of a good kid. But she's young, feeling her way around, learning the ropes, know what I mean? Now, you got anything important you want, you come straight to me—'

Donovan was still talking, wedged between the desk and the wall, when Steele walked out onto the jetty.

Mary-Beth was waiting for him by the cradle. She lifted her head, hair fanning out in the evening breeze, and smiled as he came up. She was still barefoot and Steele could smell the salt crusting her ankles again.

'Over to you,' he handed her a copy of the repair schedule.

Mary-Beth studied it and nodded. 'It's going to be tough in the time, but I reckon we can just about handle it.'

'And how did you make out?' Steele asked.

'Well, I've found you someone. He's waiting up in the cockpit now.'

'And a place too?'

She looked doubtful. 'Yes, but I don't figure you're going to like it much.'

'Let's take the driver first. Who is he?'

'He's called Marcel Hamid,' she said. 'A mix, a half-breed, French father, Arab mother – or that's his story. I met him when I was a kid at the Jesuit mission school over on Rue Dr Fleming. He'd been sponsored by some fat old priest across the bay. I guess he'd been using Marcel as a bedwarmer and wanted to stroke his conscience instead—'

Mary-Beth shrugged. 'It happens all the time here. Anyway, Marcel was maybe eighteen then, in his last semester, and he sort of looked after me. Walked me back when Don got smashed and forgot to collect me after class, that sort of thing. Later on, when he left school, he'd pitch up occasionally looking for work. If there was anything going I'd lean on Don to see he got it. Mainly because of what he'd done for me. But also because he's bright and gutsy and straight—'

She paused. 'You'd better see for yourself. At least he knows the *quartier* inside out.'

'And he wants the job?'

'You must be kidding!' Mary-Beth laughed. 'He's like all the rest round the docks. If he had any money he'd pay just to be able to say he worked for you.'

They climbed the gangplank. Marcel Hamid was standing by the steps to the wheelhouse. He stiffened as he saw them, holding himself awkwardly to attention, and flashed a nervous smile.

Steele studied him. He was small and scarecrow thin with dark olive skin, oily black hair and regular almost feminine features. A ragged fawn jacket, much too large for him with the sleeves covering his hands, hung down to his thighs, and a pair of equally outsize trousers – clerical black and probably a legacy from the priest – were knotted with string at his waist.

If his father really was French, no trace of a European ancestry had been passed onto Marcel. He had the face of the quintessential street Arab, the endless survivor, knowing, tireless, patient and amoral.

'So you're Marcel and you want to work for me,' Steele said finally.

'Yes sir.'

'Sit down.'

Steele lowered himself to the cockpit bench and Marcel dropped to his haunches.

'What can you do?'

'Anything, sir. Drive a car, cook couscous, wash clothes, show you all sights of Tangier—'

'I know all the bloody sights of Tangier.'

'Yes, sir,' the voice impassive, the English American-accented. 'I do anything, sir.'

'What do you know about boats?'

Marcel glanced quickly round the cockpit. 'I pretty good on engines, sir. Anything else I learn pretty damn fast.'

He tugged back his jacket sleeves and trailed his fingers on the boards. Squatting there, face expressionless, birdboned limbs jutting from the immense jacket and trousers, he looked like an organ-grinder's monkey resting in the shadow.

Steele thought for a moment. Then he said, 'I'll tell you a story, Marcel. When I was here before I had many Moroccan boys working for me. One day a man came to one of them. He wanted to know where I was, what I was doing, many things about me. He offered this boy money to tell him. The boy took the money and told him. Later I found out. Do you know Melouki beach?'

'Yes, sir.'

'Well, I put the boy on the *Lara* and we went round to the beach, about a mile offshore, and I asked the boy why he'd done that. The boy cried but he couldn't explain. In fact he cried so goddam much he fell off the boat. And you know what happens to people who fall into the sea off Melouki?'

'Sharks, sir.'

Steele nodded. 'Hammerheads that day. There were eighteen of them round the launch by the time they finished and it only took a minute. Afterwards the sea was red for fifty metres all round.'

Steele stopped. Marcel was watching him intently.

'You'd never forget a story like that, would you, Marcel?'

'Never, sir.'

'Good boy. You just got yourself a job. Ten dirhams a day, you sleep here on the boat and you do whatever I tell you. First off I want a car—'

Steele pulled out his wallet and tossed a charge card in Callum's name across the deck.

'Take it to the Agence Vartan on Rue de la Paix – it'll tell them who you're working for. Have them bring a Citroën DS VIII round to the Minzah tomorrow morning by eight sharp. You be there, too. Right?'

'Yes, sir.'

'And just so you don't forget,' Steele took a fifty dirham note from his wallet, folded it in four and flicked it over, 'that's to remind you – about sharks!'

Steele gave a roar of laughter, Marcel gazed at him, uncer-

56

tainly, then he started to laugh too – hesitantly at first but afterwards with more and more confidence until he suddenly bounded to his feet and scuttled away down the gangplank.

Steele watched him run along the jetty. He could have grilled the little Arab for an hour but he'd still have known no more about him. Instead he'd flatly disobeyed Wedderburn's instructions, acted on impulse, threatened Marcel with an outrageous story and then hired him for a far higher salary than was necessary.

He turned back towards Mary-Beth grinning. For an instant he'd almost felt he was Callum.

'You did fine,' he said. 'I liked the look of the little guy. Now what have you found me in Ligiers?'

She frowned. 'I just hope it's what you want. If not I've blown another fifty of your dirhams. We can check it out, it's only a few minutes walk.'

Steele glanced at the shore.

The light was fading fast now and lamps were already glowing in the buildings huddled against the coastal road, but he could still make out figures on the highway. Somewhere up there were two men on scooters, another in a 2CV van, a fourth in an old Simca and a fifth at the fixed observation post. Five of them and all waiting to lock onto him again as soon as he walked up from the yard.

He turned back. 'We'll wait until it's good and dark. There could be people up there who'd come along for the stroll without asking for an invitation.'

Mary-Beth looked at him puzzled but didn't say anything. Steele waited a quarter of an hour. Then in the gathering dusk they walked back.

The office was empty. Steel stepped inside and glanced round. There were dustcoated rollblinds above the windows which apparently hadn't been used for years. He reached over, pulled at a cord and to his surprise the blind clattered down. Then he did the same with the others and the office was sealed. Anyone watching it now would only see oblongs of cloudy light.

'Go out casually as if you were going home,' he said to Mary-Beth, 'cross the highway and wait for me a hundred yards west on the other side.'

She nodded, slipped on a pair of sandals and disappeared.

Steele gave her five minutes. Then he went out again. It was fully dark now and on the road above the headlamp beams of the traffic were patterning the dusty air with swordsblades of brilliance. He bent double, edged round the side of the platform, jumped down to the shore and still crouching, hidden by the concrete parapet that separated the sea from the land, paced out a hundred yards to the west.

He checked, waited for a solitary car, jumped up as it passed and ran across the road behind the dazzle of its lamps. Unless anyone had infra-red glasses trained on the yard they'd assume he was still inside the office.

Mary-Beth was standing within a few feet of him on the far pavement.

'Right,' Steele said, 'let's go.'

She led him through a maze of cobbled streets, the air thick with the smells of garbage and hashish, across two crowded squares and into an alleyway. Midway along the alleyway she stopped at the open doorway of a large dilapidated house.

The building was late nineteenth-century French, ornate and imposing once but reduced now to a shell of damp crumbling plaster and rotting beams. Peering inside Steele saw a hall littered with filth and hung with lines of drying clothes. Arab music wailed monotonously from transistors behind every door, a charcoal fire glowed on a landing above the circular stairs, children screamed and occasional flitting shapes, veiled women or jellabahed men, moved through the darkness.

'It's a boarding-house for migrant workers from the south,' Mary-Beth said. 'I heard about it from a friend.'

She looked at him defensively but Steele waved her on. They climbed the stairs to the second floor, walked round the landing and Mary-Beth produced a key.

'This is it,' she said.

She unlocked the door and Steele went in.

There were two tiny rooms opening into each other with a curtained-off cooking area and a washbasin and WC at the far end. The only furniture consisted of three rush chairs, a table fashioned out of tea chests and a scarlet velveteen couch leaking nylon stuffing. A low-wattage lamp glowed by the window and the rancid stench from the hall below pervaded everything.

Steele walked over to the cooking area, inspected the caked dirt in the basin and put his head through into the compartment that housed the WC. He withdrew it instantly, choking and swallowing.

'I'm sorry, but I warned you.'

Mary-Beth was still defensive.

'Sorry, hell!' Steele grinned as the spasm of coughing passed. 'It's ideal. All it needs is a guy with a gasmask, a scrubbing brush and a ten-gallon can of disinfectant.'

'There's Marcel—'

He shook his head. 'Not Marcel, not anyone who knows I've got anything to do with the place.'

'I'll get in the old Moroccan cleaning lady from home. She looked after me when I was a kid. She'll do anything without asking. I even borrowed her ID card to rent the place.'

'Clever woman!'

Steele tapped her on the shoulder and she smiled. He glanced round once more. Then they went downstairs again.

Mildew, dirt, drifting smells, music echoing behind walls, shadowy silhouettes on the landings. How many identical houses had he known over the years? He couldn't even count them now. The others might have been in London suburbs rather than a Tangier slum, with the clinging odour of boiled cabbage instead of hashish and a truculent Mrs Martin for the veiled old crone they passed on the way out.

Yet the instinct which had made him choose them all was the same. The instinct of a wounded animal for privacy and safety. This place was safe too.

Steele had taken the decision to find somewhere as soon as he walked ashore. It was a habit of living that had become embedded like coal dust in the seams of his mind. He still had no idea what he'd need the rooms for, but they were there now – a burrow, a bolt hole, a lair. Not just against Velatti. The threat of Velatti, with a long or a short gun, had been constant from the start.

Now there was also Wedderburn and his lies. They were new – and baffling.

'Right—'

He stepped onto the narrow street, deliberately shutting out the inexplicable story he'd been told in the white and silver garden with the water chiming in the fountain's bowl.

'To celebrate I'm going to buy you a drink. Where are we going to go?'

'Tangier's mainly dry—'

Mary-Beth broke off and laughed. 'Jesus, I keep forgetting. You know more about this town that I do.'

'That was five years ago. Where's the action now?'

She thought for a moment. 'There's a bar on the front, Jimmy's, not far from where you met up with me. A bunch of the travel and charter guys use it, and the *ambiente*'s usually good.'

Ambiente. Another phrase that until two days ago Steele had never heard.

Now, one more piece of mosaic in the endless briefings, he knew exactly what it meant. 'Atmosphere, colour, what the youngsters call good vibes,' one of Greville's team had pedantically explained. 'It comes from the Spanish and it's entered the lingua franca of the straits.'

'If it's got *ambiente*,' Steele said, 'then it gets our custom.'

The bar was raftered, gabled and hung with carriage lanterns, horse brasses and sporting prints. A tawdry imitation of a British country pub except that the waiters wore jellabahs and the predominant liquor smells weren't warm bitter and stout but Riccardi, Byrrh and Pernod – as always in Tangier the overlay of France imprinting everything from the cars to the architecture to the drink.

They pushed their way through the throng by the counter and found an empty table at the back. Steele started to ask her what she wanted but Mary-Beth cut him off.

'Look, this isn't one of Don's stupid stories,' she'd reddened slightly, 'it's for real. When the *Lara* was towed into the yard, I made myself a promise. I said if Ross Callum ever came back I'd buy him his first drink.'

She stopped. She was smiling, half-embarrassed and totally determined.

Steele grinned. 'Can the returning wayfarer start with a beer?'

'Long and cold with a whisky to follow? Sure, I'll get it myself.'

She disappeared into the crowd. Steele sat back and gazed across the room.

'So you're Ross Callum—'

A hand on the table, a deep tight voice, a figure leaning forward from behind Steele, a wave of brandy fumes.

'Why don't you stand up and say hullo?'

Steele swung himself slowly round in his chair and glanced up.

The man was large, very large, close to six foot four and weighing over two hundred pounds. A crumpled yachting cap was pulled down over his forehead, shadowing a square grey-stubbled chin, sweat coursed across his shoulders and his T-shirt was strained tight over bulging arm-muscles.

Steele looked back at him levelly. He knew the type, he'd known it ever since he first sailed out of a west country harbour. It was what Donovan pretended to be and failed. The old seadog, shrewd, proud, hickory-tough and belligerent. There was a difference between this one and Donovan. This one was for real – and he was blind fighting drunk.

'I'm sorry, I don't believe we've met before,' Steele said.

'Kirby. Jack Kirby.'

The man paused. The name was obviously meant to register on Steele. It didn't. For the first time Greville's meticulous briefing was inadequate.

Steele frowned. 'I've been away a long time, Mr Kirby—'

'Don't you fucking "mister" me, Callum—'

The man's other hand smashed down on the table. At the bar the sound of conversation and laughter died away.

'And don't you pretend you don't know either. The *Bernice*? The *Lochinver*? Remember them? Well, they're mine – or they were.'

Kirby stopped again. Steele was still bewildered. The *Bernice* and the *Lochinver*. Boats' names clearly, which should have reminded him of something even if Kirby's name didn't – except there was still no connection. This was a gap in Callum's past, unmapped, without reference point or bearing.

'Look, you'll have to excuse me,' Steele said, 'either my memory's listing badly or you're mixing me with someone else.'

'Don't give me that shit—!'

Kirby's knuckles whitened. He was incoherent now, goaded by Steele's calm and trapped in his own inarticulateness.

Steele didn't move. He knew that if he could sit it out for another minute or two the man's rage might ebb. It didn't. There was a half-full glass of beer on the next table. Kirby suddenly seized it and threw the liquid in Steele's face. Steele sat for an instant with the beer trickling down his chin. Then, as he started to push back his chair, Kirby gripped his shirt and started to shake him from side to side.

'You cheap bastard!' He was shouting. 'You dirty thieving bastard!'

Steele's stomach churned. Until then all he'd felt were charges of adrenalin fuelling his alertness. Now there were hot surges of anger. He braced himself, steepled his hands, drove them upwards and swept them out. As Kirby's arms were forced apart Steele heard his shirt tearing. Then he was on his feet and free.

Kirby was staggering but it would only be for a moment. Six four, two hundred pounds and murderous now. Steele glanced at the door, a rickety frame in the oak-varnished pasteboard wall. What he needed was space, not the narrow confines of the bar. He turned back, saw Kirby coming at him and butted him in the nose. There was a grunt of pain and blinding tears welled in Kirby's eyes. As he shook his head sightlessly Steele grabbed his arm, pivoted him round and launched him across the floor.

They hit the door together. The frame buckled, the panels caved outwards with a splintering crash, a section of the wall was wrenched away, and they were outside in the darkness. A baked earth yard, stars glittering overhead, light spilling from the shattered doorway, people thronging out to watch, a voice somewhere calling, 'For Christ's sake, someone telephone the *Garde Mobile*!'

Steele barely noticed. Kirby was in front of him, half-crouching, sobered by the butt to his face and the cooler air, clenched fists held forward from his body. A thread of blood ran down from his nostrils, his eyes were narrowed and furious, and on the shadowy earth he looked even larger than inside, awesomely menacingly large.

'You're going to learn something,' Steele said. 'You're going to learn to watch your language in front of ladies – and in front of me.'

He kicked a piece of board away from his feet, stepped forward, feinted low with his left hand and hit Kirby with a fast clipping right to the side of his neck. Kirby choked, stumbled, recovered his balance and lashed back at him. Steele rocked sideways, slipped inside his arm and began jolting him with both hands to the belly.

Steele didn't know how long it lasted. Three minutes, five, ten, it could have been more or less. He was dimly aware of faces ringing the walls, voices whispering, the stars wheeling across the night sky. But dominating everything there was Kirby. The man's strength was vast, he was fighting with a brutal unremitting intensity and he used every weapon at his disposal, knees, feet, elbows, teeth, even jagged fragments of wood that he'd pluck from the ground and stab at Steele's groin.

They crossed and recrossed the yard and once Steele thought he was trapped. His foot slipped, he fell to his knees, Kirby's massive weight bore down on him and he began to topple. Then he managed to plunge sideways, wriggle free as Kirby swore, lever himself up and hit out again – in the open, in the space that he needed. There, younger, faster, lighter, it was different and he began to beat Kirby savagely and systematically, jabbing again and again at his face until his lips were slashed, blood was pumping from his nose and his eyes were almost invisible behind great swelling bruises.

And finally Kirby started to go, gasping, swaying, reeling as he tried to follow Steele in the dark, until at the end he sank helpless to the earth, arms limp by his sides and head slumped on his chest, only some last defiant effort of will preventing him from falling prone. Steele stood above him, shaking and panting. Kirby offered no resistance, made no move. He just huddled there immobile with his head bowed.

'Did anyone come with this man?'

Steele looked across at the watching crowd. There were shuffles, murmurs, a stir, and then someone was pushed forward. A young man in jeans and a faded singlet, white-faced and frightened.

'You work for Kirby?'

The young man nodded nervously, ready instantly to bolt.

'Then you take him home. Tomorrow evening I'll be at the *Lara*. If he's got a grievance you tell him he can come and explain it to me then. If it's real, if I'm satisfied, he'll be paid what he's owed. But you tell him too that he'd better come sober and polite – and that goes for anyone else on the front who wants to speak to me.'

Steele wiped his face, feeling sweat and blood mingle over his own bruises. Then he turned and walked out of the yard. A *Garde Mobile* car was roaring up the coastal road, siren wailing and red light flashing on the roof. He ignored it. If the police wanted to see him, they could come tomorrow like Kirby.

He crossed the road, went down to the parapet, climbed it wearily and walked along the shore until he was a few yards from the jetty. The light was still burning in Donovan's office and the hawsers round the *Lara* grated as the launch rocked on the cradle in the night wind. Steele waited for a moment. Then he stepped down the shelving beach and waded into the sea until the water reached his waist.

He stood there with the small waves lapping against him, sluicing water over his face, feeling the salt sting harsh on the grazed skin, breathing deeply as his lungs expelled the lingering smells of brandy, sweat and dust. All day there'd been nothing except tension, uncertainty and a constant exhausting wariness. Suddenly the fatigue had drained away and instead he felt buoyant, relaxed, almost lightheaded.

Steele tore off the tattered remnants of his shirt and laughed. Not Callum – but a passable imitation even with two hundred pounds of drunken aggressive bully in a waterfront bar.

'Are you all right?'

A voice, Mary-Beth's voice, coming from behind him. Steele turned and saw the shimmer of her white T-shirt on the beach.

'Jesus Christ! I'm sorry, I forgot all about you.'

'I'm not surprised. Let's have a look.'

He waded ashore and she inspected him in the starlight, reaching out and touching the bruises with her fingers lightly, almost professionally.

'You were lucky or maybe just good,' she said. 'Some iodine, shades for a couple of days and there won't be a trace.'

'Who's Kirby?' Steele asked as they walked up to the jetty. 'And what the hell was that all about?'

'Kirby's got a yard like Don only it's over on the other side. He's supposed to be into the Spanish run, shifting liquor and cigarettes out of Gib onto the mainland, but I don't know what he's got against you. I was going to ask round after you dropped him but the police arrived and I figured it was better to cut out. Whatever it is I don't reckon he'll try that again.'

They went into the office. The second bottle of gin was empty and Donovan had passed out, lying snoring in a stupor across the desk. Mary-Beth tilted him back in his chair, put a cushion behind his head and turned him away from the light.

'He'll sleep through to morning now,' she said as she opened a battered first aid chest, 'he always does. Sit here where I can get at you.'

Steele propped himself on the desk, leant forward and winced as she dabbed his forehead with iodine. When he looked up Mary-Beth was rummaging in a wall cabinet. She pulled out a shortsleeved blue shirt and handed it to him.

'It's Don's,' she said. 'I always keep a couple here although in his case now it's mostly for when he's thrown up.'

Steele shrugged the shirt over his head. It bagged at the waist but it was clean and fairly new. By the time he'd tucked it into his belt Mary-Beth was holding a hairbrush.

Steele smiled. 'You should set up in business – full valet and aftercare service to the world's best bar-room brawlers.'

'I grew up here,' she smiled back. 'I've been seeing things like that, and clearing up afterwards, since I was a kid. Even Don until a couple of years ago. He'd go out on a Friday night and someone would haul him back looking like a truck had parked on his face. Believe me, I've handled much worse.'

Steele brushed his hair and glanced in a cracked and mottled mirror by the cabinet. Mary-Beth was right. Apart from some puffiness in his cheeks and a few abrasions round his eyes, which dark glasses would hide, it was difficult to tell he'd been in a fight.

He turned round. 'Thanks, and I really mean it. And, hell, in all that tangle you never even got your drink. Well, when you do collect it's going to be a double and on me.'

Steele smiled again and moved towards the door. It was nine o'clock and he was hungry, but first he wanted to telephone. By now surveillance must have discovered they'd lost him and something had happened. They'd be demanding an explanation. Steele didn't care a damn about that. All he wanted to know was what Kirby had against him and whether there were any other unexploded mines in Callum's past he hadn't been told about.

'Mr Callum—'

Steele stopped. 'Ross, please.'

'Yes. Look, I wonder if you'd do something for me—'

Mary-Beth hesitated. She was looking at him intently and her voice had changed, no longer casual and friendly but serious and uncertain.

'There's a friend of mine, a man. He wants to see you very

badly.'

'A man?' Steele stiffened, 'What's his name?'

'He's Portuguese, he's called Adolpho Gonsalves.'

'Gonsalves—'

The name meant nothing to him. Steele stood there for a moment. All the buoyancy of a few minutes earlier had gone, and he felt the icy knots against his ribs again. Then he pulled out the photograph and showed it to her.

'You're quite sure he isn't also known as Velatti,' he spoke slowly and emphatically, 'and he looks like this?'

Mary-Beth glanced at the photograph and shook her head instantly.

'That's nothing like him. Adolpho's much older, he's got white hair, he's completely different.'

'Have you ever seen this man or heard the name Velatti?'

'Never. Why?'

She was frowning at him bewildered now. Steele gazed steadily back. There was nothing in her face, in her wide green flecked eyes, except puzzlement.

Finally Steele put the photograph away. He'd trusted her before and he believed her now. Mary-Beth knew nothing about Velatti.

'If you ever do see him,' he said, 'or even hear his name mentioned, you find me immediately, wherever I am, and you tell me, right?'

Mary-Beth nodded.

'Okay, so why does this friend of yours want to see me?'

She hesitated again. 'It'd be better if he explained himself.'

'Can you bring him to me here or at the Minzah?'

'No,' another pause and another frown, 'it would mean going to him, I'd take you there. It's difficult, well, it could be dangerous for him if anyone saw him – particularly with you.'

'Jesus, Mary-Beth,' Steele shook his head. 'Listen, when I was here before I made a bundle of friends but also a whole crew of enemies. Some of them I don't even know, hell, you saw that tonight. You're asking me to go somewhere private to meet someone who wants to see me for reasons you're not saying, and who sounds as if he could get me into a load of trouble too. That's asking a lot.'

'I know, but I'll go right down the line for Adolpho. He's a

66

friend, the best. You'll like him.'

The uncertainty had gone and she was totally confident.

'You'll like him' – not Steele but Callum. For an instant looking at her, candid, determined, trusting, Steele felt like shouting that he wasn't Callum, there'd never been a Callum, the image she had of him was constructed from a web of lies, deceit and fantasy.

He restrained himself and instead he said abruptly, 'I'll let you know tomorrow.'

Steele went out, crossed the road and started searching for a callbox. Dimly he thought he heard a motor scooter's engine whirring to life. He paid it no attention. There were names to check up on, not one now but two, and he wasn't even very interested in Kirby any longer.

Steele wanted to know about an old whiteheaded Portuguese who needed to see him so badly and who was apparently frightened for his life. A man who, even if Mary-Beth didn't know it, might be a fly dropped on the water.

8

'Yes?'

She was wearing a housecoat, pale-blue, crumpled, beltless, the two sides held together by one hand across her waist.

'Callum,' Steele said quietly.

She responded instantly. A smile replacing the yawn, eyes, dulled a moment before with sleep, opening in delight, a hand stretching out and touching, caressing his cheek, a quick excited exclamation of pleasure. Everything so fast, so natural, so apparently spontaneous that no one watching – if there had been anyone – would have registered the brief hiatus of blank unrecognition.

'All right—'

Steele had reached for her, put his arms round her waist, swung her inside and kicked the door shut behind him. Now she moved away from him, shaking her head and yawning again.

'What time is it?'

'Ten-thirty.'

'Christ, couldn't you have waited until later?' Her voice was brittle and irritable. 'Oh, the hell with it. Put the kettle on anyway, it's through there.'

She pointed at a door and disappeared into what Steele guessed was her bedroom.

The hall was cramped and dusky after the sunlight in the street, but the kitchen was large and white with a window looking down across the north side of Gibraltar over the bay of Algeciras. Steele spotted the kettle behind a mound of unwashed plates and cutlery. He plugged it in. There was grease in the sink, a heap of dirty laundry on the floor and a bottle of gin, two-thirds empty, on the draining-board beside a lipstick-smudged glass.

'The coffee's on the shelf,' she called out, 'make it strong and black for me with plenty of sugar. If you want tea there's some in an old mustard tin somewhere. I'm going to take a shower.'

Steele heard the sound of running water. He moved the gin bottle – at least it was Gordon's and not Donovan's gasolene-scented brand – found a couple of mugs, their insides rimmed with dried sugar and coffee grounds, and began to wash them up.

Tangier at dawn had been grey, misty and briefly chill. Two hours later, when Marcel arrived at the hotel in a cream-coloured Citroën with an obsequious representative from the hire agency, the mist had lifted and the air was already warm with the heat of the coming day. Steele signed for the car and set off for the harbour to catch the Gibraltar hydrofoil.

The trip up the straits had taken fifty minutes, the boat planing high and fast over the emerald green morning sea. Somewhere among Steele's fellow passengers – tourists, businessmen and Spaniards visiting relatives on the Rock – was a member of the surveillance screen. For a while Steele tried to identify him in the crowded saloon. Then he gave up and sat watching the pale summer-dried hills of the Spanish coast.

It wasn't important that he didn't know what the man looked like. All that mattered was that he was there. After yesterday Steele had no doubt about that. The man had been behind him throughout the trip and then, joined by others when the hydrofoil docked, he'd followed Steele up the streets of the Rock to the home of Callum's mistress.

'You found the kettle?'

Steele turned. She'd come into the kitchen, still wearing the housecoat but fully awake now after the shower.

'God, I could do with that,' she picked up the cup of coffee Steele had made for her and gulped it down. 'Pour me another, would you?'

Steele spooned some more coffee into her cup and filled it with boiling water. Then he watched her as she sipped it, more slowly this time.

Louise Freitas, thirty-four, small and delicately-boned with violet eyes and dark curling hair, glistening now with drops of water. A drinker, Steele could see that, not just from the evidence of the gin bottle but in the shadowed cheeks, the slack down-pulling lines at her mouth, the smell that came off her skin. Yet pretty too in spite of the damage wrought by the alcohol,

69

almost beautiful with a fragile raddled sensuality.

According to Greville she was the only person outside the Callum team who knew the truth about her supposed lover. Looking at her Steele sensed something familiar, something he half-recognized. Suddenly he realized what it was. Her face was period, wartime, a face from an old movie set in blacked out nightclubs with air-raids and falling bombs, chance encounters and bitter final partings, a face that was defiantly chic and cynical but helplessly vulnerable too.

She could only have been a tiny child when the war ended. Yet deliberately or by accident Greville had chosen her as Callum's mistress, a woman who even thirty years later might still have just walked straight off the screen of Bogart's *Casablanca* – a woman who now belonged to Steele.

Steele shivered, lifted his cup and drank.

'Have you got a cigarette?'

He nodded and produced a pack of Camels.

'So Ross Callum's finally come back?' She coughed, wrinkling her nose over the smoke. 'And this time you're the lucky one?'

'Right.'

'Why the hell do they need him again now?' Still coughing she tapped some ash into a saucer. 'Christ, don't bother. You wouldn't tell me and I wouldn't want to know anyway—'

Steele had brought a package with him, a small square parcel wrapped in glossy paper and tied with a gaudy metallic thread. She noticed it lying on the table, paused and picked it up.

'What's this?'

'They told me to bring you something,' Steele said.

'Told you?' She smiled, 'Wouldn't it be lovely, amazing, if one day someone brought me something without actually being told? Shit—!'

She shook her head quickly and unwrapped the parcel. Inside a leather covered box, nestling on a satin bed, was a bracelet, cut and polished ovals of dark jade linked by a lace filigree of silver.

'Where did you get it?'

She was holding the bracelet up and twisting it against the light.

'Lisbon,' Steele said. 'They routed me through there on the way in. I paid a couple of hundred pounds. The man wanted three but I told him I was catching the boat and I hadn't got time to haggle.'

'Lisbon. Well, at least thank God for that—'

Louise buckled the bracelet round her wrist and tossed its leather covered box under the sink.

'It's quite pretty, it's smart, it's even fairly well-designed. It's also junk, worth about ten pounds at the most. The jade's synthetic, the silver's plated and the leather on that box is plastic. If you'd bought it here, the jeweller would either have thought Ross Callum had gone soft in the head while he'd been away – or he was dealing with someone else, someone who couldn't tell rubbish from the real thing.'

Steele flushed. 'I'm sorry.'

She shrugged. 'Save yourself the bother, I don't give a damn. I was thinking about you—'

She stopped and looked at him curiously, 'You know, somehow you don't look like one of them. Who are you?'

Steele, his cheeks still hot, didn't answer.

'All right, never mind,' Louise yawned and glanced at the clock on the wall. 'I'll call the Rock Hotel and get them to send over a couple of bottles of bubbly and some caviare.'

'Caviare?'

'Christ, you really are different, aren't you? A real country boy,' she laughed. 'Didn't they tell you about me?'

'There wasn't much time,' Steele said defensively.

Any confidence he'd briefly felt the previous evening had long since gone and the flushes kept returning.

'Well, I'm a fallen woman, that's what I am. A fallen woman of extravagant tastes which Ross Callum can happily afford to indulge in return for a few – services. And caviare happens to be one of my weaknesses.'

The telephone was in the hall. Louise went out, made the call and came back. Her mug was half empty. She rummaged on the shelf, found a brandy flask and tipped its contents into what was left of her coffee.

'At least you can tell me your name, can't you?'

She was inspecting him carefully as she drank, the colour returning to her cheeks with the brandy.

'Steele,' he said.

'And is that real or did they dye it on like they did with the ones before?'

71

For a moment Steele didn't understand what she meant. Then he saw she was looking at his hair.

'It's real.'

'My God, where did they find you?' She laughed again, not with hostility or scorn but a private amused laugh. 'A man called Steele with some plastic junk, weak knees at the thought of ordering caviare for his fancy-lady, and yet proper bright red hair – and he's not even one of them.'

The laughter stopped. She finished the brandy-spliced coffee. Then she asked, 'How long are you going to be around?'

'A week at most.'

'Well, you'd better see the geography.'

Steele followed her into the hall. There were only three other rooms. Louise's bedroom at the end of a passage, a bathroom beyond it and a little sliproom opposite the kitchen.

'I'll make up a bed for you there,' she gestured at a couch in the sliproom, 'that's what we used to do – Christ, how long ago is it now?'

'Five years.'

'The keys are still here anyway,' she handed him a set from a hook by the door. 'There are two locks, mortice and Yale. I always lock them both when I go out.'

'What about friends?' Steele asked.

'Friends?' She looked at him puzzled.

'I mean, is anyone likely to call round?'

'Oh, Jesus!' She laughed and this time there was only bitterness in the sound. 'No, no one's likely to come here – or if they do, it'll be by mistake.'

Steele glanced at the telephone. 'Can I use that?'

'You pay the bills, sir,' she gave a little bow and turned away. 'I'm going to get dressed.'

Steele dialled. The surveillance monitor answered, he identified himself, then a moment later he heard Wedderburn's voice on the line. He must have been transferred direct from the travel agency to the villa on the hill.

'What the hell happened last night?'

Wedderburn sounded angry and suspicious. Steele visualized him standing in the marble floored hall with the jasmine floating in the bowl on the table and the houseboy waiting silently behind.

'I've already explained—'

'You explained nothing,' Wedderburn interrupted him. 'You called at nine to leave two names with control. That was after you'd vanished for an hour. Three men were waiting for you on the coastal highway. You couldn't have crossed it without them seeing you unless you'd intended to. What were you doing?'

'I wasn't doing anything, for Christ's sake. I just wanted to find a drink and they must have missed me—'

'You're a fool,' Wedderburn cut him off again, 'a bloody fool. Try that once more and you're likely to wind up in a gutter with a bullet through the back of your head, understand?'

Steele didn't answer. Wedderburn didn't believe him, but there was nothing he could do about it.

'And there was someone driving your car this morning,' Wedderburn went on, 'who was he?'

'A Moroccan. He's called Marcel Hamid, he's working for me.'

'You took him on without checking?'

'I took him on because I needed him.'

'Listen, Callum,' the fury in Wedderburn's voice was edged with menace now, 'I'm warning you for the final time. You're here under Article 49. If you take one more decision on your own, I'll see you're pulled straight out, sent back and charged before a court martial. Is that clear?'

Steele smashed the palm of his hand against the wall. The blackmail again, the ancient blackmail that was still potent here in the heat at the southern end of Europe. And once more he was helpless against it.

He breathed out slowly. 'Yes.'

'Right,' Wedderburn's tone changed slightly. 'Those two names you left with control. Kirby isn't important. He bought two short haul freighters for a contract he was told he'd be given. At the last moment the contract went to someone else. He thought Callum was responsible.'

'Judging from last night he still does,' Steele said.

'He's got a British passport, the Consul's seeing him today, he won't cause any more trouble,' Wedderburn paused, 'Gonsalves is different. He's interesting—'

The name hadn't registered with surveillance control when Steele called the night before, but it obviously meant something to Wedderburn now.

'A leftwing Portuguese politician with a big following in the

. 73

south, in the rural areas. He was active in the underground opposition to the Salazar and Caetano regimes, but in the past few years since the revolution nothing much has been heard of him.'

'Then what's he suddenly doing in Tangier?' Steele asked. 'Why should he want to see me, why's he so goddam scared, and most of all – what's it got to do with Velatti?'

'We don't know,' Wedderburn said, 'but Callum would certainly have found out.'

It was a test, that was what Wedderburn was suggesting, a test that could equally well be a trap – and all Steele had as protection was Mary-Beth's untried word for the old Portuguese.

'So you want me to check it out?'

'I want you to be very careful indeed,' Wedderburn answered.

The solicitude of yesterday was back in his voice now and once again Steele found it even more unsettling than the anger.

'I'll be in touch,' Steele snapped.

He put the telephone down.

Gonsalves a well known politician and Wedderburn, who was meant to know everything that happened in the straits, couldn't answer the simplest questions about him – why he might be there, why he was so afraid, why he wanted Callum. Steele didn't believe him, he didn't even believe him about Kirby. But then he'd stopped believing him about anything on the drive down from his villa.

The man he was to trust more than anyone else. Steel swore violently under his breath. Then he went back into the kitchen.

Louise, dressed now, was making desultory efforts to clear up the mess round the sink. She'd put on high-heeled silver sandals, the silver painted on over black leather which showed through in places where the paint had scuffed away, a long soft full skirt and a low off-the-shoulder blouse edged with lace ruffles.

The effect was feminine, pretty, slightly blowsy and above all once more unmistakably period – the texture and style of the forties.

'So what are we going to do, to pass the time, I mean?' She rinsed a dirty plate under the tap and put it in the rack, 'One of the ones before was marvellous at patience, he knew all sorts of variations I'd never heard of. We used to play two-handed for hours, Demon's Delight I think it was called—'

74

The doorbell rang, interrupting her. She glanced over her shoulder and frowned.

Then she added, 'It must be the champagne. You sign for it by the way, if you didn't know. Nothing so vulgar as cash for the great Mr Callum.'

Steele went to the street door. A delivery boy was standing outside with a large package.

'Mr Callum?'

Steele nodded. 'That's right.'

'Compliments of the Rock Hotel, sir.'

Steele took the package and said, 'Give me the bill and I'll sign.'

'No, sir,' the boy shook his head beaming, 'from the management, sir, to say welcome back.'

Steele hesitated for a moment. Then he put his hand in his pocket and pulled out a five-pound note.

'Give my thanks to them – and that's for you.'

The boy nodded happily and Steele closed the door. He took the package into the kitchen and put it on the table.

'Well, what are you waiting for?' Louise came over from the sink. 'Aren't we going to celebrate?'

'Yes, sure.'

Steele opened the package, awkwardly uncorked one of the bottles inside, still cold and beaded with water from the hotel icebox, and poured the champagne into two glasses which Louise produced.

'Cheers!'

Louise lifted her glass and drank. Steele drank in return. The label on the bottle was Veuve Cliquot and the wine was clean and dry. He guessed the hotel had given him the best they had.

'Here, pour us another. You can't beat the old Widow, can you? And where's that caviare? While the bastards are paying, let's enjoy it—'

She lifted out a pottery jar, broke a wax seal and unscrewed the lid. Then she trailed her finger across the surface and delicately licked the oily black grains from her skin.

'Just as it should be, real Beluga! How shall we have it? I haven't got any onions but there's some bread and a lemon somewhere—'

She'd looked up as she was speaking. Now she broke off, gazed at Steele, reached forward and touched his face.

'What's that? I didn't notice it before.'

Her fingers were resting on a bruise above his eye.

Steele shrugged. 'I bumped into a door last night.'

'You bumped into a door!' She knew what he meant. 'When did you arrive?'

'Yesterday morning.'

'And you're new out here from home, aren't you? It's the first time?'

He nodded.

'Jesus Christ!' She shook her head slowly. 'They really are bastards, aren't they? I mean not just to me, though God knows they've screwed me up enough. But to pick on someone like you, someone who obviously doesn't have a bloody clue, and then drop them right in at the deep end without caring a shit whether they can even swim, and believe me they don't care—'

She paused, still staring at him, finger to her mouth as she licked off the last of the caviare.

'Where did they find you, Steele, and what are they trying to make you do?'

Steele stood up and walked to the window.

Below a British destroyer was nudging its way into the naval dockyards, white ensign fluttering against the sea, and above it great golden-brown birds, eagles he thought, were rising in slow circles on the morning thermals.

'There's a man called Velatti—'

Steele turned and told her.

Not everything but the outline in short flat phrases. That he'd been a soldier once. That recklessly, mindlessly, he'd done something which years later had allowed them to blackmail him back into service as Callum – the fantasy they'd been forced to resurrect as bait for the little Maltese.

The room could have been bugged. He could have been wrong about Louise's own hostility towards them. It might have been an act to test him. Steele didn't know. All he knew was that once again he had to gamble. There were too many pressures crowding in, too many lies on every side. At one level he had to believe in what he was told. In Greville, Wedderburn and the surveillance screen. They were his safety net and he was tied to them as if by an umbilical cord.

76

Yet on another deeper level he believed in nothing any longer. Nothing except Velatti. Velatti was the one constant factor in the equation, the sole figure Steele accepted without qualification. He'd seen in Kirby the bitter antagonisms Callum had been capable of arousing. Velatti was even more bitter, more obsessed with vengeance. He'd wait, watch Steele, track him, and then when he was certain he'd try to kill him.

If Steele was going to survive, he had to trust. First Mary-Beth, now Louise, maybe even others too. Not sure yet why he needed them, except they didn't belong to the department. Because whatever else, Louise was right. In the end the others didn't care. They were alternately encouraging and frightening him. Encouraging him so Steele wouldn't lose his nerve. Frightening him so he'd hurry, so the contact would be made, because only then would it be over and he'd be safe.

Even that wasn't important. Velatti meant too much. If the price of finding him was Steele's death, it was of no consequence – compared to Velatti Steele was expendable.

'And they could really get you again after all that time?'

Louise was shaking her head bewildered.

'Put it this way,' Steele said, 'they were in a position to offer me a choice. I fancied the alternative even less.'

'Less than this?'

She gazed at him incredulously.

Steele grinned. 'Now I'm out here I'm not so sure. The idea of a military prison suddenly looks almost inviting. But it's a little late to think about that.'

It wasn't too late. Theoretically he could still turn and run, just as he could have refused at the start. Only there'd been no question of that ever.

They hadn't understood why, nor would Louise. They thought he'd agreed because of the threat of Article 49. They were wrong. Steele wasn't frightened by Article 49. He was holding to something different, something they'd never know. Whatever he'd lost, however much he'd been forced to yield over the years, there were certain things that stubbornly, privately he vowed he'd never surrender.

To have refused when they came for him, to opt out now, would be a defeat even worse than accepting the blackmail. It would mean he'd finally acknowledged their power over him was total. Behind bars he'd be safe. Here in the open he was in danger, lethal danger. Yet he was still free. In spite of all the constraints and hazards he could move, make choices, even in small measure defy them.

Whatever they or Velatti did he was going to keep that freedom to the last.

'You poor crazy sod!'

Steele hadn't been wrong about her. The sympathy and anger in her voice were real, he was sure of that now. Yet for a moment he barely registered what she was saying.

He was concentrating on something else, something that had suddenly come to him, jarring, shocking, numbing his brain like one of Kirby's murderous swings. He stood quite still by the window. Then he turned. He couldn't risk telling her, there was no one he could tell, but Steele knew then with chilling absolute certainty it was the answer, the only possible answer.

'Listen, Louise,' he crossed the kitchen and interrupted her, 'I want you to think—'

He'd put the names to her before. Now he tried again. Velatti meant nothing, she'd never heard of him. Nor Gonsalves. But this time when he mentioned Donovan she nodded vaguely.

'He owns a boatyard in Tangier, doesn't he? It's where they kept the launch, I heard them discussing it once. He's got a daughter I think, some sexy little bit. People were talking about her at the club a few weeks ago.'

'The club?'

'Where I play bridge – where I used to play.'

She glanced at him sharply, resentfully. Then she shrugged.

'I'm sorry, it's not your fault. You don't even know Gib, do you? Well, it's like any little expatriate community. Nice and friendly if you're respectable and "British" and go by the rules. Chilly as hell if you don't. I got here six months before the whole Callum thing started. Until then I was welcome. Afterwards I wasn't—'

Steele nodded. The role of mistress, the night visits, Callum's reputation, the whispers and rumours and scandal – she must have been frozen out of Gibraltar society as effectively as if she'd had leprosy.

'And just as I was beginning to become acceptable again, to be "forgiven",' she smiled ruefully, 'you return and I'm back to square one. That's why I said there won't be any visitors.'

'I'll try to make up for it with a regular supply train from the Rock Hotel—'

Steele smiled. Then he went back to the list of names.

'What about Wedderburn?'

'Yes, I've heard of him. He's English, rich, he lives in Tangier.'

'That's all?'

'Well, I've never met him. He's meant to be very important, I don't know why. Just one of those people everyone knows about here.'

Steele nodded again. There was no point in telling her that Wedderburn was one of them, the most powerful, the person who ultimately decided what happened to her, the humiliations, the degradation, the enforced loneliness. Not now. Now it would just distract and embitter her more.

'What happened when they used to come before?'

The names had produced nothing and he was casting around at random, not even certain what he was searching for.

'Sometimes they'd telephone first,' she said, 'sometimes they'd arrive without warning. Mostly just one, the one who played patience, occasionally someone else with him.'

'The one on his own, did he talk to you?'

'About Callum?' Louise shook her head. 'Look, I'm the fancy lady, remember? And what does a fancy lady do? See there's drink in the house, wear pretty clothes and warm the bed – not that I ever got lucky there! That's all. I didn't need to know anything else. Funny—'

She laughed. 'I learned more about my "lover" from people outside, from the looks they gave me, from what I overheard, from the way I suddenly got credit in shops, than I ever did from them.'

'But when there were two,' Steele insisted. 'You heard them talking about Donovan and the launch. Wasn't there anything else?'

'I don't think so,' Louise frowned. 'Apart from the Indian of course, he always seemed to be causing problems. But then they generally do, don't they?'

'The Indian?'

'Yes, the one they used.'

Steele looked at her blankly. 'What do you mean?'

79

'You don't know about the Indians?' She laughed again. 'My God, they really tossed you in here without a lifebelt—'

She started to explain and as she talked Steele tensed.

The Indians. The worldwide traders, the most private of all bankers, the sources of the most secret finance, the people who would put up money against securities no ordinary lender would touch and at interest rates no ordinary borrower would consider. Callum might have had his launch, his mate, his contacts, his women, his glamour. But the final acid test of his substance, his reality, was his wealth. Not in credit cards or paper money or lavish tips but in the one currency the dirty area accepted as being serious – gold. The people who dealt in gold were the Indians.

To finance Callum's supposed deals – the cargoes he ran, the men he carried, the weapons he traded in – to give him the last imprimatur of authenticity, Greville's team had gone to the small dark men in their offices above the Queen Street stores. Without gold, without the Indians' trust, Callum would have been a man of straw. With it he was believable, he could do anything.

The Indians hadn't been part of Steele's briefing because there'd been no need. This time there weren't going to be any deals, no cargoes or men or weapons. Just Steele on his own for seven days. That at least had been the intention.

'And the one they used, Louise, what was he called?'

'Charan Desai. He's got a store between Queen Street and Blenheim Arcade. But you're not going to need him, are you? He's a shark.'

'I don't know yet what I'll need, but at least I know where Callum went.'

She looked at him puzzled as Steele laughed and filled her glass. Then he glanced at his watch. Midday. He could telephone Tangier and then catch the next hydrofoil back.

Steele stood up. 'Thanks, Louise, thanks for everything.'

'You're not going yet?'

She got to her feet too. Her voice was flat and quiet and her face had suddenly crumpled. Steele gazed down at her.

Companionship, that was what she missed most of all. The chance to talk and laugh and communicate, with the man who'd played patience, with the others in the Callum operation, even with himself returning to trample over the life she'd rebuilt in the little community – anything was better than the unendurable

80

silence of the house.

'I have to, Louise, but I'll be back—'

Steele stopped.

It was more than companionship, it was something they shared. For Louise the Callum who'd come back was different. Not another anonymous and professional functionary sent by a common employer but a man apart, separate and alone. Trapped, coerced and shackled yet still not belonging, not one of them. Instead hating and despising the faceless people she worked for as much as she did herself.

She'd recognized that immediately. Then, in the qualified explanation he'd given, in the questions, at first tentative and afterwards insistent, in the guarded and precarious trust that had grown, Steele had acknowledged the same in her. They were both different and they stood together against the rest.

Steele reached out and touched her cheek. Then he pulled her towards him, locking his arms tight round her back and feeling her shudder as she pressed against him.

'I'm very good on the hydrofoil schedules,' Louise leant away smiling, 'there's one at half-past two. It's much less crowded.'

Steele smiled back. 'My mother always warned me against crowds.'

They went into the bedroom. The blinds were drawn against the morning heat and the floor was barred with alternate slats of sun and shadow.

Lying naked on the bed in the dusky haze Louise looked much younger than in the harsh light of the kitchen. Her body was lightboned and firm, her breasts small and compact, her legs slender and rounded at the thighs. Steele watched her for a moment from the window. Then he lay down beside her. He ran his hand across her stomach, she shivered again at his touch, turned and clung to him.

Afterwards they were moving together, faster and faster until there was no corroding fear or uncertainty or the small man waiting with a long gun in the shadows. Only for an instant warmth and safety and Louise rocking beneath him, her hair brushing his face and her scent enveloping him.

'If I miss the next one I'll be stuck with the crowds again—'

Steele was dressed and standing by the door.

It was an hour later. They'd lain in silence, arms round each

81

other, calm and drowsy and still. There'd been no need to say anything. It had been a brief and temporary shelter for them both. They knew that and knew it was over and now Steele was moving out again.

'Wait a moment—'

Louise put on her housecoat, went to her dressing table and opened her make-up box.

When she turned round all the weariness that had been there on his arrival had gone, the drawn lines at the corners of her mouth and the shadows under her eyes. Instead she looked bright, coquettish, almost gay.

'That's just in case there's anyone outside waiting to see Ross Callum say goodbye to his lady.'

They walked to the front door. On the step she kissed him on the mouth,

'Come back, soon,' she smiled, 'without you there's no champagne or caviare.'

'I'm acquiring the habit. I'll be back.'

Steele walked down towards the hydrofoil berth.

The streets were hot and noisy. Union jacks hung from almost every window, policemen in shorts and bobbies' helmets blew whistles at the intersections, a sign in a shop window offered 'Homemade tea and scones', a platoon of British soldiers in familiar uniforms marched by and wheeled away to the shouted commands he knew so well.

He might almost have been at home, but Steele was scarcely aware of any of it. For once he'd even forgotten the surveillance screen behind him in the crowds. He wasn't thinking of Louise now. His thoughts were concentrated exclusively on the Indian, Charan Desai. Desai's gold had once financed Callum's voyages. Now Steele was going to use the same gold for a different purpose.

It was the key he'd been searching for when he'd taken the decision in Louise's kitchen – to turn on them all, hunt down and kill Velatti before the little Maltese could kill him.

9

There must have been hundreds, even thousands, of villages like it between the sea and the Sahara.

The road curved to the left, a sheet of stagnant water suddenly appeared, oily, metallic, throwing back the sun like a shield dropped in battle, then they were winding through the cluster of low baked-mud houses that huddled against the water's edge. There were scrabbling chickens, lean and topaz-eyed, old men propped in cones of shadow, the stench of fresh-dropped goat-dung, somewhere the chime of an almond-vendor's bell.

'Pull in under the tree,' Mary-Beth said.

Marcel nodded and swung the Citroën off the track.

A Coca-Cola sign hung by one screw above a chalked notice saying *Café* in French and Arabic. Through a beaded curtain below came the clatter of dice and laughter. A naked child with a swollen belly pattered out, looked at the car, darted back and stood half-hidden, peering between the strings of beads. Flies swarmed over the windscreen and dust billowed up from the wheels as Marcel stopped.

'We'll go inside,' she added to Steele.

Steele got out and followed her to the doorway. It was four o'clock and the afternoon heat hung fierce and still over the pale earth. They'd driven there straight from the harbour, where Mary-Beth had been waiting with Marcel as Steele told her on the telephone in Gibraltar, taking a narrow road twenty miles into the flat parched country south of Tangier.

Every few miles Mary-Beth had turned round and peered back. There'd been nothing behind them except mule-carts, an occasional ancient truck and a little 2CV van with a man on a motor-scooter trailing in its rear. The van and the scooter hadn't bothered her and Steele had said nothing.

83

'*Deux coca-colas, s'il vous plaît.*'

There was no counter inside, just a table with a rusting tin trunk beside it filled with slabs of fish-ice. The bottles Mary-Beth had asked for were produced, they drank quickly, then she led the way out through the back of the hut and they walked down a deserted street between rows of tiny apparently lifeless houses.

'It's here?' Steele asked.

She'd stopped by the last house in the street. It was like all the others, single-storied with two slit windows, a small arched doorway and whitewash flaking from the mud walls. There was no sound of anyone inside.

'Go in,' he said, 'check it out, all of it, particularly see if there's a rear entrance. Then come back and tell me.'

Mary-Beth nodded and went inside.

Steele glanced up and down the street. Still no one, not even a child. He waited, his stomach cold, his eyes fixed on the back door of the café from which he could still hear the sound of laughter. If anyone came they'd come from there – the other way there was only barren sand. He didn't think it was a trap: its very remoteness made it too obvious. But he couldn't be sure, he couldn't be sure of anything and he wouldn't be until he started to move himself. That hadn't happened yet, it couldn't until he knew more.

'There's no other door,' Mary-Beth had reappeared, 'just a window at the back. And no one else apart from him.'

'You stay there,' Steele pointed at a gap between the house and its neighbour, 'if you see anyone, anyone at all, you call me instantly.'

She positioned herself between the two walls and Steele went in.

Darkness first and he blinked, stepping rapidly to one side so he wasn't silhouetted against the street. Then the shape of a single room, a few stools, a mattress on the floor, a figure standing by a table, stocky and whiteheaded. Steele disregarded him, crossed the floor and looked out of the window, an open hole in the mud bricks. Outside an empty highwalled yard.

'Mr Callum—?'

Steele turned. The only way into the room was through the front. If Mary-Beth called he could get out by the window, cross the yard and climb the wall.

'That's right,' he said.

'Adolpho Gonsalves—'

The man came forward. He was in his late fifties and wearing an open-necked shirt and grey flannel trousers. As he reached Steele the light from the window washed over his face. A strong deeply-lined face with direct humorous eyes, a powerful jaw and a nose that had been battered out of shape like a prizefighter's. Yet there was something strange about the skin, at odds with the resolute features it covered. The texture was dead and powdery as if it had been deliberately kept from the sun.

'It was good of you to come.'

'Mary-Beth spoke for you.'

'Yes, she's a fine girl. Please—'

He beckoned Steele to sit down, sweeping out his arm with a curiously old-fashioned grace.

Steele shook his head. 'I'll stay here by the window.'

'Of course—'

Gonsalves must have noticed Steele was still gazing at his face because he paused, touched his cheek and smiled.

'I went inside first when I was fifteen. On and off I stayed there for over thirty years. I think it is never the same after that.'

Steele nodded. Thirty years in the political prisons run by the PIDE, the Portuguese secret police, under the ruthless dictatorships of Caetano and Salazar. It explained not only the pallor but also the distorted nose and the limp as he moved towards a stool.

'You will excuse me if I do not stand too. My hip is like my skin. I walk now, exercise, put it in sunlight, but still it has trouble in recovering.'

He lowered himself awkwardly, stretching out one leg at an angle to the floor.

'You wanted to see me,' Steele said.

'Yes, and naturally you have little time, Mr Callum. Well, I will not waste it. I wish to buy guns.'

'Guns?' Steele looked at him incredulously.

'I am too blunt? I appear naive? I am not the sort of person you are used to doing business with? Maybe so,' Gonsalves laughed in self-deprecation, 'yet I am serious, I promise you. I want guns and I have the money to pay for them with, not much but I believe enough.'

Steele said nothing.

He didn't know what he'd been expecting – a message to be passed, a piece of information to be given, an introduction to be offered, even a request to charter the *Lara* – but almost anything else. Not this simple offer to purchase a cargo of weapons – weapons he wouldn't have had an idea how to obtain even if he'd wanted to.

Then as he stood there bewildered Gonsalves hunched himself forward – mistaking Steele's silence for lack of interest.

'Mr Callum, I have been in prison or working underground all my life. In that time I have learned there are very few people one can trust wholly. I believe you are one. We come from different worlds. You are not a politician, I am. Yet in the end we are of the same company. Please hear me out—'

He clasped his hands, broad splayed hands with knots of scar tissue on the knuckles, round his knees and gazed upwards. Steele hesitated, then nodded.

'I am a socialist, Mr Callum. I started as one and nothing that has happened to me since has altered my beliefs, only strengthened them. And so that you understand I will tell you what happened—'

He spoke in a quiet measured voice without a trace of self-pity, without dramatization or heroics, cataloguing events which he accepted and considered normal in terms of the goal he'd set for himself – a goal which made everything else irrelevant.

Steele listened. The recruitment as a schoolboy, the work as a courier, the first arrest by the PIDE, the beatings and torture, water pumped into his mouth until he almost drowned, electricity to his testicles until he fainted only to be brought round and made to faint again. The threats to his family, the mockery of a trial when he refused to name his companions, the first prison sentence, seven years in the Lazares dungeons – built to house nineteenth-century Angolan slaves.

And then, interspersed with brief bouts of freedom when he'd try to build up the movement, to create a structure for a socialist Portugal of the future, the pattern repeated again and again over the years. The betrayals by colleagues who lacked his will-power, the suicide of his wife, driven to kill herself by PIDE threats against their children, the endless violence and sadism of the interrogations, the months in solitary confinement in the dark. Until finally the flower revolution of four years before when fascism was overthrown and Salazar sent into exile.

'That of course was a glorious time,' Gonsalves smiled. 'But even as they opened the cell doors and the girls were putting carnations in the soldiers' guns and all the bells were ringing, even then there were those of us who knew it was only the start—'

The start for a country unprepared, uneducated, for its freedom, and plunged instantly into power-struggles between its new rulers and the old fanatical dispossessed forces of the right.

'They have not given up, they never will. I have told you what they did before. Given the chance it is what they will do again.'

'And you figure a boatload of guns will stop them?' Steele asked.

'I am not that naive,' Gonsalves smiled again. 'A single boatload is a symbol as the guns themselves are symbols – symbols of strength. If they give confidence, belief to just a few villagers that what has been won can be held, then they will have achieved their purpose. I am old, Mr Callum, not in years but in health, in what has been done to me—'

He got to his feet slowly, levering himself up from the stool, still without any bitterness in his voice.

'Old and realistic. Once I hoped to take part in the affairs of the new Portugal. Now I know I am no longer strong enough. I came from the countryside, I will go back there – to the villages I mentioned. They are the ones round where I was born. Yet I will always remain a politician and I see those villages as a symbol too. One boatload of guns is nothing, yet it can also be a start, a signal to others. Afterwards there will be more, many more, until the whole country can defend itself. When that happens the right is doomed. If you like, I wish to light the signal that dooms it.'

'Look, I've been away, I'm out of touch,' Steele said, 'there are lots of others much better-equipped to sell you guns. Why did you come to me?'

'Two reasons, Mr Callum. One you know, a matter of trust. The second I learned from Mary-Beth. We have collected money, not much but all that could be given. I understand the costs, the risks, in shipping weapons and maybe for the others what we have is not enough. Yet I was told that to Ross Callum the money was not always what mattered—'

Gonsalves limped towards the window, hair suddenly daz-

87

zlingly white as the light caught it.

'Once, I believe, in Tangier you paid for an operation on a Moroccan child who would otherwise have lost her sight. Today the child sees. You will forgive me the comparison—'

He stopped in front of Steele, grave, smiling, courteous.

'But I regard our freedom as a child. I do not want its sight to be lost. Mary-Beth said you would understand that.'

Steele looked at him in silence once more.

It was the same as before, at Donovan's yard on the waterfront, at the hotel, in the bar with Kirby, on Gibraltar when the management of the Rock sent the champagne and the caviare. The legend had come back, the ghost had returned from the past, the myth was believed in again – even by this simple but strong, experienced and honourable man.

He shook his head helplessly, angrily, and said, 'How much money have you got?'

'Seven hundred thousand escudos.'

Steele made a rapid conversion in his head. Ten thousand pounds. It sounded pitifully little.

'And what sort of guns do you want?'

Gonsalves shrugged. 'Handguns, I assume, any type we can teach the people to use easily. I thought you would know the best. Does it make much difference?'

The question as frank and ingenuous as everything else and again Steele felt a furious baffled impotence. Gonsalves was prepared to entrust what was presumably the entire fund he'd collected to a stranger with no idea what he wanted or what he'd be getting – simply because the stranger was called Ross Callum.

'I'll think about it and let you know through Mary-Beth.'

Steele turned, started to cross the floor towards the door and suddenly stopped.

It had been there plucking uneasily at a corner of his mind ever since they'd left the harbour, the road twisting ahead of them in the heat through the flat barren countryside without a house, a ruin, even a telegraph pole to interrupt the emptiness. Now he'd finally made the connection and the coldness in his stomach flooded back.

'Who the hell told you I dealt in guns?'

'The knowledge is common,' Gonsalves seemed surprised, 'I remember hearing before even in prison—'

'Before isn't now,' Steele cut him off, 'before was five years ago, that's different. I only got back yesterday morning. But within twelve hours you know I'm in Tangier and you've got a message to Mary-Beth saying you want to see me—'

Steele paused. Gonsalves was staring at him puzzled and he added, 'There's no telephone between here and Tangier.'

'No, of course not. The man came at midday yesterday—'

'What man?' Steele fumbled for his wallet and dragged out the photograph of Velatti. 'This one?'

Gonsalves glanced down and waved it aside. 'No, this was a Moroccan, not a European. I assumed you knew.'

Steele wiped the sweat from his face, put the photograph away and shook his head.

'Tell me.'

'He was a young man, polite, well-spoken. He said he'd been sent by a Mr Yehuda.'

Gonsalves produced a visiting card from his shirt pocket. Steele took it. The name 'Mr Benjamin Hassan Yehuda' was engraved at the centre in roman lettering with what he guessed was the Arabic equivalent below. There was also a Tangier address, again in the two scripts.

'What else?'

'He said Mr Yehuda had heard I wanted to buy what he called a "certain commodity" and I might be interested to know you had returned. I thanked him, wrote a note to Mary-Beth and asked him to deliver it – he was going back into the city. That was all.'

'Do you know this Yehuda?'

'No. I thought he was some contact of yours. I've been here two weeks now. I'm not used to this sort of business and Mary-Beth has been helping me. We have had to be careful, very careful. Tangier is full of exiled members of the Caetano and Salazar regimes. They're like the Algerian *pieds-noirs*, bitter, brutal, dangerous. I represent everything they hate. That is why I have stayed out of the city. If they knew I was here—'

Gonsalves lifted his hands, rubbed his jaw and smiled.

'I would have more than the paleness of my skin to worry about. Yesterday, thinking Yehuda had something to do with you, I was not concerned at being found. Now I believe we have perhaps not been careful enough. I think I should move.'

Steele nodded. 'Can you find another village?'

'I may know little about guns,' Gonsalves smiled again, 'but in survival I have forty years experience.'

'Get a message to Mary-Beth as soon as you're settled again. I'll be in touch.'

Steele went out. The street was as silent and deserted as before, and Mary-Beth was still standing in the gap between the two houses. He beckoned and she walked quickly beside him towards the car.

The visiting card was in his pocket. The name on it meant nothing, but Steele hadn't the slightest doubt why it had been left with Gonsalves. Mr Yehuda knew a great deal about Callum, knew within a few hours that he'd landed in Tangier, knew he'd go to Donovan's yard, knew that a message sent to Mary-Beth would reach him, and knew too that he'd drive out to the village.

Only a very few people would have known as much as that. Apart from Wedderburn and the surveillance screen Steele could think of just one. The card was simply a formality at the end of the chain – an invitation to a meeting.

10

'Jesus Christ!'

Steele looked down from the coastal road and swore.

Below him, thronging round the office, lining the wooden platform, spilling out in excited chattering groups along the jetty, was a crowd of two or three hundred people. Bearded old men in jellabahs, peasant women from the Atlas foothills, dockers in singlets and jeans, sharp young city Arabs in threadbare suits and glistening pointed shoes, merchants with trays of food and high-smelling leatherwork, the inevitable squealing and tumbling children.

His first reaction as he got out of the car was that there must have been an accident. Then he realized: the word had gone round Tangier that Callum was back.

He glanced at Marcel. 'How long have they been there?'

'They been coming all day, sir.'

'And what the hell do they want?'

'They just want to see you, sir, mostly. Some, they say they got things to talk about from before, business and so on,' Marcel shrugged doubtfully. 'I don't know how much of that's true, sir.'

Someone must have spotted the Citroën. There was a shout, the clamour subsided briefly, faces swivelled towards the shore, then the uproar started once more and people were moving in waves towards the road.

Steele cursed again.

'Let's get on the boat!'

He ran down to the office, plunged into the advancing crowd, shouldered his way through, grinning, patting heads, clasping hands, throwing off the importunate clutching arms, stumbled across the jetty and climbed the gangplank.

'All right—'

He heaved himself panting into the cockpit with Mary-Beth and Marcel behind, and leant over the stern.

'Come here, Marcel, you translate for me—'

The crowd had swung round and was surging against the base of the cradle, calling, imploring, gesticulating. Steele lifted his hand and bellowed for silence.

'Right, you tell them this,' Marcel was hunched over the cockpit rail beside him, 'tell them I'm happy to be back in Tangier. Tell them I've come home, I'm with my friends again—'

Marcel shouted down in Arabic, there was a delighted roar in return and Steele waved laughing.

'Say I want to meet them all as soon as I can, but right now I'm busy. Anyone who reckons he's got business with me, he can tell it to you in the office – and you get the hell over there, Marcel, when we've finished. But you tell them too I can remember every single bloody dirham from before. All right?'

Steele waved again, there was another roar, then as Marcel scuttled down the gangplank he ducked into the cabin.

Donovan had already run a powerline out to the boat. A light was blazing from the cabin roof, he could see the glow of other lamps forward in the hold, and from the deck he heard the throbbing of an electric drill. The lockers under the bunks had been emptied, the brass porthole covers gleamed, and smells of varnish and fresh paint were circling in the air. Whatever else, the American wasn't wasting time.

'Well, you've got all your fan-club back now—'

The light from the open hatch was blotted out and Donovan clambered down the steps wiping his hands on an oilstained wad of hemp. Sweat was pouring from his shoulders and his face was streaked with grease.

'I heard you from the engine-hold. "Every bloody dirham"!' He chuckled. 'You want to watch it, Ross. If they've changed from before, it's only for the worse. So how do you reckon we're doing?'

'It looks like a good start,' Steele said.

'Ten men on her today, another five tomorrow. By the time I've finished with her you'll be able to take her to a ball.'

Donovan nodded contentedly. For once Steele couldn't even smell the gin fumes.

'Listen, Don,' he said, 'I want you to take a break. Just fifteen minutes and get everybody off. There's something I want to do. I'll tell you when you can come on again.'

Donovan frowned at him. Then he shrugged. 'It's your money.'

He climbed back up the steps, shouted and Steele heard the shuffle of bare feet on deck and then the gangplank creaking as the Moroccans streamed down to the jetty.

'No, not you. You stay here—'

Mary-Beth had turned to go too but he called her back. Steele waited until the boat was completely silent. Then he went through into the gallery.

Above the entrance, on the inside of the bulkhead that separated the galley from the cabin, was a copperplate engraved in black with the *Lara*'s name, specifications and launch date. Steele took a blunt knife from the sink and removed the four screws that held it to the wood. The plate came away, revealing a pale square of timber that had been protected from the galley smoke and grease. He tapped the square once, then harder and finally a hinged panel dropped inwards.

'*They were put there in case of an emergency*,' Greville had said reluctantly. '*There'll be no question of your needing to use them, but you should probably know where they are.*'

Steele put his hand into the cavity, felt it round and found what he was looking for – a heavy oilskin package. He lifted it out and took it into the cabin where he unwrapped it on the table.

There were two revolvers inside. A small Browning 9mm automatic and a powerful long-barrelled Smith & Wesson .38, together with several boxes of ammunition. He pushed aside the .38 and picked up the Browning. The oilskin cover and a thick layer of grease had protected it from the corrosion that had bitten into everything else on the boat. He wiped off the grease, worked the breech mechanism until it was turning smoothly, and filled three clips with shells. Then he dropped the gun into his pocket.

Outside, in the open, with light and time and distance, he'd have chosen the .38 for its accuracy and power. But Steele wasn't going to be outside. If he was right he'd be in a room, cramped, blocked, with perhaps little light and less time. There the small rapid-firing Browning had the advantage.

'Can you drive that Citroën?'

93

He glanced at Mary-Beth who'd been watching him – half-frowning but her eyes steady and her face calm.

She nodded. 'Sure.'

'And do you know where this is?'

Steele showed her the address on the card. He'd asked her before, on the drive back from the village, if the name Yehuda meant anything and she'd shaken her head.

'I guess I can find it,' she said. 'It's somewhere in Amalat, between the French quarter and the old town.'

'Right—'

He wrapped up the Smith & Wesson, took the package through to the galley, put it in the cavity, and screwed the copper plate over the panel. Then he came back.

'We're going over there.'

It had to be her. Marcel was keeping the Moroccans occupied. If Steele took him away they'd be followed all over the town, it would become a procession not a journey. And he couldn't telephone surveillance control. They'd call him off, tell him to wait. They didn't want him anywhere near Velatti until they were sure they could nail the Maltese on their own terms.

The only way was to pre-empt them, to go now before they knew, alone, prepared, hoping that speed, surprise and the Browning would be enough. It wasn't what he'd planned, he hadn't thought it would happen this fast, but the signposts to the rendezvous had been unmistakable and he knew he'd no choice but to keep it. At least everything then would be over.

Mary-Beth was looking up at him puzzled and uncertain.

'Listen, you said you'd go down the line for Gonsalves?'

'I will.'

'Why?'

She hesitated. 'I knew his son. Through him I got to know Adolpho. I liked him, I trusted him, I believed in what he was working for. I still do. That's all.'

She stopped abruptly. It wasn't all. There was more, Steele knew that, much more than she'd said but for the moment it was enough.

'I'm not going to kid you, Mary-Beth,' he propped himself against the table, 'I didn't come back here to do business. I'll think about those guns Gonsalves wants, but that's all. I'm making no promises. Only there's one thing I can tell you for sure.

94

Yesterday I asked you about a man called Velatti, remember?'

She nodded again.

'Velatti's after me. I want to find him before he finds me first. Until I do nobody connected with me is going to be safe. That goes for Don, for you, for everyone. But most of all it goes for Gonsalves.'

'He's in danger as well as you?'

'I figure he's being set up for me. I think he's bait. If I get hooked, he'll be swallowed too.'

'And this man Yehuda?'

'Either he's the trimmings, the bright feathers, the silver thread round the shank,' Steele paused, 'or he's another name for Velatti. I'm going to find out which.'

There was a clatter outside. He straightened up and glanced quickly at the cockpit, but it was only a hawser rattling against the hull. When he looked back Mary-Beth was smiling.

'You got me wrong,' she said. 'Sure, I'd do it for Adolpho, but I'd do it the same for you. I just wanted to know the score before we started.'

Steele grinned. 'Then let's go.'

The Moroccans, jostling and clamouring round the office, didn't notice them as they crossed the jetty. They climbed to the road, got into the Citroën and headed west towards the old town.

The house was on its own at the centre of an island of waste-land. One moment they were bumping through narrow zigzag streets, noisy, crowded and bustling. The next the streets had suddenly been sheared off, the sounds had gone and they were in the open with the house ahead of them. Tall, rambling, derelict, with crumbling walls and blind shutterless windows. A battered impermanent building like an observation-tower erected in a forest clearing by an army in retreat, and then hurriedly abandoned to the wind and rain.

'Stop here,' Steele said.

Mary-Beth braked twenty yards from the door and turned off the engine. Steele glanced through the rear window. He couldn't see the van but it had been behind them before and he guessed it was parked where the houses ended.

'I'm going inside,' he swung back. 'Somewhere behind us there's a grey 2CV van. If I'm not out within thirty minutes find it and tell the driver where I am. If you can't find it call this number

95

and pass on the same message—'

He scrawled the digits for surveillance control on an empty
pack of Camels.

'But if anything else happens, if you hear shots, if someone else
comes out and comes towards you, don't wait to see what they
want – just get the hell out of here. Right?'

Mary-Beth nodded. 'Take care.'

She reached across and touched his hand. Steele gripped her
fingers for an instant. Then he got out and walked to the door.

There was a frayed bell-pull dangling by the frame. He tugged
it down, stepped to one side, felt in his pocket and balanced the
Browning in his palm. A stray mule, without saddle or bridle,
plodded across the baked earth behind the house and in the
distance where the streets ended abruptly he could see a group
of children playing marbles, the glass balls glittering in tiny
withered hands. Then the door opened.

'*Sala'am.*'

A woman in a *haik*, the long white gown of the orthodox
Moslems, with only her eyes showing behind the veil. Over her
shoulder he caught a glimpse of an open courtyard filled with a
wild tangle of climbing plants.

'I'm looking for Mr Yehuda.'

Steele had pushed past her and was standing inside the door,
his hand still in his pocket and his back to the wall.

The woman bowed without speaking and led the way to a flight
of stairs. Steele followed her. There were three floors all with
arched landings opening onto the courtyard. As they climbed
upwards, the woman's gown rustling on the worn stone steps,
Steele glanced into the rooms that led off the landings. They were
empty and deserted. Dust had silted up in waves on the floors and
cobwebs misted the rafters. In other Arab houses there would
have been clutter, movement, cooking smells, the glow of a
brazier, the sound of flutes. Here there was only silence and the
scent of honeysuckle.

They reached the top landing, the woman opened another
door, bowed again and stood back.

Steele wiped the sweat from his hand and eased the gun
forward so that it was resting against his hip under the cloth. His
wrist was shaking slightly and he could feel a tremor at his neck.
He steadied himself, breathed out slowly and flexed the fingers

of his other hand. Then he stepped inside.

It was hot, dim and fragrant and instantly different from the rooms below. Sealed and soft with thick carpets on the floor, tapestries covering the walls, glass in the windows and embroidered curtains hanging beside the frames. Before Steele's footsteps had rung clear on the stone, now there was only a soft rustle as he walked forward.

'I am glad to meet you, Mr Callum.'

He whirled towards the voice, hand tightening round the butt of the Browning. There was a man sitting on a high stool in an alcove by the window. Tiny, hunched, wearing a black skullcap and a silk jellabah, his head shadowed by the overhanging arch.

'You must excuse me,' the man touched the stool, 'I have difficulty in moving, this takes the weight from my legs.'

Steele gazed at him, his finger curled round the trigger-guard. Then he slowly relaxed his arm and let the gun slide into the bottom of his pocket.

'Mr Yehuda?'

'Yes.'

The man tapped ash from a cigarette and held out his hand. Steele crossed the floor and shook it.

He was old, immensely old. His features were blurred and wasted, his skin had the cold pale sheen of a wild bird's egg, and his body was like a fragile bundle of grass-stems beneath the silk. Only his eyes were alive, rheumed and crusted round the lids but with fierce black unblinking pupils. His eyes and his voice – slow, hoarse, furred with smoke but resonant and strong.

Perched on the stool, knees tucked up against his chest, he might have been an ancient dying hawk in his winter lair above the ruined emptiness of the house. A hawk – but not Velatti.

'You would like something, perhaps? A whisky, a dry anis, a cup of coffee?'

He pointed at a table, his hand writhen and buckled with arthritis like a twisted tree-root.

Steele shook his head.

'A chair then?'

'I'll stand.'

He moved away from the old man and positioned himself between the alcove and the window so that he could watch the door. The gun was dragging at his jacket but he knew he wasn't

97

going to need it, and he suddenly felt both drained and savagely, unaccountably angry.

He'd been convinced Velatti would be there, he'd wound himself up for it, he'd come in tense but utterly certain, cold-bloodedly determined not even to ask questions – ready instead to end it all with the Browning latched on automatic fire through his pocket. He'd been wrong. There was no Velatti, only this strange shrivelled little man crouched on top of his stool.

Steele lit a cigarette, exhaled and looked at him through the smoke. Yehuda had known about his arrival, the boatyard, Mary-Beth, Gonsalves, the village, everything.

'I get the feeling you were expecting me,' Steele said.

'I thought it possible you might come, yes.'

'Why?'

Yehuda shrugged. 'You have been away, Mr Callum. Tangier has changed, has it not? After five years it was bound to do so. The cargoes then, the submachine guns for the Sahel, the bonded crates of Scotch, the men from Indo-China looking for employment, they are much rarer now. The markets, the commodities, the city itself, everything is different—'

He struck a match, his fingers like broken claws as he raised the flame to his mouth.

'It occurred to me that even you might feel in need of – introductions, shall we say?'

'To a supplier of weapons for an order from Adolpho Gonsalves, perhaps?'

'I will be glad if I can oblige.'

Steele paused. 'You seem to know a hell of a lot about me, Mr Yehuda.'

'Not just you, Mr Callum,' Yehuda smiled, a flicker of the pinched almost transparent lips, 'about everyone. You saw my card, surely. I am that contradiction in terms, an Arab-Jew. Such as we, and there are few of us, survive only through knowledge. It is our business.'

Benjamin Hassan Yehuda. Steele hadn't taken in the last two names until then. Now he realized their significance.

'Like knowing how to find Gonsalves, for instance?'

Yehuda nodded. 'That among much else.'

'And even if I wanted an introduction,' Steele said, 'what would the price be?'

'Price?' Yehuda's voice conveyed shock. 'We are not talking of bargains, Mr Callum. I would consider that a gift, a natural courtesy to one who belongs here as much as I do.'

His face was impassive. Steele ground out his cigarette and glanced through the window.

Distantly across the roofs he could see a haze gathering on the sea under the setting sun. It was the tarot, the dense low mist that would build up until it covered the straits like a vast white bed of pressed swansdown. Ships had already started to hoot and the far-off beam of the Tarifa lighthouse was pulsing on the Spanish mainland.

Most boats would be making for harbour now. Not Callum. If there'd been a cargo to carry he'd have sailed the *Lara* through any weather, even the blinding screen of the tarot. Except his cargoes, and the introductions that procured them, hadn't come for free. They'd been paid for in gold, the introductions, then as now, almost as valuable as the loads themselves. And most of all when the source was a man like Yehuda.

Steele turned back abruptly. 'Do you know a man called Velatti?'

'I know most people in Tangier.'

'I believe he wishes to see me. I want to see him too.'

'Mr Callum—'

Yehuda was no longer looking at him but at a tapestry on the far wall, crimson pomegranates outlined in gold woven round a silver Moorish sword.

'Let us assume I know this Velatti. But let us assume too he has a quarrel with those who employ him, that he has come to dislike and distrust them. Would he not want to be quite sure you were who you claimed to be before meeting you?'

Steele stood quite still. 'What do you mean?'

'I am speculating, of course. But publicly you avoided Tangier before. There are few, perhaps none, who would recognize you for certain now, not even Velatti himself. It would not be too difficult for another man, an intelligent well-rehearsed man, to arrive and represent that he was Callum.'

The old man stopped, smoke coiling up from his hand, his eyes still fixed on the glittering pomegranates.

Steele said nothing for a moment. He'd been right in the first place, he knew that now, Wedderburn had been right. He was being tested. The whole chain that had led from Mary-Beth to Gonsalves to this isolated decaying house was part of the test – a test that hadn't ended when he walked in the door, as he'd guessed, but had only just begun.

Yehuda was simply the vehicle, the conduit Velatti had chosen. Yehuda wanted no payment from Steele because the little Maltese was paying him – it was part of the bargain they'd made. From Yehuda Steele would be passed to someone else, someone who ostensibly had access to the guns Gonsalves wanted, and further on along the chain Velatti would be waiting. Not in a decrepit tower in the heart of Tangier, like the village that was too obvious a trap and Steele cursed himself again for believing it could have finished there. No, not in Yehuda's house but somewhere much safer, more private and remote.

Yet he still didn't understand altogether, there were whole areas of total bewildering contradiction. Yehuda hadn't denied knowing Velatti, he'd acknowledged it openly – alerting Steele, warning him, leaving him in no doubt that Velatti would strike as soon as he was satisfied he was dealing with Callum. It made no sense and he shook his head quickly baffled.

'All right,' Steele moved away from the alcove. 'So how's your friend going to be convinced?'

'My business is knowledge, Mr Callum, yours was primarily guns. I imagine anyone looking for proof would want to know if they are still your main interest—'

The stool creaked as Yehuda shifted to face him again.

'There's a man called Juan Fischer, a dealer, a broker half-Spanish and half-Polish. He operates out of the Casino in the upper square of Algeciras. I am told he is there most mornings between eleven and three. I think you would find it useful to meet him.'

'I'll go there tomorrow.'

Steele crossed the floor. The sun was dipping below the horizon and the last of the light flared on the clustered sequins of the wall-hangings. Fog-horns were booming from the straits as the tarot thickened and a shrill mechanical muezzin was calling the faithful to evening prayer.

'Mr Callum—'

Steele turned at the door. He could barely see Yehuda's head in the shadows of the arch, but a scarlet star glowed on his lap.

The old man raised his hand, ash drifted to the floor, shreds of burning tobacco spilled over his fingers.

'I spoke of quarrels. Such are common here. Velatti for example with his employers, perhaps even with you too. I have learned long since to take no part in any disputes—'

The bright embers of the cigarette must have been scorching his skin, but Yehuda didn't seem to notice.

'I have no quarrels with anyone. You might find it fruitful to remember that.'

Steele stared at the alcove for an instant. Then he went out. The Citroën was still parked twenty yards from the front door. He crossed the bare space of earth and got in.

'There's a villa up the hill,' he said to Mary-Beth, 'I want to go there right away.'

Her gave her the address and she started the engine.

Steele leant back. He'd understood exactly what Yehuda meant and the implications left him dazed. The old man had said he'd made no bargain with Velatti for delivering Callum. He was refusing payment from either side. Yehuda would only have done that if there was infinitely more at stake than a vendetta to be settled or a single cargo of arms to be sold.

He sat in silence, his mind numb, as they climbed through the darkening streets.

'No, tell him I'm waiting here.'

The houseboy nodded and padded away between the banks of white flowers and silver leaves, burnished like armour in the lamplight.

Steele stood on the paving stones inside the street door.

All he'd eaten since breakfast were a few spoonfuls of caviare. He was hungry, exhausted and this throat was dry from the airless heat of Yehuda's room. Yet even in the ten minutes since they'd left the house the confusion had dissolved, the unanswered questions had become unimportant, and he knew once again with the same total certainty he'd felt in Gibraltar what he was going to do.

The hall door opened, light from a candelabra veined the marble floor inside, then footsteps sounded on the path.

'What the bloody hell do you think you've been doing?'

Wedderburn held up the candles so the flames lit both their

101

faces.

He was wearing carpet slippers and a brocade dressing-gown over his clothes. The white patches were back on his cheeks, pale against the livid surrounding skin, and his voice was tight with anger.

'What I was told to do,' Steele said quietly. 'Looking for Velatti.'

'Velatti? You weren't looking for Velatti – you were trying to get yourself killed. You didn't report after meeting Gonsalves, you missed the six o'clock check, you went off on some hare-brained pursuit of your own. Do you know who Yehuda is?'

'No.'

'I'll tell you. He's corrupt, evil and dangerous. For you, apart from Velatti, he's probably the most dangerous man in the straits. He'll cheat you, inform on you, sell you, see that you're dropped off the nearest pier for the price of a drink.'

'Then why didn't London warn me?' Steele paused. 'Or is he like Kirby – someone else they just forgot?'

The candelabra wavered in Wedderburn's hand. Between its branches Steele could see the jade bowl on the hall table. There was a different blossom floating on the water, not jasmine but a fleshy milkwhite gardenia.

'You'd better come inside,' the silver leaves gleamed as Wedderburn turned.

Steele shook his head. 'I'm staying here.'

Wedderburn hesitated. Then he swung back and snapped, 'What happened?'

'I've been given a name. A man called Juan Fischer.'

'Fischer?' Wedderburn frowned, 'I don't know him. I'll have him checked out in the morning. Afterwards I'll tell you what to do next.'

'You'll check him out tonight,' Steele said. 'I've already decided what I'm going to do in the morning.'

He'd spoken as quietly as before. There was silence for a moment. Then Wedderburn's cheeks flared white again.

'You've decided! For the last time listen to me—'

'No,' Steele cut him off, 'you listen instead, you listen very carefully. He may be your Velatti, but this is my bloody skin. Right now Velatti's not sure who I am. Maybe he'll get tired of waiting to find out, maybe he'll shoot first and start checking afterwards. Every day that goes by he's got a bigger incentive to act. I'm going to put him out of his uncertainty. I'm going to find this Fischer tomorrow. I'm going to buy the guns he wants to sell. I'm going to set up the whole operation. Hire a new mate. If necessary put more men on the *Lara* to get her back in the water—'

Steele turned and jerked open the door to the street.

'All Tangier's going to know I'm back in business for real – and that includes Velatti. If it doesn't convince him, nothing ever will. But he'll be satisfied, Yehuda damn nearly said as much. And when he is he'll make contact. You'll get him and I'll move out. Only it's going to be done my way and there's nothing you can do to stop me.'

Steele slammed the door behind him.

It had come to him as suddenly as his realization about Velatti in Louise's kitchen. Out here Article 49 wasn't even a threat any longer. It had become hollow and meaningless. They'd chosen their Callum, they'd put him back into the dirty area, they'd exposed and committed him. If they withdrew Steele, they'd lose Velatti irrevocably. There was no way they could make someone else credible in the role after the past forty-eight hours.

He had them by the throat, every one of them, Greville, Wedderburn, the anonymous surveillance control. They were stuck with him. He'd become their albatross. There was nothing they could do now except follow where he led.

'If you leave me and the car at the Minzah, can you get a cab home?'

He was in the Citroën again. Mary-Beth nodded and headed back towards the centre of the town.

'Did you find out anything about Velatti?'

Mary-Beth glanced across at him as they stopped at a red light, and Steele realized he'd barely spoken to her since she'd driven him away from Yehuda's house.

'Not yet,' he said, 'but in the morning I'm going over to Algeciras to look for Fischer.'

'The one with the guns?'

Steele nodded.

'So you are going to help Adolpho?'

'Now wait a minute. I said I wasn't making any promises—'

He broke off.

Finding Fischer, setting up the deal, hiring a mate, floating the *Lara* – that was one thing. If necessary, now he knew about the Indian Desai, he could even go as far as completing the purchase of the weapons. But the idea of running them into Portugal had never occurred to him. There'd be no need. All Steele was after was Velatti – and he should have forced the little Maltese into the open long before then.

Steele glanced at her curiously and added, 'What's so important about these guns?'

'They matter.'

'To you?'

Mary-Beth hesitated. Her jacket collar was turned up against her neck and her hair was billowing over it, tangled, pale gold, plucked back by the wind from the open window.

'I told you I knew Adolpho's son,' she spoke very softly and quite dispassionately. 'He was called Dino. He came over here to study French in Casablanca. I met him and I went with him for a year, he was the first boyfriend I had—'

She smiled. 'I guess the first is always different. But Dino was very special. He believed in the same things as his father, he worked with him, he wanted to carry on from where Adolpho knew he'd have to stop. This spring he came to Tangier. It was about the guns, the first time I heard of them. I found a man who said he could arrange for Dino to meet someone who could help—'

She paused. 'Dino went to the place. They were waiting for him, a group of the people Adolpho told you about, men who'd worked for Caetano and Salazar. They knocked him down with a car, then they drove over him several times to make sure. He died in hospital the next day.'

'I'm sorry.'

Mary-Beth shrugged. 'He was called Gonsalves, he knew the risks. For them it was propaganda. They'd killed Adolpho's son, they'd showed how powerful they still were—'

The lights of the Minzah showed up on the right. Mary-Beth drew into the side and switched off the engine. Then she looked at him again.

'If the guns go through now, they won't have won altogether. That was why I was so happy when you came back yesterday. I didn't want to tell you before you saw Adolpho, I wanted him to

104

explain on his own. But I always told him you were the only one we could really trust and if you'd been here you'd have understood. Now you are.'

She stopped. Steele got out, called for one of the porters and told him to put the Citroën in the car park.

'I'll do what I can,' he said, 'goodnight.'

He turned away abruptly, walked into the hotel, snatched the keys from the desk clerk and went up to his room.

Callum. The folk hero, the champion of the poor and underprivileged, the one man who could be trusted, who would understand, whose word was inviolable to everyone from the Moroccan dockers to Mary-Beth to the old Portuguese socialist. And tomorrow he'd be back in business again with his launch, his mate, his guns, his gold. Except like everything else it would all be a sham, another lie, another deception.

Steele picked up the telephone and dialled room service.

'Send me up a bottle of Black Label and some ice,' he said.

Black Label had been Callum's whisky, but any other brand would have done as well. At that moment Steele wasn't interested in Callum, he wasn't even thinking about the morning and the man called Fischer and the events he'd put in train which sooner or later would bring him face to face with Velatti.

All he wanted to do was get drunk. He stood by the window looking down over the harbour and swearing viciously.

11

The cab was the tenth in the line of yellow and black Renaults on the quay.

Steele stepped back and checked the licence number painted on the door again. Fifty-seven. That and the name were the only identification surveillance control had given him.

He bent down by the driver's window. 'Pepe Lorca?'

The man nodded. 'Yes, señor.'

He had a hard flat face, dark and seamed with wrinkles, and his hands on the wheel were stubby and strong.

Steele got into the rear seat. 'Take me to the viewpoint.'

The driver pulled out of the line, circled the concrete apron and headed into the little town.

It was eight-thirty, the ferry had just docked and Ceuta, in the clear early morning light, was like a miniature Tangier. A bay, a harbour, whitewashed buildings shelving up from the quays, bare, rocky hills rising steeply behind. At first sight, watching it from the bows as the boat approached, only the scale was different – the scale and the colour of the sea. In Tangier, less than forty miles behind them to the west, the water had been turbulent Atlantic grey. Here, an hour later at the mouth of the Mediterranean, it was green, glittering and still.

The ferry had slid into its berth and Steele had scanned the front. Two baroque hotels, Spanish colonial with battlements and turrets, the main street running back from the port, the shop windows on either side filled with duty free Japanese cameras, radios and watches, a dusty road spiralling upwards in the distance. And then, lying so close to the berth that he almost missed it, a slim grey motor torpedo boat with the hammer and sickle flying from the masthead.

Across the harbour the hammer and sickle were repeated on

two vast black container towers. Steele had stiffened and gazed at them through the clouds of wheeling gulls. Seven years ago the Jewish cryptographer had stepped out of the administration block at their base, walked down to the front and the Callum legend had been born.

'This is it, señor.'

The driver drew in by a walled observation platform and Steele got out.

It had taken them only fifteen minutes to cross the town, climb the winding road beyond and come out on the summit of the hill that marked the western border of the tiny colony. Along the way they'd passed barrack blocks and barbed wire compounds, sentries at steel gates beneath the red and yellow banner of Spain, armoured jeeps and squads of marching soldiers. Greville had described Ceuta as little more than an armed camp. It wasn't difficult to see why.

Steele walked forward and looked down over the port and across the straits.

Eleven miles away the dark angular mass of Gibraltar was flanked with mist. Opposite it, on the African mainland to his left, the peak of Jebl Mussa soared bright and sharp against the sky. And as always between them, the twin pillars of Hercules of the ancient world, the sea-lane was crowded with shipping. Liners, tankers, freighters, trawlers, tugs, fishing boats, endless convoys moving in both directions – the same convoys through which in darkness, in the tarot, in the winter storms, Callum had once sailed the *Lara*.

He closed his eyes briefly. Then he turned and held out his hand.

'Ross Callum,' he said.

Lorca beamed, gapped yellow teeth showing between battered lips, and shook it firmly.

'I'm happy to meet you, Señor Callum.'

Standing he was shorter than he'd appeared in the cab, a squat thickset man with a deep barrel-chest and heavily-muscled arms. He was wearing a plaid shirt and a gold crucifix, nestling in dense black hair, gleamed through the open neck.

'So you want a job as a mate?'

'Yes, señor.'

'What about that?' Steele pointed at the cab. 'Can't you earn

107

'more money there?'

'It's October, señor, the season's over. A few *mili's*, maybe, but no more tourists, not even the local people now. They're moving out, going back to Spain. Once the British give back Gibraltar, the *moros* will want Ceuta. They've said so, they'll take it and afterwards—'

He swept out his hand in a flat chopping gesture. Then he hesitated.

'All my life I've lived with boats, Señor Callum. This is nothing,' he jerked his thumb contemptuously at the Renault, 'even if there were tourists, money, no problems, I would still sooner go back to the sea. That's a man's way to live. This is for *maricones.*'

'Tell me what you know about the sea.'

Surveillance control had rung through to the Minzah with Lorca's name the night before. The normally brisk expressionless voice had sounded angry and reluctant. Steele hadn't cared. It was late, he was halfway through the bottle of whisky, all he wanted to know was that they'd come up with someone Callum would have accepted – someone good.

'I started when I was thirteen, señor. My uncle had a small boat fishing out of Tarifa. I went there to crew for him, handlines at night and nets when the shoals were moving—'

Steele had been given the outline on the telephone. He listened now as Lorca filled in the details.

A childhood spent working as a deckhand, first on his uncle's boat and then on a coastal trawler. Next his *'mili'* – his military service which as a Ceuta native he'd done with the Spanish Legion whose base was in the colony. Afterwards fifteen years as a fitter in the naval dockyards on Gibraltar, where he'd learned to speak English. Finally, when Franco closed the Rock's border with Spain and the Spanish work-force became unemployed, he'd returned to fishing, this time on a deepsea tuna boat.

'But the catches dried up, señor,' he finished. 'What they take now, they take from offshore and the *sindicatos* control the jobs. I never belonged. But my cousin owns taxis here. For me it was that – or nothing.'

Lorca shrugged and stopped.

Steele looked at him. Then he made up his mind. Mary-Beth, Marcel, Louise, he'd trusted them all by instinct, taken them on

108

instantly without question because there was no time to probe or query or hesitate. It was the same now. The burly little man looked dour, taciturn, intransigent – a loner like the other three. Yet he'd sailed the straits on and off for thirty years, he'd been a legionaire, he knew engines, and in the hard, lined face – he'd smiled only once – Steele guessed there was more than just toughness. There was the capacity for loyalty too.

If he was right Callum himself could have done much worse.

'Do you know Donovan's boatyard in Tangier?' Steele said.

'I can find it, señor.'

'Be there by six this evening.'

'I got the job?'

Steele nodded and Lorca stretched out his hand. 'I won't let you down, Señor Callum.'

'You'd goddam better not!'

Steele grinned, they shook hands again, then they drove back to the town.

'I want some binoculars,' Steele said as they entered the main street. 'Where can I get them?'

'We go to my cousin's house, señor. He deals—'

'Not your cousin,' Steele cut him off, 'a shop, the biggest and best in Ceuta.'

Lorca glanced at him puzzled. Then he pointed. 'Mahaji's over there. He has as good a stock as anyone in town.'

Steele looked across the street. A large plate-glass window with banks of merchandise behind and the owner's name lettered above the door. Mahaji. Another of the ubiquitous Indian traders.

'Pull up and wait for me.'

Steele went inside. An old man and two assistants were serving a group of shoppers. He pushed his way through to the counter, pulled out a credit card and tossed it down.

'Give me a pair of those Zeiss 14 × 50s.'

Steele pointed at the most expensive binoculars in the window. The old man broke off from what he was doing, picked up the card, read the name and stared at him. Then he bowed.

'Of course, Mr Callum.'

He scuttled away smiling. Steele waited. Behind him the shoppers had stopped chattering and the two assistants were gazing at him open-mouthed.

'Is there anything else, sir?'

The old man had returned with the glasses. Steele shook his head, signed for them and picked up the parcel.

'My pleasure, Mr Callum,' the old man escorted him to the door. 'Any time you find yourself in need of anything, you have only to let me know.'

He bowed again and Steele went out. As he crossed the street he could hear the murmur of voices rising in excited speculation and he knew the curious stares were following him to the car.

'Here,' he got in and dropped the parcel on the front seat beside Lorca, 'a present to make sure you don't get lost on your way over to Tangier. Now take me down to the port.'

Steele leant back wiping the sweat from his face as the sun cut down between the lines of shops and the street filled with the morning heat.

It had taken him barely five minutes, but in Ceuta that was enough. From Mahaji's the word would spread out, rippling through the tiny colony until by midday everyone would have heard that Callum had been there. Not as a rumour this time, a shadowy fugitive presence, but in the flesh, a man who'd made purchases, signed his name, been seen and vouched for – just as he'd been seen in Tangier and Gibraltar, walking into the Minzah, checking the *Lara* at the boatyard, receiving the caviare and champagne he'd ordered from the Rock Hotel.

Tangier, Gibraltar, Ceuta. Three of the five ports of the dirty area that already knew beyond doubt Callum was back. Now there was the fourth, Algeciras, and Juan Fischer.

The Casino was on the eastern side of the upper square.

'*Remember that in Spain,*' Greville had said, '*Casino doesn't denote gambling in the sense you or I would understand. It's the name given to the local businessmen's meeting-place, their private club. There's one in every town and they'll gamble between themselves of course. But much more important the Casino is where every transaction takes place.*'

Steele stood by the fountain at the square's centre surrounded by orange trees, gaudily-tiled benches, plump Spanish matrons and screaming skipping children. The crossing had lasted forty minutes and he'd walked up into the town from the modern harbour. Through the open floors of a half-finished office block

110

he could see the landward face of the Rock, only two miles away now, and smoke from the industrial complex that ringed the bay between it and Algeciras streamed in grimy black pennants overhead.

He lit a cigarette, kicked away a ball that landed at his feet, stepped round a little girl sobbing over a grazed knee, and walked towards the entrance.

'I'm looking for Mr Fischer.'

'*Perdón, señor?*'

The white-jacketed waiter at the door looked at him uncomprehending. Steele took out a piece of paper, wrote down Fischer's name and handed it to him.

'*Ah sí, señor,*' the waiter nodded. '*Momentito, por favor.*'

The waiter disappeared and Steele stepped back. Beside the door a long, smoked glass window fronted onto the street. Behind it fat men in black suits and dark glasses were seated opposite each other at tables in silent concentration over games of chess or dominoes, occasionally reaching out to remove a piece from the board. In the grey twilight world they looked like immense fish feeding in some vast aquarium.

'*Buenos días.*'

Steele looked round. 'Mr Fischer?'

The man nodded.

'My name's Callum,' Steele said, 'Ross Callum. Your friend Mr Yehuda suggested I came to see you.'

Steele didn't know which of the two names was responsible, but Fischer went pale, rose on the tips of his toes as if he was preparing to become airborne, then suddenly grabbed Steele's arm and bolted across the road.

With Steele behind him he threaded his way through the crowd in the square and plunged into a cobbled street leading downhill on the far side. Thirty yards further on there was an open doorway with the word *Camas* painted on the wall and a broken neon bar sign. Fischer turned in and climbed the stairs to a dusky room on the first floor.

He didn't speak until they were sitting on a bench below a window so thickly coated with dirt that beams of light filtered through as if it had been an iron grille. There was a chipped plastic table in front of them, a few more scattered round the walls, a pair of sallow Moroccans apathetically playing cards, and

111

a bar at the far end.

'Truly I don't know how to excuse myself, Mr Callum—'

Fischer was wearing flashy gold-framed glasses with broad wings. He took them off, hands shaking, and wiped his face.

'For me personally to make your acquaintance is a delight, a privilege. But the circumstances, your sudden arrival, our good mutual acquaintance Mr Yehuda – well, you understand my position, of course.'

He raised his arm importantly and snapped his fingers to summon the barman. The only sound he succeeded in making was a limp click which the barman didn't hear over the gush of water in the sink.

Steele didn't understand, but he could guess.

Fischer was in his forties, an ill-made flabby posturing man with a balding head, furtive eyes and a long thin moustache that straggled down over a moist mouth. His suit, black like the others behind the smoked glass, was cheap and shiny, and the cigarette-case he laid on the table when the barman finally appeared was like his glasses – large, ostentatious and vulgar.

Steele looked at him with distaste. A smell came off him, aniseed, cologne and something else – greed. Yehuda had called him a dealer. He wasn't. He was a hustler, a scavenger, a grubber in the dust, a ragbag merchant who was trying to become respectable, to graduate from the small time, and who'd been terrified at the thought of what Callum's appearance in his company might have done to his standing in the Casino.

'Now what will you have? A cognac, an anis? Whatever is your pleasure.'

Fischer smiled ingratiatingly.

Steele waved away the barman and said curtly, 'I didn't come here to drink. I came to talk. And I'm not used to talking in places like this.'

'Mr Callum, please,' Fischer ordered a large brandy for himself and gulped it nervously as soon as it came. 'This is purely for convenience, so we can speak in private.'

'Then let's speak. You've got a consignment. What does it consist of?'

'Well, in general terms—'

'Not in general terms, in specifics. Numbers, makes, types, condition.'

Fischer frowned unhappily. 'It is a little difficult at this moment for me to be precise.'

'What the bloody hell do you mean?'

'I am acting for principals. If only you had given me warning, given me time to organize everything. Maybe you could come back tomorrow—'

'Tomorrow? Who do you think I am—?'

Steele stared at him. His anger was part simulated and part real.

'Listen, I've broken people's necks for wasting my time less than this. You either produce your principals right now – or you can forget about it.'

He started to rise, but Fischer caught his arm.

'Please, Mr Callum, let me consider—'

He hesitated, plucked at his moustache, fiddled with his stained tie, then he jumped up.

'I will try to telephone.'

He went over to the bar and disappeared into a cabin by the counter. Steele waited. The two Moroccans had abandoned their game of cards and were sipping tea. Fragments of Arabic drifted across the floor and in the distance he could still hear the screams of the children in the square.

'We are in luck, Mr Callum,' Fischer came back smiling eagerly, 'if we go now, we can catch them. I take you in my car.'

'Who are they and where do we find them?'

'The first is a Señor Calderón, a gentleman of much distinction. We go to his *cortijo*, his farm, in the country. It takes us maybe two hours.'

Steele thought for a moment. Then he said, 'Wait here.'

He walked to the telephone cabin, closed the door tightly and dialled.

'Go ahead.'

Another anonymous voice, not surveillance control because the Algeciras–Tangier linkup was too slow. Instead someone new, someone in the town who'd been directing the protective screen since he landed.

'Right, take this down carefully and get it over to Tangier. I'm going out into the country, to a farm belonging to a man called Calderón—'

113

There was a little window in the cabin. Steele twisted his neck round and glanced through. Fischer was still by the table, hurriedly drinking another glass of brandy.

'Whoever you've got behind me, pull them back, tell them to wait for me at the city limits. If Velatti's out there, they'll just scare him off. And if he's not I won't need them.'

'Now wait a minute. Whereabouts in the country—?'

'I don't know and I don't care,' Steele interrupted, 'if it's a set-up, that's my problem. You just do as I tell you – and God help you if you don't.'

He put the telephone down and went back to the table.

Fischer's car was an old black Fiat. They crossed the town, joined the midday traffic streaming along the Malaga highway, followed the coast for a few kilometres, then they turned inland towards the sierras.

Afterwards they drove steadily for two hours. At first the countryside was wild, oppressive and desolate with steep rock-strewn hills, dark cork forests shadowing the road, lonely valleys that sheered down from the peaks beneath soaring vultures. Later it opened out into rolling plains, pale, dun-coloured, scorched and faded by the months of summer sun, with occasional little farmhouses, most of them ruined and deserted, and always on the crest of each horizon a hill-village, gleaming white like a snow-fortress suspended in the heat.

'Medina Sidonia,' Fischer pointed at one of the villages. 'The *cortijo* is beyond.'

They circled the foot of the hill and drove for a further twenty minutes. Then Fischer turned off the road onto a track that led through an arch with a carved stone emblem, painted a deep red-brown, at its centre. Half a mile later they stopped on a baked earth courtyard in front of a long rambling building.

'A moment please.'

Fischer got out and walked over to the main door. Steele stood by the car looking round.

They were in a bowl in the hills with great sweeps of dry fissured pasture stretching up on every side, the dead grass silver now in the afternoon light. The sun was still fierce and arid but a thin breeze rippled down from the high sierras to the north. A bell sounded from the tower of a little chapel somewhere inside the building, a cluster of greyhound puppies tumbled sleepily in

114

the dust, some farmhands gathered at the entrance to a barn talking quietly in the shade.

Everything was normal, tranquil, almost drowsy. He couldn't believe Velatti would have chosen a place like this, it had the wrong feel to it, the wrong atmosphere. Yet the old Moroccan Jew, Yehuda, had been quite specific: you will find Fischer of interest. Steele casually put his hand in his pocket, feeling for a cigarette but checking the Browning at the same time. Then Fischer came back.

'Señor Calderón is over at the ring—'

He explained as they crossed the yard.

'He has a nephew, a *torero*, who goes for the winter season to fight bulls in South America. Señor Calderón himself is a breeder of repute, the bulls from this *ganadería* are known all over Spain. He is running some of them now for his nephew to practise before he leaves.'

The ring was a small brick circle, painted the same dazzling white as the hill-villages. As they reached it a wooden gate opened. Beyond on the sand inside a group of people were standing by a barrier against the curving wall. Some herdsmen, three figures holding scarlet capes, a slim young man in boots and a short black jacket, and a taller older man at the centre.

Fischer went up and spoke to the tall man. Steele couldn't understand what he was saying but his voice was respectful and the ingratiating smile was back on his face.

'Señor Calderón doesn't speak English,' Fischer turned. 'I have explained it is the same for you in Spanish. But I introduce you.'

Steele shook hands. Calderón was burly, thick-necked, with red-veined cheeks, a tight cunning mouth and a great fleshy curving nose. The Andalucian equivalent, Steele guessed, of a west country English landowner – coarse, hard-drinking, shrewd and avaricious.

The Spaniard said something and Fischer translated. 'He asks if you still have the *afición*, the love for the bulls.'

Callum was supposed to have been a follower of bullfights, Steele remembered. He shrugged and then grinned.

'Tell him I've been away a long time,' Steele said, 'I'm more at home with young heifers now – the two-legged variety.'

Fischer repeated it in Spanish and Calderón gave a roar of

laughter.

'*Queda uno. Uno bueno.*'

'They have one left to run,' Fischer said, 'A good one.'

Calderón stepped behind the barrier, beckoned Steele to stand beside him and tossed him a cape. Steele took it, feeling the weight of the heavy cloth dragging at his hands, and glanced at Fischer who was standing on the other side of the Spaniard.

'In case there is need to make a *quite*, a distraction,' Fischer called across, 'in case of an accident.'

Steele gripped the cape by its collar as the others were doing on the far side of the ring, shook it out grimly, looked over the top of the barrier and waited.

The outer gate slammed shut, another one opened to their left, for a few minutes there was nothing except a square of darkness, then something exploded out of it, a black shape, racing, plunging, grunting, travelling in a cone of dust. The animal skidded to a halt, Calderón reached over and slapped the barrier, and the animal charged.

As it hit the wood the entire frame shuddered and rocked, and for an instant Steele thought the barrier was going to shatter, pinioning them in the wreckage against the wall behind. The bull snorted, hooked savagely at the planks, its horns gouging out great splinters that whirled up into the air, and a hot feral smell came reeking up over the sound of savage remorseless battering. Then it turned suddenly and galloped away.

Steele let go of the pillar he'd been clinging to and breathed out slowly. Sweat was streaming off him, his arms were limp and his chest felt hollow. He'd never seen anything like it, the speed, the massive neck muscles, the horns stabbing and slashing like steel lances, the power and blind implacable ferocity of the attack.

'*Un toro muy bravo, no?*' Calderón was grinning at him.

Steele wiped his face, forced a smile and nodded.

Then the slim figure in the black jacket was in the ring, trailing a cape behind him. The bull whirled, charged, the cape belled out and suddenly the animal was turning again on the other side, grunting, head tossing, searching for the target before it charged once more. The matador backed off, cited and there was another flare of pink and gold.

It went on for ten minutes. The passes with the cape first. Then

116

a horseman entering, legs encased in armour, and a metal-tipped pic being driven into the animal's neck, breaking down the muscles and lowering its head as the blood pumped out. Finally the matador again, this time with a smaller cloth, working the animal more slowly, closer to him, drawing out each pass longer and longer as the bull surged forward with the same unremitting hostility.

'*Te alcanza?*' Calderón called out and the matador made a gesture of agreement.

'*Será un buén semental,*' the Spaniard glanced at Steele again, '*para criar.*'

'A fine bull,' Fischer translated, 'good stock, good for breeding, not to be killed.'

Steele nodded as if he'd reached the same conclusion.

A third gate leading into a corral was swung open and the matador began guiding the bull towards it, moving the animal forward in a series of little charges, citing each time with the cloth and then running back a few steps as it came on. He brought it past the barrier five yards away from them, positioned the animal at the entrance to the corral, flicked out the cloth for the final time – and then it happened.

The matador turned away as the bull lunged forward, the trailing cloth tangled itself round his ankle, he slipped, thrust out an arm desperately trying to keep his balance, his leg buckled and he fell face down on the sand. Instantly the bull veered away from the corral and checked.

There were urgent cries and figures started to race out from the far side of the ring. Then Steele was aware of Calderón swivelling towards him.

'*Anda, hombre, anda!*'

He heard Calderón bellowing, a hand struck his shoulder and he stumbled out from the protection of the barrier onto the open sand.

The bull was already moving towards the matador's prostrate body and Steele suddenly realized he was the only one with a cape near enough to stop the animal before it attacked. He ran forward, swirled out the cloth, the bull's head jerked up, it hesitated, then it changed direction and charged.

Steele rocked back pushing the cape away from him. He heard his shirt rip as a horn scythed past his chest, felt a jolting bump as

117

the animal's shoulder cannoned against his ribs, dimly saw blood spreading over his stomach. Then the bull was turning on him again and there was only dust, sweat stinging his eyes, an agonizing pain in his foot as the animal trampled him, vicious laboured grunting, a great dark mass tossing and heaving and goring.

The cape ripped like his shirt, one of his hands was thrown free as if it had been kicked away, and he knew he was falling, the bull, the chopping horns, the torn cloth, his body, the stench of blood and animal urine, manacled in a single flailing bundle.

'*Olé, torero—!*'

A voice shouting, laughing, Calderón's voice, a hand under his shoulder, stillness after the furious battering noise. Steele levered himself to his feet. He was trembling, panting, aching, but the corral gate was shut and the bull had vanished.

'*Un quite muy noble. Felicidades!*'

Calderón clapped Steele's shoulder and laughed again. All the herdsmen and peons were standing in a circle round him, and Steele realized that one of them must have done the same as he'd done for the matador – drawn the bull away at the last moment. The slim young man came up and gripped his hand. Over his shoulder Steele could see Fischer beaming proudly.

'Tell him I normally charge for something like that,' he said, 'but this time I'll settle for a drink.'

Fischer translated again and Calderón chuckled. '*Claro,*' he turned towards the gate, '*a la casa.*'

The house was dark and cool with stone-flagged corridors, vines rustling on the window glass, shutters pulled against the sun, and walls hung with rows of mounted trophies, the antlers gleaming grey-white in the dim light. A servant-girl gave Steele one of Calderón's shirts and a pair of trousers, and showed him to a bathroom. He showered, dressed and walked back to the hall.

'Here, Mr Callum.'

Fischer was waiting for him. Steele followed him into a study overlooking the front courtyard. Calderón was standing by a desk with a bottle in his hand. He filled three glasses and gave one to Steele.

'*Salud!*' Calderón raised his glass and drank.

Steele sniffed the wine, circling it first in the slender tumbler. It smelled chill, dry and fragrant.

'*Pesetas,*' he said, '*y amor.*'

118

He drank too. Health, money and love. Not health alone because that was the republican, the communist toast from the civil war. Money and love were what the fascists had added – the love most Spaniards would say, as Greville had explained, being an overwhelming desire for wealth.

Calderón laughed, drained his glass and offered the bottle again. Steele shook his head and glanced at Fischer.

'You tell him I came to talk business,' he said.

Calderón must have understood because before Fischer could translate he went to the back of the room, unlocked a cabinet and returned with three leather cases. He laid them on the desk, unzipped their flaps and stood back. Steele looked down, then up at Fischer again.

'These are samples?'

'Yes, señor.'

Steele picked up the nearest case and folded back the leather covering. Inside was a long-barrelled Belgian .38 revolver identical to the Smith & Wesson he'd found in the *Lara* except it had a calibrated rear-sight and a modern ring-frame at the muzzle. The second case contained a standard open-butt Mannling submachine gun and the third an Israeli FN rifle.

'How many of each?'

'Three hundred of the revolvers,' Fischer said, 'one hundred rifles, fifty Mannlings. They are a very fine consignment, Mr Callum, unused, guaranteed, surplus from Angola.'

Steele studied the guns again. Calderón was watching him, eyes hidden behind sunglasses. He hesitated, something grating at the back of his mind. Then he picked up the Mannling.

He worked the breech mechanism, checked the sights, the balance, the magazine chamber, the spring loading – all functioned perfectly. It was an adequate serviceable weapon. So was the revolver and the rifle. Steele stood back frowning. Something was still wrong, something he couldn't place. Then it suddenly came to him.

'*It's pure background of course,*' Greville with a photograph in his hand, '*but remember there's a lot of rubbish mixed up with the arms being traded down there. There's one particularly notorious model, a Mannling made under licence in Yugoslavia. The firing-pin spring collapses after a few magazines.*'

Steele reached for the submachine gun again, and turned it

119

over. A tiny stamp at the base of the trigger-guard gave a Belgrade manufacturer's name. He cocked the gun, raised the breech to his ear and squeezed the trigger. Behind the hard metallic tap of the pin he heard the spring rustle softly.

He tossed the Mannling onto a chair.

'No,' he said flatly.

Calderón didn't move but Fischer looked at him blankly. 'Is there something wrong, Mr Callum?'

'It's more than wrong, it's bloody rubbish. Who the hell does your fancy friend think he's dealing with?'

Fischer started to say something to Calderón but the Spaniard cut him off. He went back to the cabinet, returned with another leather case, handed it to Steele and spoke to Fischer.

'Señor Calderón says if you prefer we can offer you fifty of these instead.'

Steele unzipped the case and examined the new gun. It was an American version of the Mannling with the same calibre and performance, but without the history of malfunction.

'Too goddam right I prefer it,' Steele put it on the table beside the other two. 'Now what about price, terms and delivery?'

The two conferred. Then Fischer said, 'Señor Calderón says those are matters for his partner.'

'Fine. Where is he?'

'In Algeciras—'

'Algeciras!' Steele exploded. 'For Christ's sake, what the hell is this – a bloody paperchase?'

'Mr Callum,' Fischer lifted his hands plaintively, 'like I told you, if I had known in advance everything could have been arranged, he would have been here too. But we can drive back and find him.'

Steele stood for a moment looking at them. Calderón impassive, Fischer tugging nervously at his moustache.

Fischer was a cypher, a nonentity, but the Spaniard must have known. It had been rigged, everything, the whole day had been a series of tests, and watching Calderón's face Steele knew he'd underestimated Velatti once again. Velatti was more than cautious, he was obsessive, a paranoic, feeling every inch of his way like a man walking across sheet ice.

Callum had been an expert on weapons so the dud Mannling had been planted on him. That had been simple, explicable enough.

120

But then Steele thought of the bull, the slashing horns, the risk he'd taken with his life in those dizzying bruising seconds just to prove Callum knew about *corridas* too – and his anger against the little Maltese, against his accomplices like Calderón, flared up in a surge of murderous hatred.

He could feel his wrists shaking, sweat pooling on his shoulders in spite of the study's coolness, a vein throbbing beneath his ear. He gripped the Browning in his pocket and pressed the barrel against his thigh until it was almost cutting his skin. Then he controlled himself. They'd been tests and he'd passed them all. He'd go on passing them, however many there were, until he found Velatti. When that happened there'd be more than the assignment to be finished – there'd be a reckoning too for everything the Maltese had done to him.

Steele let go of the gun, stepped forward and shook hands stiffly with Calderón. Then he glanced at Fischer.

'Tell him I like his wine better than his bulls or his guns.'

He went out and got into Fischer's car.

It was dark when they reached Algeciras again. Fischer drove through the town and stopped by a building in a run-down suburb on the edge of the bay. As Steele got out of his car he saw a red lamp glowing above a door and higher still in scarlet neon a sign saying *Pasaje Andaluz*.

'I am sorry, Mr Callum,' Fischer shrugged apologetically, 'but in such places one can talk in confidence.'

They went into a long narrow room lit by revolving bulbs encased in pink cellophane shades, with strips of silver tinsel hanging from the walls and a little sunken dance-floor at the far end. The Madame of the house was leaning over the bar, immense, heavily-painted, stone-faced, wearing a flounced and spangled dress with a deep cleavage that showed vast marble-white breasts. It was too early yet for the evening trade but a group of women, none of them under forty and all almost as large as the Madame, were sitting yawning and talking spasmodically at a table near a deserted bandstand.

Fischer spoke to the Madame, beckoned to Steele and they climbed a flight of stairs at the back of the room. Partitioned cubicles led off either side of a landing, their doors open and the same cellophane-shaded lamps glowing inside over simple iron

121

beds. The air in the corridor smelt of disinfectant, orange blossom, perfume and sulphur from the discharge of the refinery half a mile further round the bay.

'If you will kindly wait,' Fischer showed Steele into one of the cubicles, 'I will fetch Señor Ybarra.'

'Is he Calderón's partner?'

'Yes, señor.'

'Okay, I'll wait. But this time we finish it, no more running around like a goddam travelling circus, right?'

'Of course, Mr Callum.'

As Fischer nodded a girl appeared at the entrance to the cubicle. She could only have been fourteen or fifteen, slender, childlike, with slanting sloe-black eyes, dark skin and long shining hair. She was wearing a plain white shift and her feet were bare.

Fischer glanced at her and then looked back at Steele.

'Listen, it takes me maybe fifteen minutes. You want to enjoy yourself? The ones downstairs, they're for sailors. They like flesh,' he cupped his hands against his chest. 'But this one's different, for special clients. Very clean, very nice, very experienced. *Quitatelo*!'

He shouted at the girl and she raised the shift to her neck. Underneath her naked body was even more like a child's, slim and firm with small uptilted breasts and long delicate legs. She moved her hips and smiled at Steele.

'She's hot, no?' Fischer leered at him, 'You take her as a present from me and my principals.'

Steele shook his head. 'I'll just wait.'

The girl's face crumpled, she lowered the shift slowly and turned away.

'Tell her it's nothing personal,' Steele added embarrassed, 'but all I want right now is a drink.'

He fumbled for his wallet, handed the girl a thousand-peseta note, Fischer translated and she smiled again, a quick radiant smile of gratitude. Then she went out with Fischer behind her.

Steele surveyed the cubicle rapidly. The bed, a cane chair, a wash-basin groin height on the partition wall. Nothing else. He stepped into the corridor and walked to the far end. There was a door opening onto a metal staircase that led to the ground. He removed the key, tossed it into the darkness and latched back the

122

lock. Then he returned to the cubicle and checked the window. It was too dark to see what was below but he guessed the drop was only eight or nine feet.

He was pushing back the shutters when he heard something tinkle behind him. He dropped the bar and swung round, crouching, flattening himself against the wall, reaching for the Browning. It was only the girl. She came back into the room holding a tray with two bottles of Spanish champagne and some glasses. Beyond her he could see other figures gathered round the doorway, a shrivelled man of about sixty, a dumpy grey-haired woman in a black shawl, a younger man with a guitar, two more girls, all with the same dark shifting eyes.

'*Quiere usted una copita*?'

The girl filled a glass and held it out to him. Steele straightened up and took it. The others came into the cubicle and squatted on the floor. He watched them warily for a moment, his hand still round the gun. The girl poured out more champagne, passed round the glasses and knelt beside the young man, who began to pluck tentatively at his guitar, the chords building slowly until he found the melody and was playing it, happily, confidently, smiling over the waxed strings.

Then Steele understood. They were the girl's family. He took his hand from his pocket, smiled and lifted his glass.

'Cheers,' he said.

The girl laughed and started to sing. Very quietly at first in a high wistful voice as if she was singing to herself, and then more strongly until after a few minutes she got to her feet and began to dance. Steele stood by the window watching. He couldn't understand the words of the song but there was an extraordinary grace in her movements, demure, precise, fingers snapping, black hair whirling round her face, the white shift flaring out as her bare feet stamped rhythmically on the floor.

He glanced at the others. They were smoking, laughing, clapping happily in time as they followed the intricate patterns of the steps. Then he drank again and grinned. A whorehouse, a young gypsy prostitute, a glass of cheap Spanish champagne, a gun weighing down his jacket – and yet for the first time since he'd walked ashore at Tangier he felt relaxed, almost content.

A moment later footsteps sounded on the landing. He stiffened, waved them into silence and Fischer reappeared.

'He comes now, Mr Callum.'

Steele pulled out another thousand peseta note, tossed it to the girl and the family filed out. There was silence for an instant, then more footsteps, firm confident steps, and Steele gripped the Browning again.

'Señor Callum?'

Ybarra was short, formal, blunt-headed, businesslike, in the regulation uniform of the Casino. Black suit, dark glasses, highly polished shoes, the same as Fischer wore except where on Fischer they looked tawdry and unconvincing, with Ybarra the effect was prosperous and assured – the equipment of a solid competent man of affairs.

'I hope we can conclude this to mutual satisfaction.'

His English was fluent and barely accented. A bilingual Gilbraltarian, Steele guessed, who'd moved to the mainland when the border was closed.

Ybarra produced a sheet of paper. 'Three hundred revolvers, one hundred rifles, fifty medium automatic repeaters. You have seen samples and you are satisfied?'

He looked up.

'Leaving aside the garbage I was no doubt shown by mistake,' Steele said, 'they'll do.'

'So the consignment interests you?'

'The price interests me.'

'The current market rate for the three models is respectively as follows—'

Ybarra read from the sheet of paper, multiplied the figures and added up the total.

'I will give you a substantial discount of course,' he finished, 'twelve and a half per cent. For the entire consignment, therefore, let us say £15,000.'

Steele shook his head. 'I'm not interested.'

'Mr Callum, you know the state of the market, the going prices, the discounts—'

'Señor Ybarra,' Steele interrupted him, 'I know in the present state of the market it's damn near impossible to unload a cargo like that. It's too small to interest a government, too big to be sold individually. I know the going price, which is roughly half what you're quoting. And you know I pay in gold coin, in krugerrand, which carries a discount value not of twelve and a half but

124

twenty-five—'

He paused. 'Now we've got three choices. We can continue to play games. We can have a drink and discuss the state of the nation. Or we can talk. I had my games today in your partner's bullring. I've already had my drink. So—'

Steele stopped. Ybarra thought for a moment. Then he said, 'Maybe we can talk a little.'

It took them ten minutes to agree a final figure of £9,000 in gold krugerrand, one third to be paid as a deposit to Ybarra's agent in Tangier, the balance when Steele took delivery of the weapons.

'And where are they?' Steele said.

'In Morocco south of Tangier. We will do the transaction in one. You pay the deposit, our agent escorts you to the consignment, then you complete.'

'Morocco's a large country, Señor Ybarra. How far south?'

'In the desert near Boumalne. Five hundred kilometres.'

'Five hundred?' Steele stared at him. 'I think we're playing games again. You expect me to shift them that distance, across the whole bloody country?'

Ybarra shrugged. 'I have many lines of business, Mr Callum, but I am not in transportation. You will need only one truck and a driver. With hire charges and gasolene I imagine it will cost you perhaps three krugerrand in all. I give you that as a last discount.'

He took off his glasses and polished them carefully. His face was expressionless and Steele knew he'd finished, there'd be no more bargaining or concessions.

Steele turned away, walked to the window and lit a cigarette. The price, the terms and arrangements were normal, even the distance in spite of his protestations was standard for an ordinary arms deal. Consignments of weapons were too hot, too dangerous to be held in cities. Until they were sold they were stored out in remote areas of the desert like the country round Boumalne.

Yet this wasn't an ordinary deal. It was an elaborate set-up engineered by Velatti, not to supply a cargo of arms to Gonsalves – the Portuguese and the guns were irrelevant – but to satisfy himself he was dealing with the man he believed to be Callum and not an imposter. Yehuda had said as much and the unseen presence of the little Maltese, scrutinizing, checking, testing, had lain unmistakably like a shadow over every stage along the trail.

Now at the end it was inconceivable he'd expect Steele to keep a rendezvous five hundred kilometres from Tangier, and relative safety, in a desolate section of the Moroccan desert on the edge of the Sahara. It was an invitation to suicide and Velatti would know it, know Steele was bound to refuse. After his letter to London when he'd disappeared neither Callum nor anyone else would walk into a trap as dangerous and obvious as that.

Steele turned and looked back. Fischer was standing at a respectful distance by the doorway. Ybarra was in the centre of the room, stiff, impassive, patient.

Then Steele said suddenly, 'Do you know a man called Velatti?'

Ybarra nodded. 'Casually, señor.'

Steele froze. 'You do business with him, business like this?'

'All of my business is private, Mr Callum,' Ybarra said calmly. 'I am sure yours is too.'

Steele dropped his cigarette and ground it out on the floor, forcing himself to move slowly, unconcernedly.

'Well, maybe you can tell me when you saw him last?'

'Of course. It was in the town this morning. We met briefly in the street. I think he mentioned he was on his way to Lisbon.'

'Thank you, Señor Ybarra,' Steele stepped forward and held out his hand. 'On the other matter we have a deal. I will contact your agent as soon as I'm ready.'

'My pleasure, Mr Callum.'

Ybarra shook hands and went out.

'I knew you would like my principals, very fine gentlemen.'

Fischer had said nothing throughout the conversation. Now he came towards Steele beaming happily, his mouth damp and complacent under the wispy moustache.

'Perhaps we have a proper drink to celebrate, no?'

'Why not?' Steele managed to grin. 'But first I want a quick word with that little lady. You wait for me in the car, right?'

He winked, Fischer laughed knowingly and disappeared into the corridor.

Steele listened to his footsteps fading on the stairs. His stomach was churning and he had to keep drying his palms on his jacket. Ybarra had seen Velatti in Algeciras that morning. It might have been another lie, another deception, another plant,

126

but Steele didn't think so. The information hadn't been volunteered – it had only come out by accident after Steele's impulsive question.

If it was true the Maltese was almost certainly still there now. It was the story about going to Lisbon that had been the blind. Velatti knew Steele would end up in the whorehouse, knew that whatever he said to Ybarra Steele would instantly reject the idea of a rendezvous in the desert, and knew too that once the Spaniard departed he'd be left isolated in darkness in the derelict suburb.

Steele stepped onto the landing. Three of the cubicle doors were shut now and he could hear muffled noises from inside, a moan, an arguing voice, the slap of a hand and giggling laughter, but the corridor was deserted and there was no sound from the stairs. He glanced upwards. There were two bulbs in the ceiling, both with bare bright filaments unshaded by the pink cellophane inside the rooms.

He unscrewed one quickly with his handkerchief, but the second stubbornly refused to turn. Steele hesitated. Then, as a door opened below and music echoed up the stairs, he pulled out the Browning and tapped the globe with its butt. There was a small explosion, drowned by the noise of the band, a shower of sparks, and the landing was plunged into darkness. Steele shook the fragments of glass from his hair, ran to the end of the corridor, kicked open the door above the metal steps and climbed to the ground.

The car was a battered grey Simca. It had crawled behind him up from the harbour when he'd walked away from the Ceuta ferry, and he'd spotted it again, stationary on the highway verge, when he and Fischer had returned to Algeciras in the dusk. Now it was parked fifty yards beyond the whorehouse on the opposite side of the road to Fischer's Fiat. Steele circled the block, raced across the street at the bisection of two lamplight arcs, jerked open the passenger door and slid down into the seat.

'Get me to the port.'

The driver was young and fair haired. He grabbed something from the passenger locker and swung towards Steele openmouthed.

'But—'

'For Christ's sake, you're meant to be looking after me, aren't

127

you? Do as you're bloody well told!'

The young man gaped, hesitated, then he started the engine and pulled away from the kerb. As they turned right towards the harbour Steele lifted his head and looked back. Behind the Fiat's windscreen he could see Fischer carefully combing his moustache.

The last ferry to Tangier was about to leave. They drew up by the booking hall, Steele tapped the young man on the shoulder, jumped out, hurried through customs, pushed his passport in front of yawning immigration officials, and reached the gangplank just as the dockers were about to pull it away.

On board he headed straight for the first class bar. He bought a large brandy and walked out onto the foredeck as the boat swung away from its berth. Apart from a few harbour employees the quay below was deserted and he was certain no one had boarded after him. He drained the glass, gripped the rail and looked over the bows.

In spite of the warm night air Steele was shivering. He finally knew where Velatti was – on the shore behind him, waiting somewhere in the ill-lit streets between the whorehouse and the harbour. Within an hour the Maltese would realize what had happened. Tomorrow he'd have to plan again and tomorrow Steele would be ready. He'd find some reason for another meeting with Ybarra. He'd cross the straits and keep the appointment – only this time there wouldn't be just a dazed young man in a battered Simca covering him, there'd be every single figure working for surveillance control in the western Mediterranean.

Steele pushed himself away from the rail. The lights of Gibraltar were receding as the ferry headed south. Halfway up the Rock Louise would be pouring herself another drink. Cynical weary vulnerable little Louise with her crumpled housecoat, her bottles of gin and her loneliness. Yet for an instant, as the lights faded on the horizon, she seemed to represent something safe, a sanctuary where he didn't have to be constantly on the alert, wary, delving endlessly for protection into the store of what Greville had taught him.

Steele swore. A voice at the end of a telephone line, worried young men who followed him in cars, a dowdy Englishwoman trying to blunt the pain of her solitude with alcohol – and he was clinging to them all like a child to a lamp in the dark.

He went back into the bar. He was still there when the ferry docked. It was eleven. He hadn't been able to send a message to Marcel to meet him with the car and there were no taxis on the quay. The shortest route to the Minzah was up through the souk. Steele walked along the harbour front and turned into the town.

The man lurched across the alley and cannoned into him when he was only fifty yards beyond the police barrier.

12

There were five of them. At first, seeing them reel and sway in the shadows ahead of him, Steele had thought they were a party of sailors looking for a last drink in one of the bars round the Grand Socco.

Even when the man crashed against him and he felt an elbow slam into his ribs, he still believed it was a drunken accident. Steele swore, heaved him away and crossed to the other side of the alley. A moment later the alley divided, he took the left-hand fork and they vanished.

In the darkness the souk was a blind twisting warren. The stalls and shops, noisy and crowded by day, were shuttered and silent. A few lamps gleamed behind curtains on the upper stories of the cramped houses, the invariable smells of Tangier – hashish, coalfire smoke and herbs – filtered down, an occasional light hung from an arch, but apart from one or two scurrying Arabs the lanes were deserted. If Steele hadn't known his direction was straight upwards he'd have been hopelessly lost within minutes of leaving the port.

He turned a right-angle corner and saw the five were in front of him again, grouped by a wall. He walked forward, came abreast of them, a match flared and there was a bellow of laughter. Then one of them leant back, seemed to stumble and suddenly plunged across the cobbles. It was a shoulder charge, the man's bone smashing into Steele's chest, and even as he toppled off balance, hurled back against a shutter, he knew this time it was deliberate.

The shutter caved inwards, glass shattered and Steele struggled upright. A window opened above his head, light spilled over the alley and he heard the brief anxious murmur of voices. Then the window clanged shut again, the light was cut off and the voices faded.

Steele stood panting on the cobbles. Something warm was running down his left arm. He touched it with his other hand and realized he'd been cut by a splinter of glass when the shutter gave way. The man who'd attacked him had returned to the group and they were all watching him from a few yards higher up the alley.

He waited sweating, bewildered and furious. He had no idea who they were, but the surveillance team should have been right behind him. There was no one else, only dim deserted tracks leading down towards the harbour.

'Hey, mister—'

The five spread out in a cordon across the alley and another of them weaved towards him laughing, his voice slurred.

'You got a cigarette?'

The man stopped and swayed in front of him. Steele tensed himself. The man's accent was thick and foreign, but Steele knew the slurred voice and the shambling gait were a pretence. He was like the others, big, dark and stone-cold sober.

'Sure.'

Steele reached for his pocket, swivelled, leant into the man, and drove his knee upwards. He wasn't fast enough. The man was turning too and Steele's knee hit his thigh instead of his groin, sending him sprawling back but not dropping him.

Steele whirled round and glanced at the other four. They were moving down towards him, no longer laughing but steady and purposeful. He checked for an instant, taking everything in, analysing and assessing. Behind him the alley wound down to the harbour. He could go back but he was more than two-thirds of the way up the hill now, they'd have the advantage of the slope and he could easily trap himself in the maze of lanes.

Somewhere ahead, only fifty or a hundred yards beyond the advancing figures, was the Grand Socco – light, people, cars, Moroccan gendarmes. He stepped back and looked to his right. There was an arch on the other side of the alley with a dark passage leading inside. If it was like the others there'd be another alley at the far end angling upwards.

He turned back again. The man he'd kicked had recovered his balance and was coming at him once more, just in front of the other four. Steele splayed out his knuckles, feinted with his leg and drove his hand into the man's face. He heard a cry of pain,

131

the man reeled away and Steele threw himself under the arch.

The passage was totally impenetrably black, the eaves of the houses on either side almost touching so that not even starlight came down. There should have been a glow in the distance where it opened onto another lane, but there was nothing – only the dense scented darkness. Steele felt his way along the walls with his fingers. Rough-cast brick, a stone coping, bars over a shuttered window, an iron-studded door.

Then more brick, a sharp angle, another bolted door, and he was working back along the other side. He stopped and swung round. He was in a cul-de-sac.

'Where's that cigarette, mister?'

There was just enough light from the main alley to see that the five were walking towards him up the passage pressed shoulder to shoulder by the constricting walls. The man in the centre struck a match, the flame flared over a craggy peering face, then the match went out and only a small dull spark glowed in the blackness.

Steele pressed himself back against the door at the end of the cul-de-sac. The men couldn't see him but he could see them, five crouching wavering silhouettes, haloed against the dim alley light. The entire souk had gone totally silent, even the small noises from the upstairs rooms had stopped and the lamps behind the curtains had been put out. All that was left was the shuffle of advancing feet, the distant hooting of a car in the town, and the eternal changeless reek of garbage.

Garbage. Steele put out his hand. A metal trash-can brimming over with paper, refuse and rotting vegetables – and saturating them all, its stench rising even over the hashish and the charcoal smoke, crude olive oil. He fumbled for the gold lighter, found it, spun the flame adjuster to maximum, and gripped the Browning by the barrel with his other hand.

The men still couldn't see him, but he could hear the sound of their breathing only a few feet away now. He snapped the flint, a lance of fire shot out and he held it to the paper. The garbage ignited and a crackling spitting sheet of flame leapt upwards. Steele lifted the can, shook it and pitched it forwards.

The light was the same for them all, yellow, brilliant, dazzling, except Steele was prepared for it and the men weren't. The can arced up like a blazing rocket, dropped and scattered bundles of burning refuse over the cobbles. As it fell Steele levered himself away from the door, hurdled the flames and launched himself at them, slashing out with the gun, kicking, butting, gouging, shouting – great roars of noise that echoed back and forth off the walls.

One of the men went down instantly as the butt of the Browning struck his head, crumpling hands to his face with blood pouring between his fingers. Another doubled over choking as Steele's boot jabbed up into his stomach. A third spun away dazed, collided with the wall and fell too, screaming as he rolled over the smouldering piles of garbage.

Steele didn't bother about the fourth or the fifth. He raced down the passage, swerved right under the arch and followed the twisting alley uphill until it opened out into the Grand Socco. There was a row of cabs parked round the circular island at the square's centre. He heaved himself into the nearest one, slammed the door and shouted at the driver.

'Take me to Donovan's boatyard on the coastal road!'

The man gaped at him over the seat. There were distant terrified shouts and through the rear window Steele could see flames rising over the souk.

'Listen,' he leant forward and grabbed the driver by the collar, 'you've got Ross Callum for a passenger. Now move!'

'Yes, sir.'

The man switched on the ignition, reversed blindly into the square, tyres squealing on the roadway, and headed for the bay.

Mary-Beth was alone in the office when Steele entered. She took one look at him and then, without saying anything, she reached for the first-aid box.

'Where's your father?' Steele slumped down in the chair behind the desk.

'He got the *Lara* in the water. He figured he was doing so well he could afford to take a break and celebrate. I found him and got him home just before he passed out—'

Mary-Beth came over with a wad of cotton wool and a dish of water.

'You'd better strip down.'

Steele stood up wearily, took off his shirt and trousers for the second time that day, and dropped back in the chair. Blood was still welling from the gash in his arm and there were dark bruises and abrasions scattered over the whole length of his body.

'This could do with some stitches,' she was sponging his arm.

'A doctor?' Steele shook his head. 'See if you can't fix it with plaster.'

She shrugged, bandaged the arm tight, washed the other cuts and painted them with iodine. Then she handed another set of Donovan's clothes.

'Keep on like this and I'll have to restock.'

She smiled and Steele grinned back. 'At least I'm keeping you in practice.'

He dressed stiffly, glanced at the telephone, hesitated, then he lifted the receiver and dialled.

Surveillance control had already broken the routine once when they'd called him at the Minzah. He wasn't going out to find a callbox now. Five men had been waiting for him in the souk. Christ knew how many more there were stationed round the town. And Mary-Beth didn't matter, she knew enough already.

Steele listened to the ringing tone, identified himself when it cut out, then he heard control's voice – brittle, strained and anxious.

'Where are you?'

'In the bloody yard,' Steele snapped, 'but where the hell were you? I thought your people were meant to be behind me every goddam inch.'

'They are. They're waiting by your car, down at the port.'

'Oh, Jesus Christ—'

Steele put his hand over the mouthpiece and looked at Mary-Beth.

'Where's Marcel?'

She frowned surprised. 'I thought he brought you up here. He went off mid-afternoon to wait for the ferries. I guess he must still be there.'

Steele swore. It had been so late he hadn't thought of checking the harbour car park.

'I just got back,' he spoke into the telephone again. 'I walked up through the souk and I got bounced. Five of them, big dark-haired bastards who looked like sailors but weren't.'

'How do you know?'

'You ever heard of five sailors ashore at eleven o'clock on a Friday night – and all of them stone-cold sober? Come on! They

134

were waiting for me, Portuguese exiles I guess. They jostled me first, then they tried to move in. I was lucky to get out. You tell your people to keep their eyes open. Now put me through.'

For the moment Steele wasn't interested in the five men. They had to be Portuguese, there was no other explanation, employees of the people who'd killed Gonsalves' son and who'd been sent to cripple him because somehow they knew he'd been in touch with the old socialist leader.

They didn't matter now. All Steele cared about was the morning and Velatti.

'What happened?' Wedderburn came on the line almost immediately.

Steele told him quickly, running through the day from his arrival in Ceuta to the attack in the souk.

'So he's finally surfaced,' Steele finished. 'He got me where he wanted, trapped in some bloody cathouse outside the town—'

'Who do you mean?' Wedderburn interrupted.

'Your friend Velatti, for Christ's sake. He set it all up and he only lost out because Ybarra saw him by accident this morning. If I hadn't discovered that I'd have walked straight into him – up the backend of some blacked-out street. But at least I know where he is. Tomorrow I'm going back there to finish it and, believe me, I'll have so many of your people round me I'll be in danger of claustrophobia.'

He stopped. For a moment there was silence at the end of the line.

Then Wedderburn said quietly, 'Velatti arrived in Lisbon three hours ago.'

'Lisbon? He's not in Lisbon, he's right across the straits from here—'

'He drove over the Portuguese border at four this afternoon,' Wedderburn cut him off again. 'At nine he checked into the Magellan Hotel in the capital.'

Steele shook his head dazed. 'It's not possible. And even if it was, how the hell could you know? He's been operating underground, Jesus, that's the only reason I'm here – to smoke him out again. What is this?'

'We've been running checks at every border post in the straits since he disappeared,' Wedderburn said. 'We didn't expect much because passports aren't a problem to him, he's probably been

135

using dozens. But today he came out into the open under his own name. He crossed the Guadiana river into Portugal. We followed him to Lisbon—'

Wedderburn paused. 'He didn't bump into Ybarra by accident. It was deliberate, so was the border-crossing. He's satisfied himself about you. He wants you to know where you can find him.'

Steele reached for a cigarette, his mind numb.

'So what do you need me for any longer—?'

He searched for his lighter, remembered he'd left it in the blazing garbage can and signalled to Mary-Beth, who came over with a match.

'Why don't you go into the hotel and pick him up?'

'Apart from certain formalities about arresting a foreign national in another country,' Wedderburn's voice was acid, 'because Velatti checked out an hour after he checked in. We don't know where he is now.'

'But he'll still be in Lisbon. Christ, the police can trace him for you.'

'The Portuguese police won't be very interested in a tourist against whom they've no reason to bring charges – even if he's still using his own name and they can find him. I don't believe he is. I think he's pointed out the direction and he's gone underground again. He'll stay there until you reappear.'

Steele inhaled, still shaking his head bemused. 'Even if you're right, how's he going to locate me?'

'He put you onto Fischer for Gonsalves. Gonsalves must have a contact in Lisbon. You're at the yard – ask the girl.'

'Wait a minute—'

Steele covered the mouthpiece once more and glanced at Mary-Beth.

'Who does your friend Adolpho deal with in Lisbon?'

She shrugged. 'Many people.'

'Who in particular, someone he really trusts, like over these guns?'

'Dino's cousin, Beni,' the answer came without hesitation. 'That's not his real name, it's what they call him, after Benfica because he's mad about football. But he was Dino's best friend and he'd handle the landing.'

'Can you reach him?'

Mary-Beth nodded. 'Sure, I can call him from here.'

'Okay—'

Steele rubbed his face and hunched himself back over the telephone.

'Yes, there's a contact,' he said dully, 'and I can get to him and no doubt there's an early bloody morning flight.'

'Eight-fifteen,' Wedderburn answered, 'Air Maroc direct. By the time you land I'll have everyone over there, even people from stations we haven't used yet. You'll have nothing to worry about, I promise you. Just let him make the approach, then give the signal—'

Steele dropped the telephone while Wedderburn was still talking.

The gash on his arm was throbbing beneath the bandage, his foot ached from the bull's trampling hoof, the other cuts and bruises grated raw and painfully under Donovan's clothes. He looked round the office. He wanted a drink badly but the thought of Donovan's Spanish gin – its gasolene scent still hanging in the air – made him shudder.

'Try this—'

Mary-Beth had been watching him. She went into the outer office, returned with a cardboard carton, pulled out a bottle and filled a glass.

'It was meant to be a homecoming present,' she smiled diffidently, 'and to say thanks for going to see Adolpho.'

The bottle was Black Label whisky. Steele took the glass and drank gratefully. Then he limped to the window and gazed over the bay through the salt-furred panes.

He'd been right about everything. The guns, the trail, the successive tests. Everything – except where it was all to end. Not in Algeciras. Not even in one of the other four ports whose geography he'd sweated to learn, whose smells and sounds and textures he was already beginning to know. But right outside the dirty area in a town he hadn't been briefed on, a town he'd never visited, whose streets were totally unfamiliar, whose language he couldn't speak, and where because he was flying in he wouldn't even be able to take a gun.

He finished his glass and cursed Velatti savagely under his breath.

Twenty-four hours ago he'd been certain he could sidestep

137

everyone, set his own traps, use the weapons as bait and shoot the little Maltese down the instant he rose to take it. He'd miscalculated hopelessly. Velatti, too wary, too devious, too clever, had never given him a chance. He'd kept in front of Steele at every step, played games with him until he was sure, now he'd made his final move – changing the terrain so suddenly and completely that even Wedderburn had been caught unprepared – and once more Steele had no option except to follow him again.

Steele pushed himself away from the window and glanced at his watch. It was almost midnight and exhaustion was flooding over him in waves.

He turned towards Mary-Beth. 'I took on a new mate this morning, a man called Lorca. Did he show up?'

She nodded. 'He arrived about midday. He stayed working with Don on the boat until eight. Then he went off to find somewhere to stay.'

'Fine. Now, can you call this Beni in Lisbon? Tell him I'm flying over tomorrow. Fix up a time and a place for me to meet him late morning.'

'Sure.'

Steele filled his glass and drained it again, feeling the neat whisky warm and fierce and dulling the aches in his body.

'Is there a blanket on the launch?'

Mary-Beth nodded again. 'We cleaned out the lockers today. I put a new one under the starboard bunk.'

'Right,' he picked up the bottle. 'I'll be staying on board tonight. Let me know when you've spoken to Beni. Then you're through – and thanks for this.'

Steele shook the bottle, grinned and went out. He was too tired to go back to the Minzah. All he wanted to do was sleep.

He walked swaying with fatigue along the jetty to the empty cradle. The *Lara* was lying moored by the stern below it, her bows pointed towards the open sea. Steele stopped. Two days before when he'd seen her first, raised on pulleys, tethered and pinioned by the steel hawsers, her cabin smashed and her paint flaking off in ribbons, she'd looked like some mutilated seabird, helpless and dying. Now, sleek, gleaming, riding low in the water with the waves rippling gently under her, she was suddenly healed, at home again and tugging restlessly for flight.

He stepped carefully into the cockpit. Before the boards

underfoot had been dead and inert. This time they were alive, supple, yielding to every move he made. He ducked into the cabin, pulled out the blanket from the locker and lay back on the bunk. Then he uncorked the bottle and lifted its neck to his mouth, swallowing steadily, blurring the pain of the bruises and abrasions even more, shutting out the morning and the fugitive murderous little man who'd be waiting for him in Lisbon.

'I got through to Beni—'

The scuff of bare feet on deck, a shadow cutting off the starlight in the hatch, Mary-Beth's voice.

'He'll be waiting at the Torre de Belém from eleven on. It's in the town centre on the bank of the Tagus, any cab will take you there.'

'Thanks,' Steele put down the bottle. 'I'll see you tomorrow.'

He turned drowsily onto his side. The shuffling went on and a moment later he propped himself up again. Dimly he could see Mary-Beth dragging something up through the hatch.

'What are you doing?'

'Fixing up somewhere to sleep.'

'Here? Come on, you get back to your house.'

She shook her head. 'I'm staying.'

She'd taken the mattress from the other bunk. Steele listened to her setting it out in the cockpit. Then she reappeared, silhouetted above the steps.

Steele peered up at her. 'Why?'

'I heard you talking. Those guys who went for you in the souk, they'll know about the yard. If they figure on trying again here, at least they'll trip over me first.'

'For Christ's sake, Mary-Beth, it's nothing to do with you—'

'The hell it isn't—'

She cut him off, came down the steps and sat on the opposite bunk, elbows on her knees.

'Look, I grew up here so first off that means I know how to look after myself. Only it's much more than that. Mostly Don talks crap, but some of what he says is true. When I was a kid I lived for this boat, I used to wait up for it night after night. I'd imagine you coming back and throwing me a line as you docked, and then next time out you'd call up and say, "Hey, Mary-Beth, I need a hand at the bows." And I'd jump down, winch us round and we'd ship out, you and me and the little guy you had then,

139

Joey, just the three of us. We'd sail off and have adventures—'

The *Lara* moved with the waves. Light drifted in from the shore through a porthole and Steele saw she was smiling.

'Well, that's how I thought of them then. Only I grew up and realized they weren't just adventures, those trips you made, they were important. The guns, the cargoes, the men into the Sahel, without them there'd be no freedom movement there now. That means without you. People like you, like Adolpho and Dino and Beni, change the way things are. I wanted to be part of it when I was a kid, but that was just a dream because I didn't understand—'

She wasn't smiling any longer and she hesitated.

'Now I do understand. Dino taught me, Adolpho taught me, well, I just learned – and I want to be part of it even more. Not for adventures, not for dreams, but because it's real. This cargo you're taking for Adolpho, I'll do anything I can to help you get it there.'

She stopped. Steele said nothing for a moment.

She'd seen the mate arrive, watched the launch being floated, heard his conversation with Wedderburn about the guns, made the arrangements for him to meet Beni. There must have been whole areas she didn't understand but of one thing she was certain – he was going to make the shipment.

'Mary-Beth, there's something you'd better know now—'

Steele broke off.

The impulse to tell her was overwhelming, but he couldn't, there was no one he could tell until it was over. They all believed in Callum, they had to go on believing, keep their dreams about him, even her. Dreams built on lies. In Velatti's case they'd created unremitting hatred. In Mary-Beth trust, absolute trust, almost something to build her life round.

Steele shuddered and turned away, huddling against the cabin wall.

'I'll speak to you in the morning.'

He heard her climb the steps and settle down on the mattress. Then he dozed fitfully.

When he woke it was still very dark and the launch was rocking softly in the water. He blinked, realized a shadow was blocking out the hatch, jerked upright and grabbed for the Browning on the floor beside him.

140

'It's all right, it's me—'

Mary-Beth's voice again. Steele relaxed. She moved and he could just make her out standing by the steps.

'Marcel just got back. There's a late ferry from Ceuta. When he saw you weren't on it, he gave up. I've given him a blanket and told him to sleep on the jetty. He'll hear if anyone comes.'

'Then you can go home now, get some rest,' Steele said.

'Hell, no, I'm staying too. But now Marcel's there I can come in out of the dew.'

Steele watched her put the mattress back on the bunk. She took off her jacket. Then she checked, looked down at him and stretched out her arm.

'You're shivering.'

He could feel her hand on his wrist. Mary-Beth was right. The effect of the whisky had worn off, his bruises ached and throbbed, and in spite of the still-warm night air his body felt icily cold.

Steele shrugged. 'It's nothing. I guess I've been away so long I'm not used to the temperature changes.'

'Maybe I can help.'

There were rustles in the dark, for an instant Steele saw her naked in the starlight from the hatch, then she was lying beside him on the bunk.

'Mary-Beth—'

He propped himself up on his elbow. Then he stopped. He couldn't think of anything to say.

How long was it since there'd been a woman in bed with him? Apart from Louise Steele couldn't even remember. It was something else he'd deliberately and clinically shut out. He didn't want to give any part of himself to anyone, not even to the Camden Town whores that the others in Mrs Martin's boarding-house would trade stories about late on Friday nights after they'd cashed in the unemployment benefits. He simply wanted to be alone, fiercely silently proud that he could do without them.

Only now, for the second time in twenty-four hours, a woman was there beside him of her own choice, and as he tentatively touched Mary-Beth's face, her breasts, her legs, Steele could feel the cold drain from his fingers, warmth invade him and the shivering stop.

Finally he managed to smile. 'Is this all part of making sure

Adolpho gets his guns?'

'Hell, I wasn't thinking of guns,' her skin moved against his face as she smiled too, 'I was remembering being a kid. I used to hear stories about all the ladies Ross Callum slept with. January nights I could only figure they did it because they were cold. I reckoned there must be an awful lot of cold ladies in the straits. I knew I was cold. I just wished he'd pick me instead of the others.'

Steele tensed. Mary-Beth wasn't lying beside him – she was with Callum. Then he heard her laughing, quietly, happily.

'All those cold ladies,' she said, 'I'll tell you something – they were even luckier than I thought.'

His arms were round her. For a moment he remained taut and frozen. Then he relaxed and laughed too.

'There aren't any cold ladies in October – anywhere!'

Steele turned and held her tight against him.

13

The Torre de Belém shimmered grey-white in the morning sunlight, a fragile pearl grey-white of age with swollen-bellied barges swinging below the turrets and the Tagus flowing dark beyond.

Steele crossed the stone bridge that linked the tower with the waterfront and walked under the main arch. The Air Maroc flight from Tangier had been an hour late in taking off and it was already midday. The heat in the traffic-clogged Lisbon streets had been dank and oppressive. Here, inside the massive walls, the air was fresh and cool and full of river smells. He climbed to the third floor, went into the ancient lookout room and crossed to an open window above the water.

There was an old uniformed warden propped against the doorway on crutches and a student sitting crosslegged on the floor, books spread out in a circle round him. Apart from them and the occasional strolling visitor the room was empty.

Steele swung himself up onto the window ledge. Almost five centuries ago Magellan and his lieutenant, Juan del Cano, had weighed anchor immediately below. With three ships, each egg-shell boat hardly bigger than the *Lara*, a crew of ninety, and only old Henry the Navigator's instruments to guide them, they'd set out to sail round the globe. Magellan didn't make it, he died halfway in the Philippines, but del Cano took over and went on.

Steele turned the page of the guidebook he'd bought at the entrance and tried to follow the words.

'We've been working all night. I've sent everyone over—'

Wedderburn's voice kept interposing. Wedderburn on the telephone just before he boarded the Lisbon flight. Crisp and urgent but solicitous and reassuring once more.

'I've even brought in our best men from Madrid. There'll be at least a dozen within a hundred yards of you from the moment you

143

land. All you have to make sure is that you don't get boxed in. Give him the chance to contact, that's all, and it'll be over. We'll take care of you.'

Steele shook his head. He'd given the initiative back to Velatti, committed himself, become an automaton again – dependent for survival not on himself but on the speed and skills of the unseen men who'd fanned out round him when he stepped off the flight. The sense of helplessness, the gathering tension as he waited, had made his mouth dry and he could feel a tightness round his temples.

He forced himself to relax, to concentrate on the portrait of del Cano on his knee. The lean, sunken cheeked man with his haunted yellow hawks' eyes who'd survived, who'd proved the impossible possible, sailing back two years later with the king's green and gold ensign in tatters but still fluttering at his stern.

'Senhor Callum?'

Steele dropped off the ledge, spun round and reached for the short switchblade knife strapped to his arm, the only weapon he'd brought with him.

For a moment he couldn't work out where the voice had come from. The warden at the door had vanished and there were no tourists in sight. Only the student was still sitting on the floor, his books reflecting the sunlight outside. Then he realized.

'Yes,' Steele said.

'I'm Beni,' the student began gathering the books together without looking up. 'This is not a good place for talking, but I chose it to meet because we have to be sure no one is following you—'

He paused and lifted his head listening. Steele looked at him across the floor. He had a young strong-jawed face with a black beard and level intelligent eyes. Then he glanced back at Steele. There were distant sounds of a group of visitors climbing the steps.

'Outside across the road there's a taxi rank,' he said. 'Right at back of the others you'll find one cab on its own. Above the wheel by the driver's window there's a vase. If it's got red carnations in it, get in and tell the driver to take you to lunch. If it's empty walk by and go to the Botanical Gardens—'

The clattering of footsteps was much closer now and Beni was speaking quickly.

144

'Give me five minutes' start, then you come after me.'

He swept up the last of the books, tucked them under his arm and went out. A moment later a group of German tourists wearing Hasselblads, fixed aggressive smiles and heavy stomachs came panting into the room. Steele waited the five minutes while they held an earnest symposium at full volume behind him. Then he went out.

He walked back over the delicate white bridge and crossed the street. There were half a dozen cabs parked in line and a single one, as Beni had said, twenty yards behind the others. As Steele approached he saw a cluster of red flowers by the wheel.

He got in and said, 'I want to have lunch.'

'Yes, senhor.'

The driver was even younger than Beni, maybe seventeen or eighteen, with the same intent eyes and serious unsmiling face. He pulled away from the kerb and there were some shouts and angry hooting from the other cabs.

'PIDE men,' he gestured scornfully, 'they think I stole a fare. Only work they can get now, driving cabs.'

As he passed the line he swerved in, almost brushing the wing of the leading taxi. Then he accelerated away with a slither of tyres and a derisory chorus on the horn.

'And there was no one behind me?' Steele asked.

The young man shook his head. 'Most of them we know now, the ones who are still active and out of prison—'

Like Beni he was referring to the opponents of the new regime, the diehard supporters of the former dictatorship like the group who'd attacked Steele in Tangier. Wedderburn's men would have meant nothing to him.

'If they'd followed you in from the airport I'd have seen them on the bridge. Nothing, just tourists.'

Steele glanced over his shoulder. The dazzling column of the tower was still just visible, its reflection stretching out across the dark water.

A few minutes ago Beni's instructions about the taxi and the scarlet carnations had sounded like a melodramatic rigmarole. Now Steele realized they made sense. With only one entrance, the narrow arch spanning the gap between the embankment and the main courtyard, the isolated tower was an ideal place to establish whether he was under surveillance.

145

He sat back in his seat. If the future of Portugal's precarious four-year-old democracy lay in the hands of either the old, like Gonsalves, or the very young, like these two, at least they were a lot more capable hands than he'd thought before.

They followed the riverfront for a while, then they turned left into the old town. There were posters, graffiti and slogans everywhere, on walls, hoardings, mail boxes, windows, trees and even benches, a glittering rainbow of confetti scattered across the city in flecks of green and white and crimson and yellow. Whatever the revolution had meant to the ordinary people, it had certainly been strong wine to the graphic artists.

'Here, senhor—'

The young man stopped at the entrance to a small pedestrian street thronged with workers in berets and coarse blue shirts taking their lunchtime break.

'Up there,' he pointed at a café fifteen yards away, 'Beni will be inside.'

'Thanks.'

Steele started to get out but the young man swung round suddenly and held out his hand.

'No, thank you, Senhor Callum,' he smiled for the first time, 'we know what you are doing for us. We are grateful.'

Steele shook hands stiffly, embarrassed. 'If I can help, I'm glad.'

Then he slammed the door and turned away. The lie, the prodigious recurring lie that dogged him at every step. He stood for an instant in the roadway, hands clenched, nails digging into his palms, revulsion and disgust churning in his stomach. Then he gathered himself and pushed his way through the crowd towards the café.

Inside was a bar counter, a row of packed wooden tables, shouting sweating waiters, the clamour of laughter and conversation, smells of wine and dust and seafood. For several minutes, blinking in the dusky light, he couldn't spot Beni. Then he felt a hand on his elbow, turned and saw the bearded face.

'At the back, senhor.'

Steele had thought all the tables were full, but there was a small one empty with two chairs tilted against it by the rear wall. He saw down, Beni shouted over the uproar in Portuguese and a waiter appeared with a bottle of vinho verde.

146

'You had no problem?' Beni filled their glasses.

Steele shook his head and drank. The young green wine was chill and sharp and fragrant. He rinsed out the clammy taste of the heat outside, and helped himself from the bottle again.

'We have to be very careful, you understand? As the economy gets worse they come out into the open, more and more of them, like creatures from under stones. They are true fascists, a very bad category of people, the worst.'

'I got introduced to a few last night,' Steele said. 'I wasn't impressed.'

Beni frowned at him for a moment not understanding. Then he nodded.

'The American girl said there was trouble. I am sorry. Here it is different,' he gestured round the café. 'These are our people. Also no one talks English. Even if they could, they cannot hear.'

The waiter returned with a platter of shellfish. Steele picked out a small crab. He cracked its shell, sucked at the flesh and gazed across the table.

'What else did Mary-Beth tell you?' He asked.

'That you had found a consignment and you were coming to talk,' Beni hesitated. 'I must be frank with you, Senhor Callum, we do not have much money—'

'Too goddam right you don't,' Steele interrupted him, 'you've got exactly seven hundred thousand escudos.'

'Adolpho told you?'

'I asked him. In dollars that's under twenty thousand. And if I had to lay odds I'd say it's about eleven to twelve on you've got it all in Portuguese paper money too, not in any convertible currency, right?'

Beni drew his finger round the rim of his glass. Then he said quietly, 'It comes from the people. It's what they have, what they can give.'

'The people? Jesus! I'm a businessman, not a bloody philanthropist—'

Steele shook his head. He kept glancing at the doorway, at the changing rows of figures by the bar, at the crowded tables round them.

'What the hell do you expect me to do with a little bundle of small denomination escudos notes?'

He was blustering now, prevaricating and playing for time,

feeling himself more and more out of his depth, more cheap and compromised, as the charade went on. It was three hours since the flight had landed. He'd lingered at the airport, told the cab-driver to slow down on the road into Lisbon, kept the appointment at the Torre de Belém, crossed the city again, met up with Beni in the café – and still there was nothing, no sign or move from the little Maltese.

'You knew what we had before you came, senhor,' Beni was looking at him steadily, 'yet you are here all the same. What can you sell us for those small notes?'

Steele closed his eyes briefly and rubbed his face, sweat trickling down his fingers.

'There's a possible cargo,' he said, 'handguns, rifles, some repeaters—'

Steele gave him the models and the quantities, reciting the list like a hollow litany in which he'd long since stopped believing. Beni listened absorbed, jotting notes by his plate on the stained paper tablecloth, his face eager, intense and alert.

'And you can deliver all those?' He said as Steele finished.

'Hell, I'm making no promises yet. Right now I'm just saying maybe.'

Beni hesitated. Then he ripped off a square of paper, sketched a section of coastline and swivelled the rough map towards Steele.

'This is a village called Albumeina in the southern Algarve down by the Spanish border,' he touched a mark on the paper. 'It has a lighthouse, three long white flashes each forty seconds. Here twenty kilometres west, is Benfeira, another village. It too has a lighthouse, yellow beams in groups of three twice every minute—'

He annotated the map as he spoke, scribbling in the names and the beam frequencies.

'Between them is a third lighthouse. There was a village once also. Now nothing. The people have moved away, the lamp is dead many years, it is a ruin. But there is still a deep-water jetty to the sea. The land, the tower, has come to a farmer. He is a friend.'

Steele studied the scrawls on the wine and grease-sodden paper, the indented rocky shore, the crude crosses marking the villages.

'And that's where you figure on the cargo being landed?' He looked up.

Beni nodded. 'It is maybe six hours in a fast launch from Tangier. We would signal in green, three shorts and a long repeated. You would navigate first on Albumeina and Benfeira. Then you would pick us up and run in. The unloading takes perhaps fifteen minutes. Afterwards we move the guns inland by mule-cart, the old way—'

He gave a rare quick smile. 'My home is near there. Like everyone round the straits we have much experience in such operations, we have lived off them for centuries.'

'And the money?'

'It is there, senhor. Of course, you may have it whenever you want. We would naturally trust you with it all in advance. But I think it is easier and safer for you if you take it when you make the delivery. That way you have no risks with customs at our borders.'

'*If* I make the delivery,' Steele said.

'Senhor Callum—'

Beni leant forward, arms crossed on the table, his face very close to Steele's.

'For you this is nothing except trouble maybe. I understand that. Yet for us it is much. You come from a country where freedom is a gift given of right when you are born. Not here. When I was born my father was in prison, my mother was arrested six months later. I never knew my parents, they died when I was a child – not for crimes but for believing things it was forbidden to believe. There were thousands like them—'

He spoke calmly, unemotionally, yet his voice cut through the uproar surrounding them.

'Now we have what they believed. There are many who would take it from us again. We will stand against those people with everything we have, but we do not yet have enough. I ask no favours, I tell you only how it is. And I will tell you too that if you help us it will be remembered here always.'

He stopped.

Steele gazed at him. He thought of Gonsalves with his mis-shapen nose, his awkward jutting hip, his naiveté and his quiet passionate conviction. Of Mary-Beth's boyfriend, the dead Dino, murdered by the same vicious laughing louts who'd set on him in the souk. Of the scarlet carnations by the driver's wheel and the young man smiling, gripping his hand, thanking him.

He shivered, pushed back his chair and stood up.

'I'll let you know through the American girl,' he said.

'I will be waiting,' Beni stood up too. 'Now it is better we separate. I am known, after last night you also. The less time we are together, even here, the less chance they have of making a connection.'

He held out his hand. Steele hesitated. Then he asked suddenly, 'You've got one other message for me?'

'Message?' Beni frowned, 'Who from?'

'A man who knows your uncle Adolpho perhaps. A man called Velatti.'

Beni thought for a moment. 'No, senhor, Adolpho has never spoken to me of such a man. I have never heard of him.'

'All right,' Steele shook his hand, 'I'll be in touch.'

He went out. There was a taxi cruising past on the main street. He hailed it instantly and told the driver to take him to the airport. Inside the departure terminal he walked over to the Air Maroc booking counter and handed the girl his ticket.

She glanced at it and looked up smiling. 'Yes, senhor, you have an open return to Tangier. You wish to book?'

'No,' Steele said, 'I'd like to change it. I want the next flight to Gibraltar.'

She flicked through the airline schedules. 'British Airways have one in half an hour. It lands Gibraltar seventeen-forty.'

'I'll take it.'

He waited while the girl endorsed the ticket.

Five-forty was twenty minutes before the shops on Queen Street closed. It would give him just enough time to get there from the airport before the Indian, Charan Desai, left his store. Desai had financed all of Callum's previous deals. He was going to finance the last one now.

Until then it had all been a matter of guesses, intuitions and hypotheses. Not any longer. Steele finally knew where the little Maltese was waiting for him.

14

The clerk led Steele through to the back of the shop and up four twisting creaking flights of stairs.

The narrow windows on the landings were coated with diesel smoke, sent swirling up the Rock from the naval dockyards by the Levanter wind, and the boards were stacked headhigh with bales. Edging his way between them in the dim light Steele saw rolled carpets from Bombay, cartons of cheap Polish watches, crates of Korean electronic calculators, beeswax candles from China moulded in shapes of dragons and junks, glazed pottery ducks from Birmingham, even Christmas cribs from Chile and Peru.

It was rubbish, all of it, tawdry useless bric-à-brac garnered from every corner of the earth – except to a man like Charan Desai. For a merchant who knew his market it was also a complete and highly profitable stock-in-trade.

'Please to go in, sir.'

They'd reached the top floor. The clerk opened a door and Steele stepped inside.

The office was as cramped and cluttered as the landings, only now the debris was paper and not merchandise. Tilting mounds of files rose almost to the ceiling, piles of invoices lined the walls, orders, advice notes and receipts spilled out of boxes and fluttered like leaves in the current of air as the door closed. For an instant Steele couldn't see Desai. Then a head appeared above a rampart of ledgers on a desk and the Indian stood up.

'How pleasant indeed at last, Mr Callum—'

Desai held out his hand. He was pear-shaped and sleek with a bland, hairless face and hard little eyes half-hooded by sleepy downpulling lids. Heavy gold links gleamed at the cuffs of a white silk shirt and an expensive English tweed jacket was hanging

151

over the chair behind him.

'After so many excellent negotiations I feel we know each other already,' his voice was warm and effusive with only a trace of the lisping Indian accent, 'Please will you not be seated?'

He swept some papers from another chair and Steele sat down.

'Now how may I be of service on your welcome return?'

Desai had cleared an opening in the barrier of ledgers and was sitting opposite Steele across the desk.

'Bridging finance,' Steele said, 'Krugerrand to be redeemed in escudos. Ten thousand pounds' worth for seven days.'

He stated it simply and directly without hesitation because that was what Desai would have expected. Steele was no longer Callum the legend, the adventurer, the benefactor of the poor, but Callum the hard-nosed businessman in conference with his bank manager. Before his assistants had negotiated the loans for him. The only difference now was that he was doing it in person.

'Escudos?' Desai frowned unhappily. 'You have been away but I tell you it has become a most sad currency, Mr Callum. It limps, falters, sometimes finds a crutch from the Americans, then staggers worse again—'

Unlike his body Desai's hands were thin and mobile. He moved one of them across the desktop now, miming with his fingers the stumbling progress of a drunk.

'Good healthy South African gold for this weak invalid, the escudo?' He shook his head. 'Mr Callum, I make no questions of your business but as a valued colleague I ask you – in this matter of ten thousand pounds is maybe your heart not ruling your brain?'

Desai might have been counselling an old friend, not someone he'd met for the first time barely two minutes before. Except, as Steele realized as he looked at him, to the Indian Callum was more than a friend – he was a tried, trusted and credit-worthy customer.

Steele grinned. 'Forget about the heart. The brain says the margins are good.'

Desai shook his head again and sighed. Then he smiled too.

'For you fame, excitement and margins, for me just Portuguese paper. Well, maybe one day things change, maybe God decides to give justice to us poor creatures who stand in the middle. Meanwhile, I fear you will find it expensive.'

152

'How much?'

'Ten per cent.'

For a single week, Steele calculated, that was the equivalent of over five hundred per cent a year. If Desai did all his business at those rates he must have made himself a very rich man indeed.

Yet it was of no consequence to Steel and he nodded. 'I'll take it.'

'And the security as before?'

In the past Desai's loans to Callum had been made as a marine mortgage, secured by the *Lara*'s ownership certificate and insurance policy. The certificate was still on the boat – Steele had seen it hanging by the copper plate on the galley bulkhead – but he didn't know whether the insurance was still in force.

'Right,' he said, 'but we'd better have new cover. I can't remember if the policy's run out.'

'That is no problem,' Desai reached for a drawer in the desk and laughed, 'of all your great British institutions there is none for which I have greater admiration than the famous Lloyds of London.'

He pulled out a proposal form, filled it in and handed it to Steele for signature.

'And the certificate,' he added as Steele scrawled his name, 'you have it with you?'

Steele shook his head. 'It's over in Tangier. You can have it tonight or tomorrow when you deliver the money – and I want it by midday.'

'By midday tomorrow in Tangier?'

'That's it.'

Desai paused. Then he leant back and laughed again.

'Truly you have not changed, Mr Callum. Hurry, hurry, hurry, just like the old days, no? Well, it shall be there. My representative brings it to the Minzah in the morning. You give him the certificate and a receipt, and we are back in business—'

He stood up still laughing, came round the desk and escorted Steele to the door.

'I am most delighted and I wish you all good fortune. Only I ask you too, please be careful. I think I am happier running my store than owning boats, even such an elegant one as yours.'

Steele laughed with him, shook hands and went out.

The light was already beginning to fade on the street and he hesitated for a moment in front of the store as the early evening shopping crowds jostled around him. He had the money, or he'd have it the next day, and the process had been easier, far easier, than he'd dared believe possible. Desai hadn't asked him a single question. Like everyone else he'd accepted Callum's return at face-value – he even knew Steele was staying at the Minzah – and he'd been prepared to trust him instantly with ten thousand pounds in gold krugerrand.

The gold, the guns, the rendezvous, they were all arranged now. All he had left to deal with before he could move were Wedderburn and surveillance control.

'Don't I rate a welcome?'

Louise was standing in the open doorway. Steele's set of keys was in Tangier – he hadn't thought he'd need them that day – and he'd rung the bell. She appeared instantly, almost as if she'd been expecting him, but this time there wasn't a smile or an embrace. Instead she stood gazing down from the step whitefaced, distracted, her mouth twitching and her hands clenched tight against her skirt.

'Yes, of course, how lovely. It's just that I – I – wasn't sure.'

The words were stammered and unconvincing, but she leant towards him. Steele put his arms round her, felt her cheek icy-cold and trembling against her own, half-carried her into the hall and kicked the door shut behind him.

'That's better, much better, that's the sort of welcome I expect—'

There was something wrong, appallingly wrong, and he had no idea what it was. All he knew was that somehow he had to keep talking, laughing, behaving naturally and boisterously.

'Right, let's not waste any time. Straight into the bedroom and clothes off. Jesus, I've been saving this lot up for forty-eight hours!'

Steele stepped back. They were in the centre of the hall with the sliproom on his left and the kitchen on his right. He chuckled and nuzzled Louise's neck. Then he suddenly hurled her sideways into the sliproom, whirled round and launched himself in a driving shoulder-charge at the kitchen door.

He still didn't know, he was still bewildered, acting blindly out of instinct. But there'd been the inexplicable shivering coldness of Louise's skin, a tiny rustle in the stillness that didn't belong to the house, a brief alien movement somewhere behind the line of light by the doorframe. He hit the panel, the door slammed back, he heard a grunt and a shuffle, then something clattered across the tiled floor and the door was bouncing back against him. Steele forced it inwards again, plunged through the gap into the kitchen and skidded to a halt by the table.

He was right. There were two men inside, big, bleak-faced, momentarily dazed – he took them in very fast – both wearing grey shirts and black cord trousers. One, the one behind the door, had been knocked off-balance by Steele's charge and was on his knees reaching for the object that had slid across the tiles – a heavy silenced Smith & Wesson. His fingers touched the butt, Steele lifted his heel and stamped on the man's hand, grinding it down over the cutting edge of the trigger-guard. The man screamed and twisted away, smearing a trail of blood over the floor.

Then the second one was coming at him from the other side, silent, purposeful, crouching, the shock gone now and a double-bladed knife circling viciously in front of his body. Steele swayed back, felt for the rim of the table and catapulted himself over it in a rolling backwards somersault. The man checked uncertainly. One moment they'd been face to face, the next the table was between them. As he hesitated Steele gripped the table again, lifted it and threw it forwards.

The man stumbled, Steele vaulted the table once more and caught his shirt. Behind them was Louise's glass cabinet. Steele spun the man round and battered his head against the shelves. The rows of glasses shattered, the knife arced away, there were new screams, and the man threshed and struggled in agony, blood spraying up the wall as the splinters lacerated his face.

'You bastards! You cheap filthy bastards!'

Steele was shouting now. He knew the people in the houses on either side might hear and he didn't care. Dimly he was aware that the two must be Portuguese, members of the group who'd attacked him in the souk. Yet it didn't really matter who they were. All he was conscious of was anger, a surging uncontrollable eruption of rage against the whole shadowy miasma of lies, evasion, deceit and unseen prowling violence that had enveloped him like a cloak since he'd walked ashore as Callum.

The man by the cabinet crumpled moaning, hands to his face,

and Steele swivelled towards the door. The first one was crawling into the hall, the broken fingers of his right hand tucked under his armpit. Steele jumped over a fallen chair, caught him by the shoulders, levered him up and dragged him to the sink. It was still full of Louise's unwashed crockery. He gripped the man by the hair and hammered his face down into the basin, smashing the piled cups and plates and sheeting the metal draining-board with more blood.

'Are we beginning to understand each other—?'

Both men were on the floor and there was blood, smashed furniture and broken glass and crockery everywhere, and Steele was laughing, panting and shaking.

'That's fine. Now tell your friends this. What I've done to you is what I do to children. Next time I might get serious—'

The second man was trying to haul himself upright, clutching one of the legs of the overturned table. Steele kicked him at the base of his spine. The man stiffened and shrieked and Steele turned on the other, jabbing him once, twice and then a third time in the groin as the anger flared again.

'Right, now get out. And God help you if I ever see either of you again.'

They were incapable of response even if they'd understood him. Steele went to the front door and glanced up and down the street. There was no one in sight in the gathering dusk. He came back and propelled them out, kicking and dragging them across the hall. The last he saw were two doubled-up figures, faces slashed and sightless, reeling down towards the harbour. Then he slammed the door shut.

'It's all right, Louise, they've gone.'

She'd locked herself inside the sliproom and he knocked quietly. After a moment the key turned and she came out. She looked at him blank-eyed and shuddering. The she collapsed against him weeping, great choking sobs racking her body.

Steele held her tight, talking to her gently, caressing her hair, comforting her, while the convulsions went on and on. Finally they faded and after a while the tears stopped too.

'I'm sorry,' she stepped back from him, shaking her head and rubbing her face. 'It was just the most terrible thing I've ever been through.'

'What happened?'

'They came this morning and they said—'

She broke off as the tears welled again. Then she controlled herself and went on, her voice still unsteady but calmer now.

'The bell rang about ten. I opened the door and they pushed their way in. They told me to telephone you at the hotel and tell you to come over here urgently. One of them had a knife,' she shuddered, 'he said if I didn't he'd start by cutting my—'

She shut her eyes and stopped again, and Steele put his arms around her once more.

'It's all over now, I promise,' he said. 'They've gone and they've had something they'll never forget. They won't be back. Did you telephone?'

Louise nodded, her head against his chest. 'You weren't there. They made me call again every half an hour all day. I'd just tried again when you rang.'

'Do you know who they were?'

'No. The one with the knife spoke English but they were both foreign. When they talked together it sounded like Spanish, although it wasn't. Portuguese maybe, I'm not sure.'

'Did they call anyone else?'

She shook her head. 'They made me sit in the kitchen and they stayed with me. Sometimes when they were bored they messed around with me. The other one kept putting his hand down my dress—'

The closed eyes and the shudder again. Then she added quickly, 'Can I have a drink?'

'Of course.'

She turned towards the kitchen but Steele stopped her.

'I'll get one for you,' he said. 'You wait in your bedroom. I want to clean the place up first.'

Louise nodded passively and walked along the hall.

There wasn't a single glass unbroken in the kitchen but miraculously a bottle of gin had survived in the shambles. Steele found a coffee mug that had also escaped unshattered, half-filled it with liquor, added a splash of water and carried it through to the bedroom.

'How's that?'

Louise was lying propped up against the pillow. She took the mug, gulped and smiled.

'Better,' she said, 'much better.'

157

'You stay where you are and finish it. I'm going to telephone. Then we'll decide what to do.'

Steele closed the door, went back to the hall, picked up the telephone and dialled.

The dizzying surge of rage had passed, but he could still feel recurring waves of anger like the swell after a storm. No longer at the two men. They were nonentities, mindless waterfront thugs, and his fury there had been exorcised as he savaged and kicked them on the tiled floor. But against what had brought them to the house. Callum. The ancient fantasy of a plump little major who'd been resurrected as himself.

He was Callum, he was inextricably twined and meshed with the fiction, imprisoned in it, hazarding not just his own life but sucking others with him into a nightmare of violence and brutality. Gonsalves on the run now from village to village, Louise being sadistically terrorized all day, Christ knew who next. And all to satisfy the murderous grudge of an employee of the men who'd created him.

Steele clenched his fingers round the receiver until he heard the bakelite begin to crack. Then he forced himself to relax. It didn't matter, nothing mattered except Velatti. That was all he had to concentrate on because once he found the Maltese he could break the cycle, free himself, free all the others caught up in it, and make an end. And he was less than thirty hours away.

'Put me through—'

He didn't even give the operator time to speak as the connection was made. There was a brief hesitation, the familiar click, then he heard Wedderburn's voice.

'What's happened?'

'I'm in Gibraltar—'

'I know that. Why? What are you doing? Why haven't you been in contact?'

The questions were snapped out impatiently and anxiously. It was seven o'clock and Steele could see him standing hunched above the table on the marble floor, white blotches of tension on his cheeks, a fresh blossom in the jade bowl by his hand, the houseboy hovering behind.

'There was a message from Velatti—'

'Velatti?' Wedderburn cut him off. 'Where is he?'

'Just listen,' Steele said. 'I was leaving the restaurant after the

158

Tôrre de Belém. A barman handed me a note. It said he'd be waiting for me inside Desai's store here on Blenheim Court at five forty-five—'

Steele had worked it all out on the plane, even rehearsing the words he'd use.

'I knew your people were behind me, there wasn't time to call before the flight left, and the place was public and safe. So I went there. I waited fifteen minutes. Then a kid came in from the street with another message. The meeting was cancelled. I'd be called at the hotel tomorrow and a new place would be arranged—'

The story was at least plausible and Steele could sense Wedderburn listening intently as he absorbed it.

'I left the store and walked to Louise's house to telephone you,' Steele went on, 'there were two men there, Portuguese, the same as the bunch who jumped me before. They'd been holding her all day. This time I bounced them first. They'll be somewhere near the docks now if the police haven't picked them up. Even if they have, those bastards aren't going to be talking. But I want a guard on this place, a double-guard round the clock until we've finished. Understand?'

'Now listen, Callum, this second message, was it written like the first?'

The anxiety in Wedderburn's voice had vanished. Now Steele knew he was confused. Velatti should have been in Lisbon and Steele had said he wasn't and Wedderburn could only believe him.

'No, it wasn't. But I'm not talking about messages now, I want guards for Louise.'

'Oh, she'll be looked after. What concerns me—'

'What bloody concerns me,' Steele snapped, 'is that she might have had her face slashed off today, not to mention other parts of her. Now you get some people up here fast.'

'I'll have a couple of men there within an hour,' Wedderburn said.

'Right. I'm staying until they arrive. Then I'll take the boat back to Tangier. As soon as I get the call in the morning I'll let you know. I'll be in touch tomorrow.'

'We haven't finished yet—'

'Of course we've bloody finished,' Steele interrupted him,

159

'Your little friend's either playing games or something's scared him off. Either way there's nothing we can do. He wasn't in Lisbon, he's not here now, he may be in Tangier tomorrow. That's what he's said and that's what we've got to believe. Or have you any other bright suggestions?'

There was silence for a moment. Wedderburn was trying to take it all in, digest it, analyse the implications. He might even be suspicious of Steele but the situation was the same as before – he was committed to Steele now and forced to accept whatever he was told.

'If you're up to anything, Callum, and that isn't the truth—'

Wedderburn was suspicious and he was still helpless and Steele cut him off again.

'I'm up to nothing,' he said. 'You seem to forget it's my bloody skin hanging out on the line, not yours. I just want to find the bastard and cut out. I'll call you from the hotel.'

He put the receiver down and turned away smiling. Then he walked back to the bedroom.

'How are you feeling?'

Louise was still propped against the pillow. The mug was empty and there was a little colour in her cheeks now, but small tremors kept rippling over her body.

'Improving, but another of these would help,' she smiled and held out the mug.

'A small one for the patient, but give me fifteen minutes and I'll have some real medicine.'

Steele grinned, took the mug and went out.

He made her another drink. Then he called the Rock Hotel and ordered. Afterwards he set about clearing up the kitchen.

The bell rang as he finished. Steele went to the door, signed for a package from the beaming delivery boy who'd arrived when he was there before, gave him another five-pound note, and took the carton through to the bedroom.

'How about this to complete the recovery?'

Steele had asked for a pair of champagne glasses to be put in with the order. He filled them and handed one to Louise.

She drank and said, 'By any chance is there anything to go with it?'

She was laughing now and her eyes were bright with an almost childish excitement. Steele reached into the package for the jar of caviare, but she held out her hand and stopped him.

'It's a party – make it a surprise.'

She closed her eyes and leant back against the bedhead, her mouth half-open. It was a form of shock, Steele guessed, delayed shock brought on by the drink after the ordeal of the day, that had taken her back into a childhood world of candles and parties, treats and surprises. He broke the seal of the jar, scooped out some caviare with his fingers and put it to her lips.

'Like this it can be anything I want. Marzipan or cinnamon toast or the little chocolate dolls we had at Christmas—'

He was right. She was eating slowly with her eyes still shut, using the taste to conjure up other safer flavours from the past.

Steele looked down at her, small, fragile, vulnerable, and the anger came again, mixed with loathing this time, at what had been done to her, at the people like Wedderburn who'd expose her to the Portuguese and then casually dismiss the experience because it was of no consequence in relation to Velatti.

'Except it's really best of all just as it is—'

She opened her eyes suddenly. The laughter had gone and the fear was back on her face.

'Don't leave me, Steele.'

'I'm not going yet—'

'But you are later, aren't you? I heard you on the telephone,' she sat up and caught his hand. 'Don't go, not tonight.'

'Louise, I'm not stepping out of this house until I know you're safe. There'll be two men here round the clock until it's over. Nothing like today is ever going to happen again, I promise you.'

He finished lamely, embarrassed by the meaninglessness of what he'd said and feeling he was just another in the long procession of people who'd let her down. The men would come, he'd make sure of that, but in a few brief days they'd leave and she'd be alone as before – shut away in the silent little house until she was needed again.

'Over?' Louise dropped his hands. 'It's never over. Please—'

She held out her glass and Steele filled it. The shock had passed, even momentarily the fear, although that would return. Now there was just a weary resigned cynicism.

'You think I drink too much, don't you?'

Not only cynicism but defiance too in the way she swung round and gazed at him, chin lifted and mouth firm. A stubborn spark of

161

courage that must have sustained her through all the solitary days and nights.

'If I was you I'd probably drink a damn sight more.'

Steele grinned, trying to make a joke of it, but she shook her head.

'No, you're right, I do. At least I'm bloody well entitled to—'

She stopped, turned away and gazed out of the window, where a cluster of lights glowed from the tip of the Rock against the darkening sky. Steele sat on the bed beside her. One of its legs was shorter than the others and the mattress creaked and rocked like a boat.

'Why are you here, Louise?'

'What do you mean "here"?' She asked, 'Here in Gibraltar or here involved in all this?'

'Both.'

'They're the same really. I suppose it started when I came back from India—'

She broke off and glanced at him warily.

'Why do you want to know? Because I'm a little drunk and you think if I talk I'll forget, and then you can go away without me noticing, without causing any trouble, is that it?'

Steele shook his head. 'You said I wasn't one of them. I'm not and you're not either. I told you about me. I want to know about you too.'

'Me?' She laughed quickly, derisively. 'Well, I'm a teaplanter's daughter. That's funny for a start, isn't it, like something out of Somerset Maugham, only fifty years out of date? But it's true. I grew up in India and when I was eighteen my parents sent me home, to a secretarial college near Cambridge. The first week I met a boy called Johnnie and it was like in stories, spring punts on the river and parties—'

Louise paused.

Steele knew Cambridge, not the side of the city she was talking about, the green lawns, the undergraduates, the ease and the gaiety. But an electronics factory on the outskirts where he'd worked for six months as a forklift truck operator after the marina scheme folded.

'We got married,' her fingers plucked at the counterpane. 'Christ, how silly can you be, how naive, like there's no midnight and it all goes on for ever. Five years, that's what I got. Johnnie

162

joined the Foreign Office. I never even knew what he did except he had to be away a lot travelling. Then one day the bell rang. We had a little house then at the far end of Chelsea and I went to the door—'

Her voice slowed.

'There was a man there, a rather nice man with an umbrella and a bowler hat. I thought he was a rather grand insurance salesman. He wasn't. He said he came from Johnnie's department and he told me, very kindly, Johnnie was dead.'

She stopped again and Steele asked quietly, 'What had happened?'

'Oh, the explanation was there'd been a "car accident" in Prague. There always is an explanation, isn't there, but a car accident – Christ, how unimaginative can you get! Only I believed him, I'd have believed anything right then. I just knew someone had taken the world and broken it and it didn't really matter how or why—'

She'd caught hold of his hand once more, threading her fingers between his, and he could feel her grip tighten, bone pressing against bone, nails digging into his palm.

'How many times do you think that's happened, I mean if you could count them all? Just this century from the First World War onwards – the ring at the door and the nice man asking you to sit down. But that's in wars, in the past, not now. The bastards!'

Tears came now, hot bitter tears, and harsh sobs racked her thin ribs. Steele put his arm round her shoulder, feeling her body shake and smelling gin fumes mingling with the wetness.

'Let me be—'

She pushed him fiercely away. Then a moment later she reached for his hand again.

'I'm sorry,' she steadied her voice and the tears stopped. 'Every time I think I've really forgotten something happens and I remember that day, and it's the self-pity I hate. You don't think I'm full of it, do you?'

She looked at him anxiously.

'No, of course I don't.'

'Well,' she shrugged, 'the same nice man cabled my parents and they cabled back saying they were coming home immediately. The plantation was up in the hills near Darjeeling. They chartered a light plane to get out like they always did—'

She was utterly composed now.

'The plane crashed taking off. They were both killed too. A month afterwards the government expropriated the estate. They said my father had been evading taxes and they refused to pay compensation—'

In a single month she'd lost everything, husband, parents, inheritance, and at twenty-four found herself destitute.

'And you know what? I couldn't even type, I never finished the course!' The quick laugh again. 'Then they offered me a job. They weren't nice any longer. They were the people who'd killed Johnnie, that's how I saw it, and I hated them, everything they stood for, because by then I knew what he'd been doing for them. But I took the job, not just because there was nothing else, but for those—'

She pointed at the window. It was fully dark now and the sky was brilliant with stars.

'They gave me a ticket so I could come down here to see what it was like. I landed in the evening and they were just coming out, thousands and thousands of them, clear and bright like they hadn't been since I left India. And I just stood on the runway and I decided, yes. They made me do three years in London, then they sent me back. I've been here ever since—'

There was a pack of cigarettes on the pillow. She pulled one out and Steele lit it for her. In the flame from the lighter he saw she was smiling, a defensive self-mocking smile.

'So now you know. It sounds pathetic, doesn't it?' She drew on the cigarette and the tip glowed, 'So bloody naive I never even knew what my husband's job was. And I end up working for the same people, running what they call a safehouse, all because I liked the stars—'

The sound of the bell ringing in the hall interrupted her. She listened for a moment. Then she glanced at Steele, her face a white blur in the darkness.

'Is that those men?'

Steele nodded. 'I guess so.'

'Well, I'm all right now. You can go, I won't mind. Christ, I shouldn't, I'm used to it. Just fill my glass again first.'

Steele emptied the bottle into her glass and went to the front door. There was a man outside, short-haired and broad-shouldered in plain military denims, and another dressed the same standing behind.

'Sergeant Lawton, sir,' the man in front said, 'dock police.'

'You know what to do?' Steele asked.

'Keep a sharp eye on this place round the clock.'

Steele nodded and returned to the bedroom. Louise had turned on the light and was sitting in front of the dressing-table, gazing into the mirror. She glanced round startled as he came in.

'Was it someone else?'

Steele shook his head. 'Just two sturdy naval policemen who'll be out there as long as you want.'

'Then what—'

'Am I waiting for?' He finished, 'I'll tell you. A shower first, then dinner. And as I don't want to keep that messenger boy running around, I figured Callum and his lady might go out on the town—'

Steele grinned. 'I decided on a change of hotel for the night after all.'

'Why, Steele, why?'

Midnight. There was no Levanter cloud and the same stars, the stars that had brought Louise to the Rock, were still raining down the sky in great dazzling constellations, more brilliant, more glittering than before.

'Why—?'

Steele echoed turning from the window. Louise was in bed – he could just see her face, a pale oval framed by her dark hair against the pillow – but he was still dressed.

'Because when it comes to spending the bastards' money, two of us can do it faster than one.'

Louise laughed. 'Certainly after tonight it's going to take a year in a convent to make me respectable again—'

They'd started with cocktails at the Rock Hotel. Then they'd gone to what she said was the best restaurant in the colony, where Steele ordered more champagne, the most expensive on the list. Finally they'd ended drinking French brandy in a little nightclub – surrounded, as everywhere else, by the curious stares and murmurs of the other guests.

'There was still the late ferry,' she added.

'The view's better in the morning.'

Steele grinned and came towards the bed, swaying slightly as he walked.

The drink had made him lightheaded and for a moment longer he was even more strongly aware of the elation he'd felt all evening. For a few hours he'd thrown everything off, he'd been in the open with no invisible surveillance network surrounding him, no angry worried Wedderburn at the end of a telephone line, no shadow prowling behind them all. Instead just Louise, pretty, laughing, talking, and eagerly attentive waiters, and the sense of confidence, of safety that money and reputation brought – Callum's money and Callum's reputation.

He hadn't been Steele tonight, he'd been Callum – and not the menaced hunted Callum he'd been forced to play before but the old Callum, Greville's dream, rich and dominating and successful.

The feeling went the instant he sat down on the bed.

'We spent it, Louise, and that's it.'

'Are you trying to tell me about midnight? Don't! I'm an expert on when the clock strikes—'

She smiled, sat up and propped herself against the bedhead.

'Why with me, Steele? Why not with almost anyone else, with that blonde girl across the straits for instance?'

'What do you mean?'

He blustered, reddening in the darkness. Then, as he realized Louise couldn't have known about the night before, he saw she'd noticed something and was laughing again.

'I should have guessed! Who isn't going to want to sleep with the great Ross Callum? Well, I'm meant to have shared him with others before, so I suppose I can do it now. But why spend the last night here?'

Steele didn't answer for a while. Then he said slowly, 'Because we're the same, you and I. We come from the same place, we know the same things, we stand against the same people. All the others are different.'

It was true. From the beginning he'd recognized her as another of the same kind, the same tribe. Callum was a harlequin mask. Without the mask, and in her company alone he hadn't had to wear it, they were equal, losers both of them, on the retreat, surrendering ground reluctantly but inevitably inch by inch, and yet somehow managing to survive, always refusing to concede the last few yards, the last private patch of mind and heart.

166

That was why he'd stayed with her. He'd said it was the last night, meaning his last night in the dirty area. Then, in light and warmth, surrounded by other diners, buoyed by the champagne, the morning had seemed distant. Not now. Now it was only hours away and he knew the night might be the last one in another sense.

'Come to bed—'

Louise pulled back the sheet and moved to the other side. Steele undressed and got in beside her.

'I'll tell you something, Steele. Midnights aren't important. We spent the money, but that doesn't matter. What matters is that we had it. That's winning a little and however short it was, you can make it last a long time.'

Steele turned his head to look at her. She was lying close against him, warm and relaxed. She hadn't been talking about money alone, he knew that, but before he could ask her what else she meant Louise held out her arms and pulled him over her. They made love more slowly this time yet with a fierceness and intensity that left them both exhausted. Afterwards Louise fell asleep instantly.

Steele didn't sleep. He lay on his back, cold all night in spite of her warmth, watching the stars and waiting for the dawn.

15

'How far?' Steele asked.

Marcel, the little driver, was perched on a cushion behind the wheel. He glanced down at the kilometre register and calculated.

'About 300, sir.'

'Ask him what time he reckons we'll get there.'

Steele was in the back of the Citroën with the Spaniard's agent in the passenger seat beside Marcel in front. The agent, a fat nervous sweating man who smelt of cologne and kept spitting the husks of coriander seeds through the open window, spoke a little French and less English.

Marcel talked to him in Arabic for a few moments and said, 'Difficult to say, sir. He knows only to Benawhaziz. After we look for a village, Goulahmanah, and then a guide. He thinks maybe another eight hours.'

Steele looked at his watch. Four o'clock. Another eight hours would mean midnight. He sat back and gazed out of the car, feeling the hot afternoon air parching his skin.

They'd left at twelve. Until an hour ago they'd been travelling through the harsh mountainous landscape of northern Morocco, scorched and arid in the autumn heat. Somewhere ahead there were more mountains, rimming the Sahara, but for the moment they were in desert. The sand stretched out in front, flat and barren, towards a rimless horizon, with the road nothing more than a faint imprint of tracks as if a great feather had been brushed across the waste.

Occasionaly white-painted oil-drums marked its course. Once they'd passed a policeman standing incongruously by one of them as if he was on point-duty in the wilderness. As they went by he pulled out a notebook and wrote down the Citroën's registration number.

168

Steele leant forward frowning, but Marcel shook his head unconcernedly.

'Tomorrow he sends it to Rabat for checking,' he said. 'They check and they find nothing – naturally, because they have no records for cars. The records are all still kept in Casablanca. So they file it and forget it.'

'They won't investigate any further?' Steele asked.

'No, sir. It gives them something to do, that is all. Otherwise they are sitting scratching their arses—'

Marcel said something to the agent who chuckled and nodded in agreement.

'*Shamahdi*, very rude word, sir,' Marcel grinned happily at Steele in the driving mirror, 'what all Arabs call each other. Means we are the most stupid, idle, greedy people in the world, worse than pigs. My Christ, are we not right too!'

He went on grinning for a long time.

Steele had tried to sleep before. He closed his eyes and tried again now, and still it wouldn't come. The heat, the bumping of the chassis over the ruts, the sprays of grey sand from the wheels, random particles pricking his face like wasp-stings, everything conspired against it – most of all the restless churning of his mind.

He'd dozed fitfully at last in Louise's bed as the night ended. Then at five she'd woken him with a cup of coffee. Three hours afterwards he was back at the hotel in Tangier. An hour later Charan Desai's representative had arrived, another Indian, young, punctilious, formal and unsmiling. The transaction took only a few minutes. Marcel had brought the *Lara*'s ownership certificate up from the launch. Steele handed it over, the Indian counted out the gold – one hundred and twenty-five coins packed in a canvas belt – and Steele signed a receipt.

As soon as the Indian left Steele called Ybarra's agent. The conversation was stilted and confused until Steele summoned Marcel to the bedroom. Then, with Marcel translating, he made the arrangements. They'd pick the agent up by a kiosk on Rue Dr Fleming at midday, Steele would give him one third of the weapons' purchase price, and the three of them would leave immediately in Steele's car for Boumalne to complete the deal.

Next he telephoned Wedderburn. He was going to stay in his room, Steele said, until Velatti made contact. Then he'd call back

169

and consult. Wedderburn, his voice sharp and strained now with the growing tension, agreed. Finally Steele sent Marcel to wait for him with the car in a small square off the Place de France.

After that it was easy. The surveillance group were scattered along the Rue de la Liberté in front of the hotel. Steele walked out the back, circled round to the square and thirty minutes later they were on their way. At the earliest it would be mid-afternoon before Wedderburn checked the hotel again and by then they'd be deep in the countryside to the south.

Steele reached down and checked the guns again. They were both on the floor by his feet hidden under his jacket. He didn't know which he'd take when the moment came, the Browning or the Smith & Wesson – that would depend entirely on what he found at Boumalne. He couldn't even start to make a plan until they arrived. All he knew, with an utter unshakable certainty, was that somewhere in the desert ahead Velatti was waiting for him, and that somehow he would fire before the Maltese.

He sat slumped back against the seat, hazy with fatigue, his mouth raw and dry, his head aching, gazing at the low dunes and the white shimmering sky but seeing nothing except the mournful staring eyes in the photograph Greville had handed him.

Darkness came very quickly. One moment there was the same glaring light they'd driven in since morning, the next the sky was black and thick with stars and the headlamp beams were wavering in front. Steele had no idea how Marcel managed to follow the track but he drove on steadily for another two hours. Then the agent spoke to him and he stopped.

'Benawhaziz, sir—'

Marcel pointed through the windscreen and Steele saw a line of lights a mile away in the dark.

'We go in and find someone to take us to Goulahmanah. Then he says we look for another guide who knows where we go.'

Steele nodded and Marcel drove on.

Benawhaziz was a small rambling town huddled beneath a red sandstone fort, once an outpost of the French Foreign Legion and now in ruins. They drew up in the main square and the agent disappeared behind the bead-lined doorway of a café. A few minutes later he returned with an emaciated Arab youth who wedged himself into the front beside Marcel and they set off

170

again.

It took a further hour to reach Goulahmanah. The intervening countryside was still desert but occasionally Steele glimpsed rows of low hills and once in the distance a rocky plateau. Then suddenly there were more lights, tallow lanterns and charcoal glowing in cooking pots, and they were in the middle of a village and Marcel was braking.

'This time I go with him, sir,' Marcel turned off the engine, and he and the agent got out.

Steele unfolded a map. The village was too small to be shown but he guessed they were somewhere east of Boumalne. Directly ahead, only thirty kilometres away, were the Almajin mountains, the last barrier against the Sahara. Beyond them there was nothing but sand. He tossed the map aside and waited, listening to the night wind and the small sounds coming from the baked mud houses behind the braziers.

'This is the man, sir—'

Marcel had reappeared with the agent. Between them was an old hunchbacked Arab, even smaller than Marcel and shuffling sideways like a crab. The youth had vanished and the old man tucked himself into the front in his place.

'He says it is half an hour from here,' Marcel slammed the door. 'The road is not good but he thinks we can make it in this.'

'Wait,' Steele leant forward and tapped him hard on the shoulder, 'before we start I want to know exactly where we're going, what it's like, who's going to be there. You ask the old boy and our other friend here, too.'

'Yes, sir.'

There was a lengthy conversation in Arabic between the three of them, the old man whistling and snuffling as he spoke. Then Marcel turned round.

'It's an oasis, sir,' he said, 'a small one, they don't even have a name for it, just the water. The blue men use it, the *turegs* coming up from the south with their caravans to trade. They cross the desert but they don't come no further, they don't trust. This one—'

Marcel pointed at the agent.

'He says the guns arrived here a month ago. His friends bought them and the owner has been waiting since to be paid. He gives

171

the owner money, the owner gives him the guns, then you give him money and afterwards we get the guns. I think it is truth, sir. It is the way these businesses are done.'

Steele nodded.

That explained why, to his surprise, the agent hadn't deposited the gold coins in Tangier, but instead had brought them with him. They represented the Spaniards' purchase price. The balance Steele was due to pay would be their profit on the deal.

'How many other caravans are there at the oasis?' he asked.

'None, sir. They don't come now until the rains start, next month maybe.'

'Tell him I'm looking for a man, this man,' Steele produced the photograph, 'ask if he's seen him in the village or at the oasis – or if he's seen any other European.'

Marcel showed the photograph to the old Arab, there was another conversation, then Marcel shook his head.

'No, sir. He sees no one since last year.'

'Any cars recently?'

More Arabic and again Marcel shaking his head. 'No, sir.'

Steele hesitated for a moment. 'All right, we'll go on. But I want to stop a full half-kilometre before the oasis. You make sure he understands that.'

Steele slipped on his jacket, put the Browning into the right pocket and the Smith & Wesson into the left. Then he hunched himself forward with his head low and his elbows resting on the backs of the front seats.

The track was worse than the old man had described, fissured with ruts and strewn with jagged pieces of sandstone, and it was over an hour later before they stopped again. Steele snapped at Marcel to cut the lights, got out and knelt on the sand by the open door.

'Where's the oasis?' He said as Marcel came round towards him.

'Right in front, sir.'

Marcel pointed but Steele could see nothing except the even black line of the desert.

'Listen,' he pulled Marcel down beside him, 'I want you to go forward with the old man. The other stays in the passenger seat – and tell him I'll blow his brains out if he moves. You check the whole place out. Make a full turn round the oasis, look for car tracks, above all find out how many people there are and who they are. Then come back.'

Marcel gazed at him. 'You think something wrong, sir, maybe someone waiting for us?'

'Too goddam right I do. The man in the photograph.'

'I go see, sir.'

Marcel stood up. Steele heard Arabic again, then the fading shuffle of feet in the sand, and afterwards silence.

He stayed kneeling by the car door. The fatigue had gone, his head had cleared and he felt once again totally alert and prepared, almost eager for the confrontation. He'd followed the deviously-laid trail to the end, he'd finally taken the initiative and now he was ready – ready not just for Velatti but to settle his own debts, to make the Maltese pay for everything he'd subjected Steele to throughout the week.

The wind raised spirals of dust that spun away into the darkness, an owl planed low towards him, saw the car and sheered up, starlight reflected on the underside of its wings, then Steele stiffened. There were two silhouettes against the sky and he could hear the scuff of feet again.

'Just one caravan, sir,' Marcel was crouching by him, 'maybe four or five men, but they all from the south, no Europeans with them. I go all round twice and there's nothing, not even car tracks. I don't think there's anyone else there.'

Steele stared into the night, his mind churning once more. Velatti had to be there, it was impossible he wasn't. He'd have seen the headlamps and hidden, waiting for Steele to show himself. It was the only explanation and there was only one way to prove it.

'We'll all go,' Steele got to his feet, 'the fat one and the Arab in front, you alongside me behind. Now let's move!'

For ten minutes they followed the tracks left by Marcel and the old man. Then a sheet of water gleamed ahead of them, surrounded by palm-trees and patterned like the owl's wings with myriads of stars, and suddenly there was no longer sand underfoot but reeds and thick grass. A moment later Steele saw the outline of tents, the heaving shapes of pale-bellied camels, tethered by webs of ropes to the trees, the glow of charcoal fires and the movement of figures squatting behind the flames.

'It is this one, sir.'

173

Marcel touched Steele's arm. The agent and the old man were standing by the entrance to the largest tent. Steele hesitated. He could smell the strong ammoniac scent of fresh dung and hear the camel bells ringing. Then he lifted the Browning from his pocket, prodded the agent inside and ducked under the leather flap behind him.

A copper brazier, a dazzle of green, scarlet and gold tapestries on the floor and lining the tent walls, a mound of embroidered cushions, a falcon with a crimson leather hood nodding on an ebony perch, an old man sitting cross-legged at the back and a boy beside him – Steele absorbed it all with a single sweeping glance and as instantly dismissed it. He was looking for something else and what he was looking for wasn't there.

'We make a greeting, sir,' Marcel guided him forward, 'then we let them do their business.'

The agent had already introduced himself to the cross-legged old man. Steele stepped round the brazier, dropped the revolver back into his pocket and held out his hand.

'Enchanté, m'sieu,' he said.

The man was in his late sixties but still immensely, ferociously strong – Steele's hand ached as he gripped and held it between his two. His face was teak-coloured, lined and scarred, his nose curved down like the falcon's bill between vital black eyes, and a heavy grey beard jutted out from his chin.

He let go of Steele, threw back his head and laughed, gold-capped teeth shining amidst yellow stumps in his mouth. Then he glanced at Marcel and spoke in Arabic.

'He says you are welcome,' Marcel translated, 'but in his house you will not need a gun – only an appetite for all he can offer you.'

Steele nodded and sat down on one of the cushions. The boy offered him a glass of mint tea, sweet and scalding hot. He sipped it slowly, the glass burning his fingers, as the agent and the old man started to talk.

'This is a rich man,' Marcel said, 'he has many slaves. Often he travels with six or more. But a Polisario patrol killed four when he was crossing the desert. He needs money now to buy more. He is telling the fat one that is why he sells the weapons so cheap.'

Steele wasn't listening. His hand was back in his pocket and he was watching the entrance, a slit in the tentwall to his left, an

174

aperture behind the old man, his glance moving steadily between the three openings. Velatti would choose his time and appear through one of them, perhaps only a gun would appear, but he'd be there, he was there now, in the darkness outside, and Steele knew it with as much certainty as if he could see him.

'They finish, sir—'

The agent was standing and Marcel was getting to his feet and Steele stood up too.

'We say goodbye, then we conclude our own business with the fat one at the car.'

Steele shook hands with the old man again, felt again the crushing grip, heard the Arabic phrases of farewell, saw the falcon lift a threatening taloned foot as he passed, then they were outside by the star-shimmering water with the camel bells still chiming and whisps of charcoal smoke blowing against their faces.

'This is the path, sir.'

Briefly Marcel had taken charge. He led the way proudly, scurrying birdlike across the sand as they left the damp rustling grass of the oasis and came out onto the desert. Steele followed him, head down, tramping blindly in the footprints they had made earlier. The Arab guide had disappeared, the agent was panting somewhere to his rear, and he could feel exhaustion flooding over him again. He tried to shake it off, clenching his nails into his palms and forcing his eyes to focus on the track.

He could not be wrong. He'd misjudged the precise moment, that was all. There'd been too many people in the tent, the transaction had happened too fast, they'd been surrounded by the old man's followers. Velatti would still come. All he needed was space and a little more time – and Steele would give him both here in the open desert.

'Tell him to shut up—'

They were by the Citroën, the agent was babbling and Steele rounded furiously on Marcel.

'If I hear one more word from him he gets his gut kicked in.'

'Yes, sir.'

There was a whispered conversation and Marcel turned back to Steele, his face frowning and uncertain.

'He understands, sir, he understands pretty damn good. But he says you can have the guns now, any time you want. They're back of the big tent in crates. You pay him the money and he does anything you say. That's what he says, sir.'

Marcel broke off. Beside him the agent pulled out a handkerchief and dabbed at his face, mopping away sweat in spite of the early morning chill.

'We're staying here until daylight,' Steele said. 'He can sleep in the car, he can sleep any bloody where he wants. But nothing happens until dawn.'

The agent shrugged helplessly and got back into the passenger seat.

'You think this man still comes, sir?' Marcel asked.

'We're going to give him the chance.'

'Then I watch with you.'

Steele sat down by the back of the car, where he could see the track leading to Goulahmanah. Marcel squatted beside him and they settled down to wait.

The night passed and the first wash of pale lemon coloured light spread over the eastern horizon, and Steele knew long before then that he had been wrong, fighting against the acknowledgement to the end, willing Velatti to appear as if he'd been an ally not an enemy, closing his eyes to prolong the darkness and give him one final opportunity. Then the sun lifted and the vigil was over. The Maltese wasn't coming. He'd never intended to be there.

'What we do now, sir?'

The agent had got out of the car and was babbling excitedly at Marcel again. Steele climbed to his feet and stood swaying with exhaustion.

He rubbed his face and tried to concentrate. He hadn't made any plans, he hadn't even brought the rest of the gold with him. Everything should have finished last night. It hadn't and all he could do now was return to Tangier, put himself ignominiously back in the hands of Wedderburn and the surveillance network, and wait impotently for the end.

'First you tell him this—'

Steele was forcing himself to think. The guns at least might be saved. He didn't know for what purpose but they were all that was left to be salvaged from the disaster, and they might still have some use as a bargaining counter.

'He's not going to like it, but he's going to swallow it. The

176

money's in Tangier. I'm not paying the balance until the guns are there too – and he's going to help us shift them. Is there a car hire agent in Benawhaziz—?'

Marcel nodded.

'Right. We'll go back there, leave the Citroën, hire a truck and load up. Then we'll all head for Tangier. Tell him if he doesn't agree the deal's off. His friends don't get their money, he doesn't get his cut, and they all finish up with a bunch of weapons they've paid for but can't sell. See how he likes that idea.'

Marcel translated and for ten minutes the agent argued, complained and shouted, sweat pouring off him as he waved his arms frenziedly. In the end he sullenly agreed, heaved himself into the car and slammed the door.

It was early afternoon before they were on the road back north. Between them Marcel and the agent located an ancient ten-ton fruit truck, which cost all of Steele's remaining dirhams to hire for the journey. They drove it to the oasis, loaded the crates into the back, scattered some empty orange boxes over them and set off with Marcel at the wheel and the agent sitting cursing under his breath beside him.

Steele stretched himself out on a narrow bunk behind the seats. For a few moments he felt an overwhelming sense of bitterness, depression and failure. He'd staked everything, he'd miscalculated and he'd lost. Then, numbed and dizzy with fatigue, he slept.

'Mr Callum.'

Marcel was shaking his shoulder. Steele sat up. It was dark and he glanced at his watch. Almost midnight again. They'd stopped once in the early evening to eat, but apart from that he'd slept throughout the entire drive.

He leant forward and peered out. 'Where are we?'

'Tangier, sir,' Marcel said. 'It is a wharf that belongs to this man. He says he waits here while we get the money. Then we take the guns and go – we can bring the boat up to the side. I do not think he is very happy, sir.'

Steele looked at the agent. He was hunched in the front seat, glowering and chewing nervously on his handkerchief at the same time.

'How far's the hotel?' Steele asked.

'Maybe eight kilometres, sir. We are on the bay east of the

yard.'

'Then what the hell does he expect us to do – walk?'

'He says we can take his car, sir,' Marcel smiled, 'I do not think he has much choice. He is a very unhappy man indeed.'

The car was parked inside a pair of iron gates at the end of the wharf. The agent unlocked the gates, Marcel drove out and the man returned to the truck.

'Wait a moment—'

They were circling the bay towards the town and Steele realized the boatyard was just in front of them.

'Pull in by the office. If we're going to have to move those guns we'll need Lorca to get the *Lara* under way. He was going to leave a note inside saying where he's staying.'

Marcel drove down to the waterfront and drew up by the office. Steele got out and walked round to the front of the building. The yard was silent and there was no traffic on the coastal road. He reached for the office door, checked and turned round. There'd been a sound from the jetty, a sharp splintering sound.

Steele stepped onto the wooden platform and hesitated, puzzled as he heard the noise again. Then he suddenly started to run towards the launch. The head and shoulders of a man were silhouetted above the cockpit – a man raising what looked like a sledge-hammer against the stars.

Steele was wearing rubber-soled boots and his feet made no sound on the stones. He reached the iron cradle, stumbled over something, gripped the stanchion and pulled himself upright. There was a huddled bundle at his feet, limp and inert. For an instant he thought it was a sack of caulking wadding. Then he saw a glistening puddle and the outline of a face, white and blurred in the shadow.

He crouched and turned the face towards him. It was Pepe Lorca, the mate he'd hired in Ceuta. The back of his skull had been smashed in and he was dead.

Steele cautiously pushed his body aside and stood up again. The man wielding the sledge-hammer was only eight feet away but he still hadn't heard him. Steele listened. He could hear the man grunting with effort between the blows and then, from inside the cabin, the same splintering noise. There were two of them. They'd killed Lorca and now they were wrecking the launch.

He gathered himself and jumped, hurdling the stern rail and landing in the centre of the cockpit. The man began to turn as Steele's feet hit the deck, but he was far too slow. Steele used the planks like a springboard, bounced forward and drove his head into the man's face. The man was hurled back, the cabin overhang slammed into the base of his neck and he collapsed instantly unconscious.

'*O que passa*?'

The call, quiet and uncertain, came from below. Steele flattened himself against the cabin wall by the open hatch. Apart from a scuffle, a bump and the clatter of the sledge-hammer on the deck, there'd still been no noise.

'*Luis, cue passa*?'

The question came again, more urgently now. Steele tensed. He recognized the accent, Portuguese, and the same flaring anger that he'd felt in Louise's house welled over him. They'd attacked him, they'd menaced and terrorized her, now they'd set out to destroy the *Lara*.

Footsteps sounded on the flight of stairs up from the cabin. The second man's head came into sight, he peered round the cockpit, saw his companion and began to open his mouth. Steele bent his arm, swivelled from the waist and slammed the point of his elbow into the man's jaw. There was a crack like a muffled pistol shot and fragments of teeth pattered down on the boards. The man slumped over the stairs and lay twitching as convulsions shook his body and blood pumped out across the deck.

Steele stepped back and listened again. Waves were lapping against the boat, the mooring hawsers grated on the stanchions, a distant taxi hooted in the town. That was all – there was no one else. He dragged the man into the cockpit, climbed down to the cabin and switched on the light. A second sledge-hammer was lying on the floor and the inside was a shambles – the porthole windows shattered, the table chopped to splinters, the lockers hacked open.

He moved towards the galley, froze and whirled back. There was someone else, another crumpled bundle pitched over the starboard bunk, half-hidden beneath torn cloth, broken glass and shreds of wood. He could see blue jeans, a spill of yellow hair, a limp wrist dangling above the boards.

179

Steele kicked the debris aside and lifted her up. Mary-Beth's face was grey, her lips swollen and cut, and her shoulder wrenched out at an angle from her body. But she was still breathing, small laboured breaths, and the pulse in her wrist was throbbing. He laid her down on the port bunk, ripped open her shirt and listened to her heart. It was beating strongly. Steele closed his eyes for a moment in relief. Then he flung himself into the cockpit, leapt ashore and sprinted towards the car.

'Marcel! I want you!'

He jerked open the door, Marcel tumbled out and they ran back together along the jetty. The two men were still motionless on the deck. Steele kicked one of them savagely and jumped down into the cabin.

Marcel hadn't said anything until then. Now, seeing Mary-Beth lying unconscious among the wreckage, he gazed at Steele wide-eyed.

'What happens, sir?'

'Trouble,' Steele said, 'bad trouble. Just do as I tell you—'

He half-lifted Mary-Beth, eased off the rest of her shirt and ran his hands over her body. She'd been badly beaten round the face and there were dark bruises on her breasts, but as far as he could tell none of her bones were broken. The dislocated shoulder was the worst injury. It was bearing down on her lungs and hampering her breathing.

'Help me turn her over—'

With Marcel at her legs Steele rolled Mary-Beth onto her face. The shoulder-blade was jutting out and discolouring her skin. He gripped the bone, manipulated it between his hands and pressed hard, levering it backwards and forwards. She moaned and coughed and saliva trickled over the bunk. Then he found the socket and the bone clicked back into place.

'On her back again—'

They rolled her over and Steele listened once more. Her breaths were steadier and deeper now, and the pulse in her wrist had slowed. He spread a blanket over her and stood up.

'Right, now we'll clean up the rest of the mess—'

There was a hand-hauled trolley on the jetty at the foot of the cradle, which Donovan had been using to transport equipment out to the launch. Steele dragged the two Portuguese across the cockpit, heaved them over the stern rail and tugged them onto the carriage platform. Then he and Marcel, sweating and panting, pulled the trolley a hundred yards along the stoney shore.

'Go back and wait for me by the cradle—'

Marcel vanished. Steele glanced up at the coastal road. It was too late for cars and there was no sign of any pedestrians. He tipped the two men off the trolley. One of them, the one whose jaw he'd shattered with his elbow, squirmed as he landed on the pebbles. The other sprawled out like a beached starfish, silent and limp.

Steele looked down at them. They'd be found by the police in the morning, as the other pair must have been found in Gibraltar, and they'd end up in some Moroccan prison. Only it wasn't enough. They'd declared war on him, a silent brutal war waged in sadism and viciousness that swept up as victims everyone whose life he touched. Now they were going to learn that the war was being carried back to them on their own terms.

He searched through the pebbles until he found a larger rock cast up by the tide. Steele balanced it carefully in his hand, lifted it and held it raised over the leg of the man who was still twitching beneath him. Then he hesitated.

He wanted to cripple them both, smash their kneecaps so they'd never walk again. Only it wasn't him who'd inflict the damage and take the vengeance. It was Callum. And he knew, even as the rage coursed over him, that what he intended to do was something Greville's cavalier laughing creation would have despised. Callum had no need of vengeance. Callum was secure in himself. He could look after his own without descending to the gutter-level of those who pitched themselves against him.

Steele hurled the rock away. Then he turned and hauled the trolley back to the jetty.

'All right, Marcel, that's it—'

He was standing by the cradle again. He and Marcel had wrapped Lorca's body in a length of tarpaulin and stowed it away in the hold. He could decide how to dispose of that in the morning, when he was thinking, functioning again.

'What about Mary-Beth, sir?'

'She's going to be all right—'

Steele had just checked on her. She'd passed from unconsciousness into sleep, and now she was breathing evenly and quietly.

181

'You wait in the car, Marcel. We're not moving from here until it's light. If you see or hear anyone, lean on the horn and keep leaning. I'll be in the launch.'

'Yes, sir.'

Steele climbed back on board as Marcel scuttled away into the darkness.

He spent the next thirty minutes cleaning up the boat, and pitching the rubble of broken glass and wood over the side. The cabin was the most badly damaged. The men had obviously started there together, and the one on deck when Steele arrived had just moved up to tackle the superstructure. Luckily the wheelhouse and the engines hadn't been touched.

When he finished he examined Mary-Beth again. She was still sleeping deeply. He bathed her face, turned out the light and sat down on the other bunk by the open hatch, with the revolver beside him and one of the sledge-hammers at his feet. There were still more than five hours to morning. Somewhere in the town the rest of the Portuguese group would be waiting to find out what had happened at the yard.

It was the second night running he'd sat up. This time he was fresh and alert after the long sleep in the truck. He listened to the waves and the distant hooting of ships in the straits, his mind working restlessly again. He tried to still it, to relax, but his thoughts kept spinning and tumbling in meaningless circles. He was trapped and helpless, and every move he made left only a worse trail of violence and destruction.

Another half-hour passed, once a bus rumbled along the road, otherwise there were only the night sounds of the sea and the grating of the mooring ropes. Then suddenly Steele stiffened. He could hear a splashing by the bows, a clatter and the launch started to rock as if someone was climbing aboard.

He picked up the Browning, reached swiftly for the sledge-hammer with his other hand, and backed down the cabin aisle until he was standing by Mary-Beth's head. He stood beside her listening. There was someone on deck. He could hear the drip of water followed by the quiet scuff of feet.

The steps moved overhead and sounded again, closer now, in the cockpit. Then a shape appeared at the hatch and a figure climbed slowly down the stairs.

'Mr Callum—?'

Steele gazed at the weary oval face, the melancholy eyes, the hunched shoulders framed by the starlight. Then he lifted the Browning and aimed at the man's chest.

'Please, I ask you to wait. My name is Velatti. I wish to talk to you.'

16

Velatti must have swum to the launch because his dark suit was sodden and water was pooling round his feet.

He stood wearily by the steps, even smaller than Steele had visualized, a pale huddled little figure with his chest heaving, his mouth half-open as he panted, and his arms hanging limply by his sides. The oval face, the melancholy eyes, the thinning hair, plastered flat now across his forehead, were all exactly as in the photograph.

Yet there was something that didn't fit the image Steele had carried in his mind – the exhaustion of a broken man at the extreme limits of his resources, the presence of illness in his shaking body, an edge of pleading desperation in his voice. Something so bizarre and contradictory, so alien to everything Steele had expected, that for a moment he stared at him dazed.

Then Steele said, 'Stay where you are.'

He lowered the sledge-hammer onto the bunk and came forward slowly with the Browning still aimed at Velatti's chest.

'No, no. I have nothing – look.'

Velatti took a deep labouring breath, lifted his arms and crossed them behind his head. Then he turned and bowed himself against the cabin wall.

It was the attitude of someone who knew the techniques of searching, who expected to be searched, and Steele searched him thoroughly, holding the gun hard against his back. His legs, thin and goose-pimpled under the wet cloth, his groin, his chest, his pockets, his armpits. There was nothing. No wallet, no keys, no money, not even a handkerchief, least of all a weapon.

'Keep your hands where they are and sit down with your head on your knees.'

Steele backed away as Velatti lowered himself to the bunk. All of his movements were hesitant and painful, like an old man testing his limbs after an operation. He dropped his head onto his knees and Steele walked, quickly this time, to the foot of the steps.

Logically, from everything he'd been told, everything he'd planned and prepared for since he started, it had to be a trap, there had to be someone else on deck. He listened and he could hear nothing except the slapping of the waves.

'Mr Callum—'

Steele spun on his feet levelling the revolver again, but there was still only the small bedraggled man with one hand outstretched now.

'Please may I sit straight,' he heaved himself upright and slumped against the slashed oilskin cushion. 'I fear I will faint otherwise. And I give you my word of honour. There is no one else. I came alone, I am alone.'

Steele hesitated. Then he reached for a towel hanging by the galley bulkhead and tossed it into his lap.

'Thank you.'

Velatti dabbed at his neck. More water was spreading out on the bunk and the cabin smelt of harbour sewage.

Steele watched him. He was still listening for sounds on deck, still holding the gun, still tense, wary and ready to fire instantly without question. Yet he sensed already with a chilling confused certainty that he hadn't been told the truth. The truth was different, utterly different, and he knew that whatever the explanation he'd been deceived and lied to from the start.

'She has been hurt?'

Velatti had noticed Mary-Beth. Steele glanced at the other bunk. She hadn't moved when he switched on the light and she was still lying motionless.

'Yes,' he said.

'Because of me?'

Steele shrugged. 'Not directly. She was attacked on my account. But as I only returned because of you, it comes to much the same, doesn't it?'

'I am sorry, truly sorry,' Velatti paused. 'If you have a cigarette I would be most grateful.'

His English was faintly accented. Steele reached carefully across his body with his left hand and dropped a pack of Camels and a new lighter on the bunk.

'What did they tell you, Mr Callum? That I was sick, perhaps? Well, in a way I have been, maybe I still am. The strain of it all has been like nothing I have ever known—'

Velatti lit the cigarette, inhaled and coughed, colour welling over his cheeks as he struggled for breath and then ebbing, leaving his skin even more translucent white than before.

'Or that I was disloyal, greedy, opportunist, a blackmailer making threats? I will tell you. I have never been disloyal. I am not greedy or an opportunist. I believe I am incapable of blackmail. But threats, yes, those I did make. Did they tell you of them?'

They. Their common masters, Velatti's and Callum's, and now Steele's.

'They told me you had a grievance,' Steele said, 'you thought I'd wronged you and you wanted to meet me.'

He'd meant to give nothing away, answer no questions, until Velatti had told his story, but he suddenly changed his mind.

Velatti had been ill, Steele had no doubt of that at all. It was evident in the withered body, the trembling hands, the eyes that glazed over and gazed unseeing at the light. Yet it wasn't the illness he'd been prepared for, an illness charged with energy and hate. This was the result of shock, a traumatic shock to the mind with the same effect as a massive coronary attack on the physical system. It had left him drained and wasted, too tired for guile or deceit.

If Steele was going to hear the truth from anyone, he'd hear it from him. There was nothing else left for Velatti to tell. All Steele would keep back was the final separate truth about Callum.

'I wanted to meet you? It was true, it was what I begged them,' Velatti sounded surprised, 'but a grievance against you, never. Why should I?'

'It was rather more than a grievance. They said your request for a meeting was a prelude to killing me.'

'They told you that? Oh, my God!' Velatti shook his head in disbelief. 'I told them you were the only man I would trust and they turned it upside down, they said I wanted to kill you. And you believed them, that's why you were followed all the time – you thought you were being guarded against me?'

186

Steele nodded, and Velatti went on shaking his head numbly for a while.

Then he asked, 'Did they tell you about Lorenz?'

'Lorenz?' Steele frowned. He'd heard the name somewhere but not in connection with Callum. 'No, I don't think so.'

'You would remember if they had. But I understand now, I think I understand it all—'

Another spasm of coughing shook his chest and he leant forward heaving.

Steele waited. He understood nothing yet except that he'd been fed more lies, more grotesque and deliberate distortions, than he'd believed possible even five minutes ago.

'Mr Callum,' Velatti pushed himself up, 'I will not ask any more what you have been told. I cannot fight that. All I can do is say in my own words what happened and afterwards leave it to you to decide. But whatever decision you make I tell you now I will accept it. May I—?'

He touched the pack of Camels. Steele nodded and he lit a new cigarette from the butt of the last one.

'I work of course for the same department as you. That at least you know for sure. I do not hold a high position but it is a responsible one and I have never wanted more. Most of the work is routine. Delicate and unusual perhaps to outsiders but to us whose profession it is, still routine. That again you know. And I flatter myself, no, I take pride, a legitimate pride, I believe, that I have always been good at what I do—'

Velatti inhaled, his hand, still shaking, cupped round the cigarette so that the glowing tip lit his birdclaw fingers. So far, apart from the professed lack of ambition, he was describing himself as Greville had described him.

'Occasionally I am instructed to do something which is not routine. It happens maybe once or twice a year and it happened two months ago. I was told to charter a boat. I have done it before. Down here it is not unusual, well, as you yourself know the *Lara* was a classic example. The instruction carried a very high operational rating, in fact the highest I had ever dealt with. That was unusual. More unusual still I was told to make the arrangements in conjunction with a member of the Moroccan internal security service—'

Velatti glanced up. 'After twelve years I know every member

187

of their security service. We have them on record just as they have us. Also I speak Arabic. I met this man. He introduced himself as a full colonel. I had never heard of him and his name was not on our files. Then, after he had spoken for a time, I realized he was not Moroccan, but Lebanese. The accent is quite different—'

He looked at Steele as if the information should have meant something. Steele stared back at him blankly. This had nothing to do with anything he had been told and he was totally lost now.

'I assumed the boat was for some joint mission,' Velatti went on, 'I could not imagine what nor why I was working with a Lebanese, but I have never asked questions and I did not do so then. So we chartered a boat, this man and I, an eighty-ton coastal freighter operating out of Casablanca under a Liberian flag – the size, the registration and so on were all specified. We used an agreed cover, of course, but the details are not important except one. The freighter required a deck and engine crew of six. We were each to engage three locally—'

Velatti broke off and gazed at one of the shattered portholes.

Then he added quietly, 'I am a homosexual, Mr Callum. I am not proud of it, indeed I am ashamed and I prefer to use the true word queer, not gay, because it is what such as I are. Six months before this I met a sailor here, a young Arab. He was, he is, a very beautiful boy. I fell in love with him—'

The statements were made simply and slowly but Steele could see in Velatti's face the intense effort he was going through to get them out.

'He had no work and I engaged him as one of the three hands I had to provide. It was a good job, well-paid and I had no doubts about what I had done. I didn't declare our relationship, but I did not need to. It was irrelevant and there was no one to tell. That should have been the end of it. I had completed my role in the assignment, the young man had work for the length of the charter, and I returned to my normal business. And yet—'

He hesitated again. The words were coming with more and more difficulty now, and he was clenching his interlaced fingers so hard – the last cigarette was hissing in a puddle on the boards – that Steele could see spots of blood on the backs of his hands where his nails were cutting the skin.

'For this I make no excuses, nor will I forgive myself as long as I

188

live. I can only ask that you try to understand. I am not young. I had never felt for anyone before as I felt for this young man. I thought he was perhaps my final chance, that if I lost him I would not find anyone again. Loneliness, growing old, failure with people, those are things you above all do not know. Yet I know them and they were the cause—'

Velatti unlocked his fingers and raised his hand in a small tired gesture, both denigrating and acknowledging what he saw as his weakness. He was neither asking nor expecting sympathy, but Steele felt a sudden quick surge of pity.

'I gave him that job without thought. Then I began to wonder what it involved, knowing what our work so often involves – danger. Not just for us but for anyone else concerned. It preyed on my mind. I imagined him hurt, even dead, and I selfishly left alone if he died. In the end I could stand it no longer. I decided to do something that had never even occurred to me before. I decided to find out the boat's mission—'

He fumbled for another cigarette and then started to talk again, more quickly now, tripping over and missing phrases as if all he wanted to do was to be finished.

Steele listened, incredulous at first as Velatti's voice slurred and wavered, and then with a growing mesmerized fascination that had nothing to do with himself or Callum – only with the story the little Maltese was telling.

The department's command post for the western Mediterranean was housed in the headquarters complex at North Front Gibraltar. Velatti's rank gave him access to the library, archives and general services areas, but not to the operations room – only Wedderburn and his chief planning officer were allowed there. Yet he knew the room must contain a complete brief for the mission of which the boat charter was only an element.

Velatti went over and based himself temporarily in Gibraltar, ostensibly to work on a research project in the library. It was a week before he got his chance. The duty officer, knowing Velatti as a colleague and accustomed by then to him working through the lunch hours, asked him to watch the control desk for fifteen minutes while he went out. The man left, Velatti went to the desk and removed the master key set.

Then, hazarding his entire career, he unlocked the operations room door. He found the brief almost immediately. By the time

189

the duty officer returned he'd read it, returned the keys and was back at his desk – staring disbelieving at the wall.

'I came back here that evening,' Velatti said, 'I stayed up all night. Three times I went out and walked in the town, not knowing where I was going. My mind would not accept it, I tried to convince myself I'd made a mistake, in my haste I'd become confused and read it wrong. But in the morning I knew it was true—'

What Velatti had read were the arrangements for an exchange – an exchange so extraordinary that Steele was still groping to understand its implications minutes after Velatti had finished.

In return for the release of West Germany's most notorious terrorist leader, Dietrich Lorenz, the joint Lebanese-Palestinian military command, which had financed his attacks, were guaranteeing the destruction of the entire year's opium crop on the slopes of the Bekaa valley.

Lorenz – and Steele knew instantly now why he'd recognized the name – was currently serving a life sentence for murder in Stuttgart's Wohnheim prison, after being convicted of a series of bomb explosions in which twenty-seven people had died. He'd be moved secretly from the prison, brought across Europe and held for two days on the chartered boat in international waters off the Spanish coast, until the destruction of the opium fields had been confirmed. Then he'd be handed over to the Lebanese.

And all the arrangements, from the moment Lorenz left Stuttgart until his release, would be handled by the department.

'Of course, it makes sense for everyone,' Velatti went on again, 'Lorenz in prison is an embarrassment to the West Germans, a constant invitation to the other members of his gang to mount further outrages and try to secure his freedom. To the Arabs naturally, they get back one of their most effective and vicious commandos. And for the rest of us, well, as you know the narcotics industry is now the biggest source of finance for cross-frontier crime throughout Europe. Espionage rides on the back of that finance. Destroy a year's crop from Bekaa and you reduce the year's funds by fifty per cent.'

'And why make the exchange here?' Steele asked.

Velatti smiled for the first time, a diffident private smile.

'I do not know where you have been,' he said, 'but you have been away and perhaps forgotten. Here because it is the gateway

190

to the Arab world, the logical place for such a transaction. Equally logical that we should handle it. We have a vested interest in seeing the opium destroyed. We have Gibraltar as a base, we are stronger, more experienced, than anyone else in this part of the world. But most of all because it is the place where bargains like that have always been made—'

He pushed against the rim of the bunk, stood up and lifted his legs in turn, shaking them painfully to keep the blood circulating.

The dirty area. Velatti hadn't used the phrase but that was what he'd been talking about, and Steele finally understood what it really meant. It was only in the dirty area that such a pact could have been conceived, and only there that it could be implemented.

'Traditionally our work does not allow for personal feelings,' Velatti was supporting himself from the bulkhead rail, 'that is, I think, necessary and in my case it was certainly true. I never made a judgement until then. Only there can come a moment when everything you have lived by breaks down, and you are forced to choose. It happened to me. I made my choice, my decision. You can probably guess why.'

Steele nodded. He had guessed as soon as he realized who Lorenz was, and he remembered the long catalogue of wanton slaughter. The bombings, the murdered hostages, the torture and terror, directed nominally against Germany – but in reality against Israel.

'You're Jewish,' Steele said.

'I am Maltese first, I am British equally and second, but last, for always, like all my people, yes, I am Jewish—'

The strain on Velatti's arms was too great. He let go of the rail and slid back onto the bunk.

'I broke faith with myself and all I believed in to find out what this operation was. Stupidly, vainly, in fear for a young boy, that was my only reason. But once I knew and had decided, I could not go back. I told Mr Wedderburn what I had discovered, that I could not be part of it and it must be stopped. He dismissed me. I flew to London and it was the same. I asked for you, they denied me a meeting. Finally I came back here. I wrote a letter, then I went into hiding.'

'What did you say in the letter?'

'What could I say?' Velatti shrugged. 'I made threats, yes,

threats that I would expose what they were doing. Maybe I could have carried them out. How do I know? You spend all your life working for certain ideas, believing in them absolutely, and then suddenly you find you have to betray them because they are being betrayed. How do you reconcile those two? I do not know. I wrote, I calculated they would believe in my threats at least enough to hesitate, and I asked again for you.'

'And when I came back?'

'We never met before. I could not be sure at first it really was you. So I asked help of a friend—'

'Yehuda?'

'Yes.'

Steele rubbed his face, thinking of the tiny shrivelled old man perched on his stool at the top of the house with his deep hoarse voice and his black hawk's eyes.

'Why him?'

'How much you have forgotten, Mr Callum,' the vague fugitive smile again, 'you do not remember who counts, who has power, in Tangier? Mr Wedderburn and Hassan Yehuda, those more than any other two people. It makes them of course enemies, they have been so for years, even in your time. In a sense Mr Wedderburn had become my enemy. If you like I went to the other camp.'

'So with Yehuda's help you laid a trail for me? The Portuguese, the guns, the brokers in Spain, even the Goulahmanah oasis – all to find out if I was the man I claimed to be?'

Velatti nodded. 'I was satisfied long before Goulahmanah, before you went to Spain even. But I could not approach you. You were surrounded night and day by those men. If I tried to come near you I knew I would not be given even a chance to talk. But by tonight time had almost run out.'

Steel frowned. 'What do you mean?'

'At dawn this morning, yesterday morning it is now, Lorenz arrived on the boat. He stays there all tomorrow and tomorrow night. But the next morning the deal is completed and he is handed over.'

'And you swam out here tonight?'

Velatti nodded again. 'I could think of nothing else. You had gone south, I knew you would be back by daylight, I guessed you would come to the yard. But in daylight I couldn't move and even

192

at night there might have been someone on the jetty. So I waded out from the shore and swam round. I was going to wait in the hold. Only you were here already.'

Steele put down the Browning at last. There was no need for it, there never had been any need for it. He took a cigarette from the pack he'd thrown Velatti, lit it and walked to the hatch.

Outside there were still only stars and the ripple of water and the hull creaking as the *Lara* tugged restlessly at the mooring lines. He gazed into the darkness. He knew everything now, everything except the answer to the one question that concerned him alone.

'Tell me,' Steele glanced back, 'from the moment you knew what was happening you wanted me. Why?'

Velatti spread out his hands and looked up at him. There was an expression of puzzlement on his face, but for once his voice was totally confident.

'You are Ross Callum. You risked everything before for one of my people. If anyone would understand the wrongness of what is being done now and stop it, it could only be you. You are different from all the others. I trust you.'

Mary-Beth woke then. She lifted her head from the bunk, blinked and looked slowly round the cabin. She apparently didn't notice Velatti and focussed on Steele.

'Did you get the guns?' She asked.

Her skin was still chalk-white, the bruises on her lips were swelling into puffy lumps, and her eyes were filmed with anxiety.

Steele hesitated for only an instant. Then he flicked his cigarette out into the water, walked over and looked down at her.

'Sure, I got them,' he said. 'Did you ever really think I wasn't going to?'

He touched her cheek gently and smiled.

17

Steele balanced himself on the stern. Behind him in the cabin Mary-Beth was asleep again and Velatti was changing into a dry pair of jeans he'd found in one of the smashed lockers.

The time was short, desperately short, but he gave himself a moment longer, a moment of stillness and quiet with the night wind fresh on his face and only the distant chime of bells in the silence.

He felt no anger. That belonged to the past when he'd been shackled, pinioned and manipulated, and he'd raged blindly, helplessly at what was being done to him. Now he knew. He'd thrown off the cramping web of lies and in place of rage he felt a soaring sensation of freedom. Not just from the last few days but a freedom he hadn't experienced in years.

He'd allowed himself to be beaten down. The army, the long chain of business failures, the bitter sting of bankruptcy at the end. When they came for him he'd finally given up, lost all belief and hope, abandoned any trust in himself – except for a last spark of stubbornness that stopped him from whining like the rest of Mrs Martin's lodgers.

Twelve years and suddenly they were gone, they might never have existed. The confidence had returned, the vigour and certainty, and Steele laughed aloud in the darkness.

Freedom – and a cold implacable resolution. There was vengeance to be taken for what had happened, the last form of vengeance they could ever have expected – a vengeance they had created for themselves. They had made Callum. Mathieson, Greville, Wedderburn and the rest of them. They believed he was their property, a mechanical puppet that would walk or stand still, appear or vanish as they chose to pull the strings.

They were wrong. The little Major's fantasy had become real,

194

had acquired flesh and blood, assumed a mind and will and purpose. They'd succeeded only too well. Callum was alive and beyond their control. Steele knew what Callum would have done – and he was going to do it.

For vengeance first and yet for more than vengeance. There was keeping faith too with everyone who'd believed the lies and put their trust in a man who until now hadn't existed. More than their trust, their own hopes and beliefs, even their lives. Mary-Beth, Gonsalves, the young Portuguese in Lisbon, the dead mate Lorca whom he'd known for barely an hour but who'd been killed because of him.

He owed something to them all but most perhaps to Velatti, who'd thrown away his career, his future, his lifelong beliefs to try to thwart a wrong greater than them all, and who'd held on, sick, hunted and alone, only because he believed with a passionate trusting conviction that Callum would feel the same.

Steele jumped onto the jetty and ran towards the office. Lorenz was the goal but first there were the guns.

'Come on! Get up—!'

He'd suddenly remembered on the launch that Donovan was probably asleep in his chair. He was right. The American was slumped over the desk with his mouth open, snoring and reeking of gin. He must have passed out earlier in the night and lain there ever since, oblivious of what was happening on board the *Lara*.

Steele tugged at his shoulder, but Donovan merely rolled over and went on grunting and snoring. Then he glanced quickly round the office. There was a fire-bucket in the corner, half-full of dirty water with drowned flies and ancient cigar butts floating on the surface. Steele snatched it up and hurled it over him.

'Jesus Christ!' Donovan was on his feet bellowing with the water cascading down his face, 'What the hell's going on—?'

He clawed at his eyes and peered blearily at Steele.

'Shit, it's you! What the Christ is this, Ross?'

'Shut up and listen—'

Donovan was swaying, still half-asleep. Steele caught his shirt and shook him fiercely. Then he told him what he'd found when he arrived at the yard.

'Mary-Beth? Is she all right?'

He was awake now and he stared at Steele bemused, fearful, only partly understanding.

195

'She's been hit around the face,' Steele said, 'but she's sleeping now and in the morning she'll be fine.'

'Jesus, I must get her to the American hospital—'

Donovan plunged wildly towards the door but Steele gripped his elbow and jerked him back.

'You leave her where she is. On the launch she's safe. But move her out onto the streets and Christ knows how many more of those goons are waiting for us. Understand?'

Donovan gazed at him bewildered again. Then he nodded.

'Right,' Steele went on, 'now for the *Lara*. Is she seaworthy – I mean for a trip across to Portugal and back?'

'Sure. You could take her across the Atlantic if you wanted.'

'Not me – you.'

'What do you mean?'

Donovan was gaping at him once more.

'Don't you ask any bloody questions,' Steele snapped, 'just answer mine. Can you sail that boat over to Portugal and find a harbour in the southern Algarve – I'll give you the bearings?'

'Hell, I don't know—'

Donovan scraped at his jaw. Then he suddenly drew himself up, sucked in his stomach and jabbed out his hand aggressively. Steele could smell the gin again and seen the inflamed red veins in his eyes.

'Listen, are you trying to make a monkey out of me? Sure, I could take her to Portugal, I could sail her any goddam place even with my eyes shut.'

'That's fine,' Steele said, 'because we're leaving inside an hour. Where can we take on fuel?'

'We're what—?'

'Fuel I said, for Christ's sake. Where are we going to find a depot open at this hour?'

Donovan thought for a moment frowning. 'There's an old guy across the bay called Lebas. He stays open all night for the fishing boats. But we can't just—'

'You're going back to sea, Don,' Steele cut him off. 'This is the big one and we're going to do it together. Now get out to the launch and start checking the engines. By the time I return we've got to be ready to move.'

Steele tapped him on the shoulder and grinned. Then he propelled him out of the office.

Afterwards he searched his pockets until he found the piece of paper on which he'd written down Beni's telephone number in Lisbon. He found it, folded inside the map which the Portuguese had drawn in the restaurant, and dialled. The ringing tone went on for several minutes. Then a sleepy voice answered.

'*Esta la?*'

'Is that Beni?'

'Yes. Who is this?' The voice was alert now.

'Callum,' Steele said. 'Listen carefully. I've got what you want but we've had problems with your friends. I'll have to leave here right away, I need to be well clear by daylight. If I get lucky I'll cross and lie up tomorrow off the Guadalquivir estuary until dusk. Then I'll come in sometime after dark. Can you set it up your end?'

Beni hesitated. 'It will be difficult but I think so.'

'You'd better goddam know so.'

'All right, I will be there. You have the signals?'

Steele glanced at the map. 'Green, three shorts and a long repeated. And you keep repeating them too, every five minutes from the moment darkness falls. You're clear on that?'

'Yes.'

'Right. Keep your fingers crossed and I'll see you tomorrow night.'

'Good luck, Mr Callum, and thanks.'

Steele put the telephone down, turned out the light and hurried round to the front of the building.

The rest of the gold was still in his room at the Minzah, hidden in the tank of the WC. Before he hadn't been concerned about the surveillance group. He thought the oasis had marked the end and it didn't matter when or where they locked onto him again. Now it had all changed and he was risking everything by leaving the yard. There was no choice. Without the gold they were helpless. He couldn't redeem the guns and he'd have nothing with which to pay for the fuel.

Steele opened the passenger door and slid into the seat. Marcel, hunched over the wheel, woke instantly, coming out of sleep alert and bright-eyed like a cat.

'The hotel,' Steele said, 'double back, take the long way round and stop in the Place de France. Don't use your lights until we're in the town.'

'Yes, sir.'

Steele listened intently for the sound of a van or a scooter as they circled on the road and headed east. He heard nothing. Marcel swung right, drove across the deserted city and drew up in the Place de France. There was still no one behind them and Steele sat for an instant puzzled. Wherever they thought he'd gone, they should have left at least one person to watch the yard for his return. If they hadn't, if they'd concentrated everyone round the Minzah, he was trapped.

He got out and said, 'I'll be back in fifteen minutes.'

If he wasn't back in fifteen minutes it wouldn't matter – nothing would matter any longer. Marcel nodded and Steele walked down the side-street that led to the hotel's service entrance.

The kitchen door was half-open and a shaft of light cut down onto the cobbles. He stepped inside and blinked at the glare. A Moroccan servant boy was swabbing the tiles. Steele gave him a casual wave and walked confidently between the gleaming ovens. It was the route he'd taken two days earlier. He passed the store-rooms, crossed the laundry area and came out into the main lobby.

'My key, please.'

'Of course, Mr Callum.'

The night clerk, who'd been dozing on a stool, jumped down and reached for the board behind him.

Steele waited. He was standing by the reception desk, visible through the main glass doors to anyone on the street outside. If they were watching now was the moment they'd see him. He could feel sweat gathering at the base of his neck.

'You would like me to take you up, sir?'

The clerk handed him the key smiling. Steele shook his head abruptly, snatched the key and crossed the hall to the stairs. There'd been no sound from the street and he climbed the flights in bounds, bewildered but shaking with relief. His room was on the third floor.

He unlocked the door, switched on the light, stepped forward and stopped.

She was sitting in the chair by the window, a bottle of gin on the ledge beside her and a glass in her hand. Her eyes narrowed and flickered as the light went on but she hadn't been asleep. She was fully-dressed, the curtains were drawn back and Steele knew she'd been gazing out at the stars above the straits. She'd been crying, he could see that too. The tears had gouged ugly runnels in her make-up and her face was pale and haggard.

'Louise, what the hell are you doing here?'

He shook his head dazed.

'I'm sorry, Steele, I'm so sorry—'

She stood up and came towards him, walking stiffly like an automaton, her voice slurred and quiet and toneless.

'You see, they said if I didn't they'd take away everything. I said I didn't know, but they went on and on—'

She broke off and Steele asked, 'If you didn't what?'

'Tell them—'

Louise held herself together for a moment longer. Then she collapsed against him shuddering and weeping and the glass dropped to the floor.

'You've got to explain, Louise. What happened?'

Steele pushed her gently but firmly away and held her by the arms.

'It was the evening after you left,' the words came out choked with sobs, 'a man came to the house, a big man. I know his name but I've forgotten it—'

'Wedderburn?'

She nodded. 'He said you'd disappeared and you must have told me where you were going. I pretended I didn't know anything, but he kept on for hours. He said if I didn't tell him he'd take away the house and the job and I'd be on the street. I tried, Steele, I promise—'

The tears were flooding down her cheeks again, blinding her. 'He was terrible, but I held out. Then early yesterday morning he came back with some men. They didn't say anything, they just started moving out the furniture. They emptied the bedroom and I looked at it and I couldn't go on—'

'So you told them I'd gone south to the desert—?'

Louise nodded again helplessly.

'And what happened then?'

'He said they were going to find you. He was angry, furiously angry, and he told me I was coming over here with him. I was so frightened I didn't argue. We came over and he said I was to stay in your room until you get back. Then I was to telephone. Oh,

Steele—'

She fell against him again. This time Steele let her stay there sobbing into his chest.

He could guess what had happened now. Wedderburn had moved all the surveillance people out to watch the roads into Tangier from the south. That was why there'd been no one at the yard or the hotel. They'd missed him because they'd been looking for the distinctive Citroën, not an anonymous old truck. And Wedderburn had used Louise simply because he was short of men – everyone else would be needed for the exchange operation.

'You sit down—'

She was shaking less now and he guided her to the chair. Then he went into the bathroom.

He'd told Marcel fifteen minutes and ten of them were already up. The canvas belt containing the rest of the coins was where he'd left it in the WC tank. He buckled it under his shirt and came back into the bedroom.

'You don't blame me, Steele?'

Louise was on her feet again. The tears had stopped and the hysteria had passed. She'd wiped her face, smearing the wet make-up even more grotesquely over her cheeks, but her eyes were steady now and she was staring at him intently.

'Of course not. Hell, I'm a ship in the night and life goes on. I'd have done the same with that at stake. Just give me a couple of hours before you telephone and we're quits.'

He smiled but she shook her head quickly.

'Life doesn't go on,' she said, 'not that one. They conned me and I believed them because I was so scared I wasn't thinking straight. I am now. You think they'll take me back, they'll ever trust me again, after what I did? I broke the one rule that's unforgivable – I lied to them. I'm finished there, it's all over.'

Steele looked at her.

He couldn't think of anything to say. Louise was right. Once she'd served her purpose, once the exchange was completed and they'd found him, they'd get rid of her instantly and without compunction. She'd proved herself unreliable and for that in their world there was no forgiveness. She had twenty-four hours at most and then she'd be without house, without job, without anything.

200

'I won't telephone, now or in two hours or ever,' her voice was very calm, 'I let you down, I let myself down, but I've learnt and I'm going to try never to do it again. I don't have any money. If you can lend me a little, I'll find some way of paying you back. If you can't it doesn't matter. Either way I'm leaving now.'

Steele reached instinctively for his wallet, checked and gazed at her again.

There'd been no pleading in her voice and there was no fear or uncertainty in her face now – only an acceptance of another defeat and a stubborn defiance towards the consequences that would follow. Steele knew the look and knew the effort it took to sustain, the searing uncompromising effort when all one wanted to do was break down, yield everything and beg hopelessly for pity. He knew too what he'd realized before in her house – that they were both of the same kind.

'You'd better come with me.'

He caught her hand and headed for the stairs.

Steele heard the sound of the launch's engines as Marcel pulled in by the office, a low deep growl in the darkness. When he reached the cradle the water was churning and bubbling white at the stern, and the mooring ropes were quivering wire-tight as if any moment they'd snap and the *Lara* would arrow out across the bay.

He lifted Louise and swung her on board, beckoned Marcel to follow, and finally jumped over the stern rail himself. As he stepped down into the cockpit Donovan's head and shoulders appeared through the engine-room hatch.

'How about that for the sweetest goddam noise you ever heard—'

Donovan heaved himself up onto the deck. His arms were glistening with black grease and his face was scarlet and sweating from the heat below, but he was chuckling too, a slow confident chuckle of pleasure.

'And the lady's only thinking about it. You wait until she sees some blue water and starts to shift. I tell you, Ross, we'll be flying so high we'll need an air certificate.'

'How's Mary-Beth?'

Donovan shrugged. 'The kid's still sleeping. I guess she'll be okay. But if I ever lay my hands on any of those bastards—'

'You just get us over to Portugal,' Steele said. 'You'll do them more damage that way than you could with a pair of sawn-off scatterguns. Cast off as soon as you're ready—'

He turned towards the cabin. 'Use Marcel as your deckhand. We'll take on the fuel first, then we've got a cargo to pick up.'

He ducked under the hatch as Donovan clambered up into the wheelhouse calling for Marcel.

Mary-Beth wasn't the only one asleep, so was Velatti – a grey-faced little bundle curled on the other bunk with his knees drawn up against his chest and one fragile wrist dangling over the floor. He must have collapsed with exhaustion as soon as Steele left. He'd managed to pull on the dry pair of jeans, but the belt was still unbuckled and he was naked from the waist up.

Steele draped a blanket over him and looked at Louise. She was standing in the centre of the aisle between the two splintered stumps which were all that was left of the table.

'So you're really going ahead, Steele?'

He'd told her in the car what he was planning to do. It had sounded improbable enough then. Now, with Mary-Beth and Velatti stretched out insensible between them, it must have seemed absurd, an act of lunacy.

He nodded. 'If the crew doesn't mutiny.'

'The crew?' She smiled. 'So far I've counted two fancy ladies, one of them a stretcher case, an Arab kid the size of a small monkey, an old man with what looks like a serious heart condition, and an engineer who smells like a distillery. Is that the crew – Callum's crew?'

Steele grinned. 'It's what the press-gang came up with.'

'And with them you're going to run that cargo of guns into Portugal, and then try to stop the exchange on the other boat?'

He hadn't even thought about Lorenz yet but he nodded again, not smiling any longer.

'Were you figuring on trying to prevent me?'

'No,' Louise turned briskly towards the galley, 'I just wanted to know how many I'd be catering for. Right now one third of your complement's unconscious. If I can repair that stove and brew some coffee, I might be able to get them back on their feet.'

She stepped past him and disappeared under the galley bulk-head.

Steele lifted his head and listened. The sound of the engine had

202

changed and he realized they were under way. He climbed up to the wheelhouse and stood beside Donovan.

The launch was a hundred yards out from the shore, and he could see by the town lights to their left that they were moving north-east across the bay.

'How's she handling?' Steele asked.

'Sweet as sugar,' Donovan said, 'like I told you, when you picked this one you got yourself a princess—'

He eased out the throttle slightly, the bows lifted and the *Lara* surged forward with fans of spray curling out on either side.

'When she decides to travel there's still not more than a dozen boats in the whole straits who can live with her.'

In the light reflected from the navigation dials Donovan's face was absorbed and alive. He was no longer the failed posturing yard-owner but back in his fantasy world, at the controls of the fastest launch in the dirty area about to head out for open sea. Except now briefly the fantasy had become real and Steele knew that for as long as it lasted Donovan would think of nothing else.

Steele leant over the instrument panel and watched the northern shore of the bay coming closer in the darkness.

Fuelling took an hour. Then, with the tanks full, they crossed the bay again and berthed against the wharf where he and Marcel had left the agent sitting inside the truck. Steele hauled himself up from the stern and walked over to where he could see the driving cabin silhouetted against the sky.

The agent was still slumped in the passenger seat, sullen, white-faced and shivering. He jerked upright as Steele appeared and gaped through the window, his mouth twitching in fright until he saw who it was.

Steele opened the door, tossed the canvas belt onto the seat and said, 'Count them.'

He watched the man check the balance of the purchase price. Then, as he nodded in agreement, Steele reached out and took the belt back.

'Not just yet. You're going to lose some weight before you've earned it—'

Steele turned and called softly, 'Marcel! Don! I'm bringing the truck up as close as I can. Then with our fat friend's help we'll form a chain.'

He swung himself up behind the wheel, drove the truck to the edge of the wharf so that the tailgate was directly above the forward hatch, and they started to unload the crates.

It was another hour before all the guns were stowed away in the hold. As Donovan heaved the last crate inside Steele glanced at his watch. Four-thirty, ninety minutes before daylight. He threw the belt over to the agent, who was propped panting and sweating against a bollard, and jumped down onto the deck.

'Right, we're shipping out,' he said as Donovan lumbered back into the cockpit, 'if the lady wants to show her style, now's her chance.'

Donovan wiped his face and grinned. 'You just hold goddam tight onto your hair.'

He climbed back into the wheelhouse, the engines throbbed, Marcel unleashed the mooring-ropes, and the launch swung out into the bay.

Steele edge along the narrow walkway beside the cabin roof and stood at the bows, gripping the handrail and bracing his feet against the deck as the boat gathered speed. Until now they'd been no more than another coastal vessel using the busy harbour waters. But within minutes they'd register on the radar screens of the Moroccan coastguard ships as a craft heading for the international sea-lanes.

He angled himself forward into the wind, his eyes streaming and his skin stinging from the driven spray. The bows reared up, the launch began to plane, and he felt the hammering vibrations as the hull sliced through the waves. If they had been spotted there would be flashing signal-lamps, a siren wailing, the flare and detonation of a warning shot.

There was nothing. Only darkness and foam and pitching stars and the launch leaping and crashing and occasionally blurred glimpses of a horizon heaving between a black sky and a blacker turbulent sea. Steele stayed there for fifteen minutes, chill, sodden, half-blinded by the wind-hurled water, his shoulders wrenched and twisted as the boat plunged, lifted and dived again. Still there was nothing in front and finally he heard the engine sound change again.

He worked his way back to the cockpit. They were in international waters and Donovan was throttling down as the launch cut into the Atlantic swell. If the coastguards had picked the boat up on their screens the *Lara* had been too fast for them. All they could do now was impotently patrol the offshore boundaries as the radar-blip vanished to the north.

Steele smiled and lowered himself into the cabin.

'Well, I've resurrected the stove but so far the Lazarus act hasn't worked on these two—'

Louise handed him a mug of coffee. Mary-Beth and Velatti were still lying motionless on the bunks.

'What do I do now? Pray or give up and toss them overboard?'

'You can drop them over the side if they haven't come round by dusk—'

Steele grinned and sipped from the mug. The coffee was hot and black and strong.

'Give them a chance for another twelve hours.'

Louise smiled back at him. 'I'd do it right away, but you're the captain.'

Steele drained the mug and went back to the wheelhouse.

Twelve hours. At dawn they were in the middle of the mouth of the straits, with the African coast astern and Cape Trafalgar coiled in mist rising ahead. An hour later Donovan throttled down again to conserve fuel and changed course so that they were running almost due west. They'd crossed the straits and now they were following the Spanish shore. Steele could see a cloud of smoke above Cadiz off the starboard bow in front and a long line of shipping stretching across the horizon to their rear.

Four hours later still Donovan swung the launch head-on into the small waves and cut the engines altogether. Cadiz had disappeared behind them and they were lying off the Guadalquivir estuary to the north, a wilderness of dune and marsh that reached back sixty miles inland almost to Seville. The Portuguese coast was somewhere just out of sight immediately ahead.

They lay there all day, rocking slowly in the light swell as the morning's heat grew and then faded with the afternoon. Steele shared the watches with Donovan and Marcel, but they saw nothing except caravans of migrating eagles overhead and once a solitary horseman on the shore. Mary-Beth woke briefly at midday and then slept again. Velatti never stirred.

'You're quite clear?' Steele asked.

Donovan nodded. 'Hell, yes—'

It was evening, the light had almost gone and Steele was in the wheelhouse with Donovan studying the charts of the Algarve coastline.

'From here we'll run west-north-west, that's five degrees off this morning's course,' Donovan's finger moved across the map, 'I reckon maybe two hours. Then we'll pick up the Queixal lighthouse. After that I can do it by sight. We angle south-west and follow the shore. We get a fix on Albumeira, then we run in. If we see Benfeira we've overshot. But between the two we should get them, green, three shorts and a long—'

He looked up. 'No problem unless that builds.'

Donovan pointed at the perspex canopy. Steele turned and looked out. The sun had set but in the dusk he could see patches of low mist gathering on the southern horizon.

'Tarot?' He said.

'Too goddam right. Mainly it stays inside the straits, hell, you know that. But once or twice a year in the fall it'll spread right out as far as Portugal. We're fall now and that one's got the makings of a bastard. If it starts to drift we're screwed.'

The patches were tangling and thickening as Steele watched. He'd seen the tarot once before, from the window of Yehuda's house, and he knew from Greville what it could do – blind the surface of the sea worse than a nineteenth-century London fog.

Steele turned back. 'I want that cargo landed and that's not all I want tonight.'

'Then we'd better shift.'

Donovan flicked on the ignition switches, the wheelhouse quivered as the engines fired, then the bows tilted up and a wake of white foam flared out behind them as he engaged the screws.

Donovan's guess was right. Exactly two hours afterwards Steele spotted a distant light flashing in front of them. He timed the pulsing beam against his watch and checked the chart. It was the lighthouse at Queixal, a promontory jutting out from the Portuguese coast. Donovan had seen it too. He spun the wheel and they began to run south-west parallel to the shore.

'Albumeina—'

It was fifteen minutes later and Donovan's arm was out-stretched. Steele peered forward. There was another light wink-ing off the starboard bow.

'I'll have to take her in. They won't have the power of the fixed beams, they'll probably be using car batteries. If we stay out here we'll miss them. We can either throttle back and make like we're

206

a fishing-boat. Or we can take it on the burst. I figure it's evens either way, but you're the skipper.'

Donovan turned the launch towards the shore.

Steele glanced back. The tarot had been rolling up on them ever since they left the Guadalquivir estuary. Now the dense wall of mist, still creeping forward, was less than half a mile astern. Two hundred feet above it the stars glittered cold and brilliant in the night sky. But between the sea and the mist's ceiling there was only dank impenetrable greyness.

Steele hesitated. For the moment they were still in international waters. Yet within seconds they'd have crossed the offshore limits and entered the territory patrolled by the Portuguese coastguards. In any other conditions they should slow right down and pretend to be a fishing-boat heading in for port. But if the tarot overtook them before they picked up the signal they were finished.

'Give her everything,' Steele swung round. 'Every bloody thing she's got.'

Donovan reached for the throttle controls and levered them back.

For an instant the *Lara* seemed to hesitate. The hull shuddered, the stanchion at the bows wavered uncertainly, the deck rocked and trembled. Then the full power drove into the screws, the cloverleaf blades bit at the water and the launch rose – lifting herself above the sea like a bird taking flight.

Steele stumbled and clutched at the instrument panel. The noise was deafening, a dizzying hammering roar, and after a moment he could see nothing through the screen except soaring sheets of foam. The roar grew louder and the launch started to plane, its keel hitting the wave-tops with cracks like gunfire. Vaguely he was aware Donovan was laughing. He swayed again and gripped the panel harder, numbed, shaking, feeling only the surging speed vibrating through him.

'There—!'

Donovan shouted and cut back the engines. As the boat slowed the screen cleared. Steele let go of the panel and peered out.

They were less than five hundred yards from the shore, a line of low rocky cliffs directly ahead in the darkness. For a minute Steele couldn't see the light. Then he picked it out, a steady green

207

pulse just above sea-level off the port bow. He quickly scanned the sea on either side. There was no sign of any other boat heading out towards them.

'Didn't I tell you she could still fly?' Donovan was beaming. 'And we're spot on too.'

Steele clapped him on the back. 'You just earned yourself a new master's licence—'

He turned towards the steps. 'They'll be signalling from a jetty. Take her in slow from here and berth her. I'm going to check they're all right below.'

Both Mary-Beth and Velatti were awake now. Velatti was yawning and blinking, and Steele guessed he'd only just come round, woken by the uproar of the last ten minutes. But Mary-Beth was sitting up drinking a mug of coffee.

Steele went over to her first.

'How are you feeling?'

'Sore—'

She touched her face. The bruises on her mouth and round her eyes had swollen and blackened, and she winced painfully as she lifted her arm.

'But better,' she smiled, 'a hell of a lot better.'

'How come you were on board at that hour?'

She shrugged. 'I figured with you away someone should keep an eye on her. I spelled it with your mate. He went off for a late dinner and I guess I just wasn't fast enough. I heard them on deck but they jumped me before I could get up.'

'And you did that after you knew what they'd tried to do to me?' Steele shook his head. 'You idiot, you bloody idiot—'

He stopped and grinned. 'Thanks anyway. It was a good try.'

Steele heard a bump. He lifted his head and listened. The engines stopped, there were voices outside, then footsteps sounded in the cockpit. They'd reached the jetty. A moment later Beni appeared through the hatch.

He held out his hand. 'We are glad to see you, Senhor Callum.'

'No trouble?'

Beni shook his head. 'We have fishing-boats out, seven of them. They are in touch by radio. If there is any movement by the coastguards, they tell us. So far there is nothing.'

'And the unloading?'

'They have already begun, senhor—'

208

He gestured towards the hold. Steele listened again and heard the crates being moved behind the forward door.

'We will need maybe fifteen minutes. Then you are clear. Also with the tarot I think you have no problem on the run back.'

'I'm leaving you a passenger, someone you know,' Steele turned to Mary-Beth. 'On your feet, lady—'

He caught her hand and pulled her up. She was frowning and he knew she was going to protest bitterly.

If Callum belonged to anyone he belonged to her. She'd dreamed about him as a child, waiting up night after night for the *Lara* to come back with him aboard. Then he'd returned to the dirty area and the dream had come true. She'd found him a cargo, she'd taken care of the repairs to the launch, she'd held him in her arms when he was exhausted and wounded, she'd kept faith throughout – even standing guard over the boat and almost being killed when he went down into the desert.

Now at the end he was leaving her behind and Steele could see the pain in her eyes as she realized what he meant to do.

'Listen, Mary-Beth,' he said, 'We've got a date, remember? A date for a very large drink. I'm just making damn sure at least one of us keeps it.'

He smiled, kissed her quickly on the cheek and handed her to Beni. 'Take her up and let me know as soon as you've got all the crates off.'

Mary-Beth hadn't moved.

'I waited five years for the first drink,' she said, 'I haven't had it yet. This time I'll wait ten. If you're not there when they run out I'll still be waiting.'

She swayed unsteadily. Beni gripped her arm and helped her up the steps. As they vanished Steele suddenly remembered Louise. He swung round looking for her.

'No, Steele—'

She was standing in the entrance to the galley and she was smiling, but her face was set with the same obdurate determination he'd seen before – only this time it was utterly inflexible.

'You've got your mutiny. I may not have a date but I'm not moving – not in five years, ten, never.'

Steele gazed at her for a moment. Then he realized it was hopeless. He could truss her, bind her, carry her ashore, and he knew she'd somehow still break loose and fight her way back on board before they cast off. Louise had made her decision, she was going to see it through to the end, and there was nothing in the world he could do to stop her.

'In which case you'd better make with some more coffee,' he glanced at his watch. 'We've still got the last job to do.'

Steele sat down opposite Velatti. The little Maltese had wrapped the blanket round himself and was perched shivering on the bunk.

'This boat where they're holding Lorenz,' Steele said, 'you said you'd memorized the bearings of its position?'

Velatti nodded. 'Of course. I memorized everything, it is what I am trained to do. The latitude—'

'Wait a moment—'

Steele searched his pockets for a piece of paper. Velatti watched him, blank-eyed, confused, still dazed and weary in spite of the long hours of sleep.

'I do not understand,' Velatti managed to prop himself forward, 'I believe we are in Portugal. By morning they will have completed everything. For why do you still wish to know?'

Steele looked up. 'They can't be more than four hours away and there are six left before dawn. We've got darkness and tarot and God knows what, but it may still just be enough. Now give me those bearings, because in ten minutes we ship out for the last time.'

18

Steele stood in the wheelhouse staring intently down at the chart.

Velatti's memory was photographic and even after a few minutes Steele knew every detail from the brief about the exchange. The boat was called the *Virgen de Africa*. She was lying eight miles out to sea off the little port of Sanlúcar de Barremeda west of Cadiz. At the *Lara*'s cruising speed it was little more than three hours away and unwittingly they must have passed almost within sight of the boat as they hugged the Spanish coast that morning.

On board, apart from the captain and crew of six, there would be two parties of four, each representing the different sides. Wedderburn would be leading one group, the Lebanese Colonel the other. Lorenz was to be held under joint guard until a radio message arrived confirming the poppy fields' destruction. As soon as it came through the *Virgen de Africa* would put out for the centre of the straits, rendezvous with a waiting Arab patrol-boat and Lorenz would be handed over. The deadline for the message was 6 a.m. Mediterranean time – daylight.

Steele lifted his head.

The tarot had finally caught up with them and mist was swirling round the launch in thick damp coils. On the jetty just below the level of the wheelhouse sparks flared and bounced in the greyness as the hooves of laden donkeys clipped the flint cobbles. Dim shapes in ragged shirts passed across the foredeck as they heaved up the last crates from the hold, and in the distance he could hear the rumble of carts heading into the hills behind.

He clenched his hand and smashed it down on the map, crumpling the sector where he'd marked the *Virgen de Africa's* position. Fifteen men, at least eight of them armed and wary, he could count on that, and all he could muster in reply was an Arab youth, a gin-sodden helmsman, the frail and bemused Velatti, Louise and himself.

The deck below him creaked and Steele glanced down. Beni had jumped into the cockpit. He was holding a battered satchel and as Steele watched he vanished through the cabin hatch.

Steele stood quite still, his mind racing. A possibility had suddenly occurred to him, a wild outside possibility that would need all their co-operation, speed and skill. He didn't even know if they'd be prepared to risk it, but if they were with the darkness and the tarot it might conceivably work.

Beni reappeared and Steele leant out and called urgently.

'Up here—'

Beni climbed the steps and came into the wheelhouse.

'We have finished, Senhor Callum. I have left the escudos on the bunk—'

'Listen, Beni,' Steele cut him off, 'those fishing-boats, how far away are they?'

'They are spaced out in a half-circle round us, about two miles each from here.'

'What speed can they make?'

'Fifteen knots maybe.'

Steele calculated quickly. It would mean an extra hour on the journey, but they'd still have two in hand before dawn.

'And their skippers,' he asked, 'what sort of men are they?'

'Just fisher-people from round here, people we know and trust,' Beni was looking at him puzzled. 'I do not understand what you mean.'

'Beni, whatever you think you owe me nothing. I've brought you the guns, you've paid and that's it. But I haven't finished tonight, I've something left to do. With the help of you and those boats I might still be able to handle it. Without you I haven't a chance—'

Beni listened as Steele explained what he wanted in short urgent sentences.

Then he said, 'You wish us to escort you out there?'

Steele nodded. 'They'll have radar. If they pick up the *Lara* alone they'll instantly be suspicious, they may even get under way when they see we're on course for them. But if we're hidden in a small fleet of fishing-boats, they'll have no reason to suspect anything.'

It had come to him when he saw Beni and remembered the radio. In the tarot with visibility at zero the *Virgen de Africa* would have to depend on radio too. A single boat which couldn't identify itself would trigger every alarm signal on board the other. But a flotilla using Portuguese fishing wave-lengths could be ignored.

Except that was only half of what Steele needed.

'And then,' Beni went on, 'you want us to arrange a collision, an accident?'

'Right,' Steele said, 'not serious, a heavy bump from the leading boat as if it was drifting out of control should be enough – anything so long as it creates a diversion and draws them to one side.'

'While you come out of the tarot and board from the other?'

Steele nodded again. Then he waited gazing at Beni as the Portuguese stood for a moment frowning in silence.

It was more than an outside possibility, it was a final reckless gamble – and not just for him but for the crew of the fishing-boat that staged the collision too. They were unarmed and if the men on the *Virgen de Africa* opened fire as they wallowed alongside, they'd be helpless. Yet it was still a chance and in the night, the mist, the confusion that would follow the crash, it could come off.

'Senhor Callum,' Beni glanced up, 'you say we owe you nothing. I do not agree, but I speak only for myself. I will ask the others.'

He turned, his face expressionless, and clambered down the steps.

Steele had noticed the radio receiver when he came up from the cabin, glinting in the starlight at the foot of the jetty. Now there were no stars, only rolling clouds of moist haze, and he lost sight of Beni before he even reached the *Lara*'s stern. He stood looking down into the cockpit, the boards below wavering as the mist rippled over them.

He had made his bid. He had drawn on the past, on the legend, on everything Callum had come to represent. If the fishermen agreed it wouldn't be because of this one trip alone, but for all they believed he stood for. They were the true inhabitants of the dirty area, warring across the centuries against authority and oppression, surviving for generations by smuggling and piracy, as Callum was supposed to have survived. Their acceptance now would mean they acknowledged him to be of the same company.

Then he saw Beni returning. He climbed back up the steps, his head and shoulders furred with droplets of water.

'They meet us in twenty minutes three kilometres offshore—'

Beni held out his hand smiling. 'They ask me to say that for you, Senhor Callum, they would sail to the other end of the Mediterranean.'

Steele opened his mouth to reply, but he could think of nothing to say. Instead he shook hands, hesitated for an instant looking at the young Portuguese, then he swung round and shouted for Donovan.

Out at sea the mist thickened and thinned rhythmically as if it was being stirred by a vast bellows overhead. Sometimes it was so dense that even the foredeck vanished and the wheelhouse seemed to hang suspended like a glass bubble in the air, surrounded by impenetrable white smoke. Then an eddy of wind would cross the surface, the whiteness would dissolve into grey and occasionally they would glimpse stars or the shadowy silhouette of one of the fishing-boats in arrow formation ahead before the haze closed in again.

Steele rubbed his face, wiping off the moisture that accumulated every few minutes, and peered out. Donovan, navigating by instruments, was at the wheel to his right and Beni behind him at the controls of the *Lara*'s radio. From every side over the steady throb of the engines he could hear the echoing foghorns of other craft using the straits, the deep distant call of a tanker, a tug's repeated hooting, the sharp warning klaxon of a trawler, the rising and falling wail from a freighter.

He glanced at his watch. It was half past three. They'd left at midnight and it had been the same ever since – the churning blinding grey-whiteness, the rustle of water at the bows, the far off clamouring horns, the tense silence inside the wheelhouse with Donovan frowning in concentration over the dials and periodically Beni speaking quietly to one of the skippers in front. Now, if Steele's calculations were correct, they were only thirty minutes away.

'Senhor Callum—'

Steele turned. Beni's hand was raised. For a few moments the Portuguese listened into the earphones. Then he looked up.

'It is the *Virgen de Africa*,' Beni said, 'they say they have an

214

engine breakdown and are lying with sea-anchors. They ask who we are and tell us to keep clear of their position.'

'What's Paolo saying?'

Paolo was the skipper of the leading boat. Steele had glimpsed on his bridge at the rendezvous point off the jetty, a stocky barrel-chested man who'd waved and grinned as the *Lara* drifted alongside before they set off.

Beni listened again. 'He tells them we are surface trawlers out of Albumeina staying inshore until the tarot lifts. He says we are on a course recommended by the coastguards.'

Steele nodded. They had worked it out while the two boats jostled against each other at the start. From now on Paolo would be truculent, obstructive and helpful by turns, buying time all the while, as they came closer. Finally he'd agree to change course, only the instructions would be deliberately garbled as he passed them on to the other boats and the third in line to starboard behind him would turn the wrong way – shearing into the *Virgen de Africa* amidships.

'I'm going down to the cabin,' Steele said, 'I'll be right back.'

Louise and Velatti were sitting opposite each other talking. They looked round as Steele jumped down through the hatch. Then Velatti stood up.

'You have come for these?' Velatti asked.

He was ·pointing at a pair of the American Mannling submachine-guns which Steele had removed from one of the crates while they were lying off the Guadalquivir estuary. He'd loaded them and left them in the locker under the port bunk.

Steele nodded. 'We're almost there.'

'You have prepared two, Mr Callum.'

'Right—'

Steele stopped. He'd taken a second Mannling not for anyone else – there was no one else – but so that he had a reserve in case there was a malfunction in the gun he'd chosen for himself. Only now as he stared at Velatti he realized what the little Maltese was thinking and he was amazed.

In the past few hours while Steele had been in the wheelhouse the man had changed almost out of recognition. The exhaustion had vanished, shrugged off like a coat, the passive resignation had gone from his face, his hands were no longer trembling, his eyes were direct and steady.·He was like someone who'd been paralyzed by a private lonely despair and who'd suddenly cast it off, recovered energy, belief and purpose, and walked out to stand firmly in the open again.

'Mr Callum, I will come with you,' Velatti said, 'I do not know what you have in mind, but you will need cover. I am experienced with weapons, I can give it. You have seen me in a way I have never been before. Now I am as I was. We will do this together.'

He smiled and Steele shook his head bewildered. Then he understood. Velatti was like the rest of them, like Donovan most of all. Callum had returned, the talisman had come back, and Velatti like all the others had been touched by the magic.

'You know how to work this model?' Steele handed him the second Mannling.

'Yes. I have been checking it. I have used it often in ranges.'

'As soon as the collision takes place,' Steele said, 'Donovan's going to lay us against them on the port side. By then they should all be milling around on the starboard deck, trying to figure out what the hell's happened. I'll go on board and you follow – only you stay by the deck-rail. I'll head for the cabin—'

According to the brief there was only one cabin on the *Virgen de Africa* apart from the crew's sleeping quarters, a large communal messroom where Lorenz would be held throughout the two days.

'If Lorenz is there I'm going to pull him out and bring him back. You make sure no one crosses the deck between us. Anyone who appears, you cut them down. Once we've got him onto the *Lara* Donovan will turn on the power. It shouldn't take more than a couple of minutes in all. Right—?'

Velatti nodded.

Speed, surprise, the mist, the chaos after the collision, Donovan's ability to bring the *Lara* alongside and hold her there, Lorenz's presence in the cabin, the reactions of the others on board – it was a fragile structure of intangibles pasted together with spit, string and the cold implacable anger Steele had felt as he stood on the launch's stern in the Tangier darkness, an anger that welled over him again now.

'Wait for me in the bows.'

Velatti went out and Steele turned towards Louise. She was standing too, pale, eyes shadowed with tiredness, somehow remote and withdrawn. It was no longer her battle, it never had

216

been her battle. She was the salaried mistress of a man who did not exist – except suddenly he'd been made real, her role was the same and the make-believe wars of the past were being fought again in blood and pain and vengeance.

She blinked. Then she shook her head, reached out and touched him gently on the cheek. Afterwards she smiled. Steele swung round and climbed the steps without speaking.

'Senhor Callum—'

He was in the cockpit and Beni was shouting down from the wheelhouse.

'They are ahead, maybe two hundred metres. Paolo is telling the others to turn. In a moment the collision boat changes course.'

Steele gestured in acknowledgement and raced towards the bows.

Velatti was already there, kneeling by the stanchion. Steele crouched beside him. The mist was billowing over their heads and drifting back along the deck in thick wavering plumes. From the left, the right and immediately in front he could hear the engines of the fishing-boats churning, slower and rougher than the *Lara*'s. The launch was moving steadily at the centre of the invisible little fleet like a barracuda delicately cruising through a shoal of bass.

Then suddenly there were confused shouts somewhere ahead, the urgent hooting of a foghorn, and an instant later the sound of splintering wood followed by a series of jarring grating bumps. At the same moment the *Lara*'s bows lifted slightly and the launch surged forward into the greyness. Steele gripped the Mannling and balanced himself on the balls of his feet. Now it was up to Donovan.

The shouts came closer and louder, the foghorn was booming incessantly, and the grinding buffets were echoing back nearer and nearer through the mist, and still he could see nothing except the blinding greyness. Then the launch's prow cannoned against something, the engines were throttled back and Steele glimpsed a fog-haloed lamp swinging beneath a bridge.

'Now!'

He was already propelling himself upward as he shouted. His feet touched the deck of the other boat, he heard Velatti scramble up behind him, he stumbled, then he plunged forward over the freighter's hold towards the cabin.

The door was half-open, swinging back as he reached it. He kicked it in and stepped through. There were four men inside clustered round a porthole with their backs to him, peering into the darkness where the fishing-boat had just sheared away. As the door slammed back against the wall they all turned.

'Stay where you are!' Steele swung the Sterling in an arc. 'Anyone moves as much as a finger and you all go.'

The men froze. Two were European, two olive skinned and probably Lebanese. Steele hadn't seen any of them before but one of the Europeans was unmistakable. Much younger than the other three, in jeans and an open-necked shirt while they were wearing suits, with long yellow hair, awkward rawboned shoulders and a blank shuttered face from which his eyes stared out small and feral and lifeless.

Steele remembered the face from photographs now, recognized it from Velatti's description, but he'd have known it anyway even if he'd had nothing to go on. It was weak, confused, violent and cunning – the face of a psychopath. Lorenz.

'You,' Steele jabbed out the gun at him, 'over here—'

Lorenz moved slowly to one side, his head lowered and his eyes never leaving Steele's.

'The rest of you raise your hands and put them behind your necks. Then turn round, kneel down and put your heads on the floor—'

The three did as he told them. Steele stepped back and listened. There were still shouts outside but fewer now and from the bows he could hear the sound of a winch being operated. Everyone else must still be on the starboard deck, but with the fishing-boat clear someone would return any second.

'I'll be covering you for three minutes. If you even breathe before then I'll fire. Come here—!'

The others were bowed motionless over the cabin floor. Lorenz moved towards Steele as Steele beckoned with the gun again. He stopped two feet away, Steele spun him round, jerked his shirt out of his jeans, and slid the barrel up between the cloth and Lorenz' back.

'That goes for you too. You try anything at all and you catch a burst in the lungs—'

He didn't know if Lorenz understood any English but it didn't

218

matter. The German knew guns and the message was clear enough. With the Sterling trapped inside his shirt and Steele's finger round the trigger, he'd blow off the top half of his body if he tried to break.

'Now move—!'

Steele pressed the muzzle against his spine and propelled him towards the door.

Outside, under the cabin overhand, he tugged Lorenz to a halt and looked over his shoulder. Velatti was forty feet away, hidden by the mist that was swirling across the deck. Behind the Maltese, if Donovan had managed it, the *Lara* was still nuzzling the boat's stern. To Steele's left, screened by the cabin and the bridge, the crew seemed to be investigating the damage caused by the collision. Apart from the rumble of the winch there were voices speaking in Arabic and the tap of a hammer on metal.

In front there was nothing except the tarot and the shifting deck. Forty feet. Steele breathed out, wiped the sweat from his palm, gripped Lorenz by the elbow, his nails cutting into the German's forearm, and started to drive him forward again.

As he moved footsteps clattered on the iron walkway round the cabin. Steele checked and whirled towards the noise, levering Lorenz round with him. A silhouette appeared in the haze, and walked quickly forward without seeing them. Then a moment later the man stopped abruptly. He was two yards from the cabin door and he'd finally spotted them in the light spilling out from inside.

For an instant Steele gazed at him. It was Wedderburn. Steele hesitated a second longer. Then, as he pivoted and heaved Lorenz wildly out onto the deck, he heard a rustle behind him. Something crashed against his back, he staggered, a hand chopped down on his wrist, and the Sterling slipped from his grasp. Dimly he realized it was one of the men he'd left in the cabin. He toppled, twisting as he fell, gouged at the man's face and heard a scream of pain.

'Run, Lorenz, for Christ's sake, run!'

The shouts came from Wedderburn. Steele climbed panting to his knees. Still only one of the three men had come out of the cabin, the one who'd tackled him from the rear, and he was lying moaning by the door with his hands to his eyes.

Lorenz was standing confused in the twilight greyness between the cabin lamp and the coiling mist. As Wedderburn called he blinked, shook his head uncertainly and lunged forward. Steele searched desperately for the Sterling, but it had slid out of sight across the heaving deck. He scrambled upright and watched helplessly as Lorenz stumbled away between the hatches.

Then suddenly there were more footsteps, running this time, and another silhouette appeared through the tarot from the stern – a small thin silhouette with the gun glinting, hard-edged and black, at his waist. He slipped, recovered his balance, stopped in front of Lorenz and jabbed the muzzle into his ribs.

'Mr Callum!' It was Velatti shouting, 'Quick, I am covering you!'

Steele leapt over the hatches and raced towards him. The *Lara*'s bows were only a few feet behind where Velatti was standing, his gun alternately resting against Lorenz and tracing warning semi-circles across the hold.

Steele reached them, caught Lorenz' arm and twisted it up behind his back.

'You speak English?' Steele said.

Lorenz mumbled and nodded.

'Climb up on the rail and sit with your legs over the edge.'

The German clambered over the deck-rail and sat hunched on the top bar above the *Lara*'s forehatch. Steele glanced round. There were more shouts now from the area round the cabin and the shapes of blurred figures on the bridge. He turned back, put one hand against Lorenz' spine, lifted the other and held it angled flat in a rigid wedge of bone behind Lorenz' ear.

Then Steele pushed him forwards. As the German fell Steele struck downwards, driving his flattened hand into the side of Lorenz' neck. Lorenz went limp in the air and tumbled unconscious onto the deck below.

At the same instant guns erupted from the bridge and the mist was shredded by the whine and crackle of automatic fire. Velatti gave one burst in return. Then, as the line of flame was still flaring out from the muzzle of his Mannling, he lurched, coughed and crumpled against the rail.

Steele knelt and lifted him in his arms. He could feel blood trickling over his hands and quick gasping tremors as Velatti tried to breathe. For a moment Velatti seemed to be smiling. He opened his mouth, struggled to speak, then his head fell back and his arms dropped lifelessly to the deck.

Steele rolled him over the gunwale into the sea. Then, with the tarot still churning round him and the gunfire raking the deck at random, he threw himself down onto the *Lara* and shouted frenziedly for Donovan.

19

'Back her off!'

Steele seized the wheelhouse rail and hauled himself panting upwards. Donovan engaged the propellers in reverse, the launch throbbed and began to move backwards.

Steele peered through the canopy. The *Virgen de Africa*'s stern vanished and they were isolated in the mist again. He could hear the clamour of shouts from the direction of the bridge, but the shooting had stopped.

He swung round. Beni was still listening into the radio earphones. Steele tapped him on the shoulder.

'What's happening?'

'Paolo's told them all to stop. The ones on the other boat, they're shouting and cursing at him. Paolo's shouting back,' Beni smiled. 'In shouting he's very strong.'

Steele turned back to Donovan. 'Take her forward on the other beam until you spot one of the fishing-boats. We're transferring Beni.'

Donovan nodded. The *Lara*'s engine sound changed, he swung the wheel and they moved slowly forward again. A moment later the riding-lights of one of the Portuguese boats appeared in front of them, rocking from side to side as the boat wallowed motionless in the water.

'Okay, Beni,' Steele tapped him again, 'that's it. We're going alongside.'

Beni took off the earphones. He looked at Steele. Then before Steele could say anything he held out his hand.

'No, Senhor Callum, the thanks are from us.'

Steele gripped his hand and Beni jumped down into the cockpit.

He climbed onto the stern and shouted in Portuguese. There

was an answering call, the *Lara* edged closer, the two boats nudged each other, and Beni leapt onto the other deck. He turned and waved quickly. Then he vanished.

'Right,' Steele said, 'get clear of the rest of them and give her power.'

He climbed down the steps and shouted for Marcel. The little Moroccan came scrambling up through the hatch.

'Give me a hand.'

Steele walked round the cabin roof. Lorenz was lying inert on the foredeck, still unconscious from the blow to his neck. Steele caught him under the shoulders, Marcel lifted his feet and they dragged him into the cabin.

'Twine,' Steele said.

Marcel produced a ball from a locker and Steele lashed the German's wrists and ankles. He heaved him through into the hold, slammed the door and turned round. Louise was gazing at him white-faced from the entrance to the galley.

'We lost Velatti,' Steele said bleakly, 'they got him right at the end—'

The roar of an engine starting somewhere behind them in the darkness interrupted him. Steele's head jerked up, he listened intently for an instant, then he raced back to the wheelhouse.

They weren't clear of the other fishing-boats yet and the launch was still inching through the mist. Donovan had glanced back and was listening too. As Steele reached him another burst of noise echoed across the water. The second engine had fired.

'They're getting under way?' Steele asked.

Donovan nodded. 'Sure as hell it's not one of the Portuguese.'

'What speed can they make?'

'She's one of the new ones. They're built for fast short haul jobs with big Yamahas to drive them,' Donovan shrugged. 'Unloaded like she is I'd guess maybe fifteen knots. We've got seven over her. Only that's not going to help—'

He pointed at the fuel gauge.

'If we run at full we'll be out of gas before we make port. I'd allowed fifteen too and even then it's going to be goddam tight—'

The last blip on the inner southern vector of the radar screen disappeared. Donovan opened the throttles, the bows lifted and the *Lara* surged forward.

'I reckon that's the maximum, Ross,' Donovan was already

223

easing the control levers back, 'You're the skipper and if you say more, I'll give it to her. But it's going to be a suicide run. They'll have a fix on us now. Doesn't matter how far ahead we get, they can track us. Then soon as the gas goes, they can take all the time in the world to come up.'

Suddenly the earphones crackled. Steele hesitated. Then he picked them up and put them on. A voice was speaking through the rustle of static.

'This is the *Virgen de Africa* calling the motor launch *Lara*. We have an urgent message for you. Come in please *Lara*—'

Steele listened as the call was repeated three times. Then he answered.

'This is the *Lara*. What do you want?'

'We have a message for your Captain—'

'You're talking to the Captain.'

There was a brief pause and another voice came over the air.

'Listen to me very carefully, Steele—'

'The name's Callum,' Steele cut him off.

The static was lighter now but Steele would have recognized the new voice whatever the level of interference. Wedderburn. In his mind Steele could see him standing by the radio operator's table on the bridge. Tall, heavy-shouldered, florid-faced with anger as the two white patches burned high on his cheeks.

'It doesn't really matter what you call yourself now,' Wedderburn went on, 'I'm simply going to tell you this. Whatever you thought you were doing, you're finished. I've already radioed my people on the shore. We can track you from here by radar. If you head for any port they'll be waiting for you. And if you try to lose them or make a landfall anywhere else I'll alert the coastguard, the police, everyone. Morocco, Spain or Gibraltar, it's going to be the same. There's nowhere left for you to go—'

Wedderburn paused and Steele wiped his face, rubbing off the coagulating beads of mist and sweat.

'You've just one chance,' Wedderburn added, 'you've got Lorenz with you.'

It was part-statement and part-question.

'I've got a psychopath,' Steele answered, 'who's been convicted of twenty-seven murders and who's just caused a twenty-eighth – this time by you.'

'I want Lorenz back,' Wedderburn ignored him. 'You can stop

224

your engines now, we'll come alongside and you can hand him over. If you do that I'll allow you to continue to Tangier and take the morning flight out. If you don't you can try to find somewhere to land or cruise until you run out of fuel. Either way you'll be picked up. Wherever it is you'll be charged with piracy, and I'll see that you and everyone else on board spend the rest of their lives in prison—'

Wedderburn paused again. 'I'll give you five minutes to choose.'

The static flared again as Wedderburn flicked off the microphone.

Steele put down the earphones. He went to the back of the wheelhouse platform and stood outside in the darkness with the mist swirling round him. His brain was churning dizzily, and he suddenly felt drained and numb.

He hadn't made any plan for what would happen if they got Lorenz. Vaguely he'd assumed Velatti would know what to do, but he hadn't even been thinking of it when he boarded the ship. All that mattered then was to stop the transfer, and smash back at Wedderburn and all the others for everything that had been done to him.

Now Velatti was dead and they were trapped. Donovan had been right about the radar, but Donovan hadn't known the rest of the story – Wedderburn and the men in the five ports and the significance of Lorenz. On his own Steele would have killed the German without compunction, run for harbour and taken his chance against Wedderburn's threat. He wasn't on his own. He had Louise and Donovan and Marcel with him. He couldn't put them at the same risk, not for the sake of a private vengeance and an unspoken promise to the little Maltese.

Steele gripped the wheelhouse rail, shaking in helpless frustration. Then he tensed. There was a tiny apartment in the Ligiers slum, an old man perched like a crippled hawk on a stool at the top of his house, and something else – something in the configuration of the waterfront near the boatyard.

He swung back towards Donovan. 'How long before we make Tangier?'

'If we hold this speed an hour,' Donovan said.

Steele glanced at his watch. It was just after four. An hour would leave them fifty minutes of darkness before dawn.

'We'll be coming in from the north-west so we'll have to swing round the Hakir mole, right?'

'Sure,' Donovan nodded.

Steele frowned. It was coming back to him, but he still hadn't found the link. The Hakir mole. A stone breakwater built out across the bay to service the deep-draught cargo ships when Tangier had been a freeport.

'What's the clearance on the bridges?'

Suddenly Steele had remembered. The mole wasn't an unbroken line of boulder and concrete – it was interspersed by spans of steel bridging.

'Depends on the tide. Eleven foot at the ebb, six if it's running full,' Donovan glanced at him puzzled, 'You figuring on a short cut tonight? No way. It's at flood. We'd shear off the whole goddam superstructure.'

Static crackled again in the earphones as Donovan finished. Steele hesitated. Then he picked them up.

'This is the *Virgen de Africa* calling the motor launch *Lara*—'

'We're receiving you.'

Wedderburn came on the air immediately. 'What's your answer?'

'You can have Lorenz,' Steele said, 'only you can have him my way. If you think I'd let you come alongside out here in the dark with that bunch of thugs, you must be insane. I'm going into port, to the boatyard. I want the Consul there in person. He's going to escort me and anyone else I say to the airport. I'll hand over Lorenz as soon as I see him on the quay.'

'I said you were to hand him over now—'

'You don't get him now,' Steele interrupted, 'you get him like I said or not at all. I'll tell you something. If you don't want him my way I'm going to put a slug in his head, pitch him overboard and take my chances. Figure it out. I've got nothing to lose.'

There was silence for an instant. It was a stand off and they both knew it, and Steele knew too that Wedderburn had no choice but to agree.

'If you're planning anything,' Wedderburn's voice was harsh with fury and uncertainty now, 'I promise you this – you'll never get out of the area.'

'You just do what I tell you,' Steele said, 'and you'll get your psychopath.'

226

He turned away from the microphone. He'd barely spoken during the earlier conversation, but Donovan had been listening to what he said this time. Now the American was gaping at him bewildered.

'This is what we're going to do, Don—'

Steele explained. The numbness and exhaustion had gone, and his own anger had returned.

'They don't know who's on board,' Steele finished, 'Marcel can just vanish in the streets, you'll have to hide up somewhere on the front until morning. But there'll be nothing to connect either of you with what's happened. Okay?'

Donovan frowned for a moment. Then he grinned, 'Hell, Ross, this is the way I always knew it would be. I'll be fine.'

Steele tapped him on the shoulder. 'Keep her steady on course. I'll get them ready.'

He went out. The tarot was clearing quickly with the approaching dawn and he could already see the lights of Tangier glowing off the port bow. There were lights behind them too, the lights of the *Virgen de Africa* following the launch a hundred yards astern.

Steele ducked into the cabin, called Marcel and Louise together, and briefed them in terse urgent sentences. Then he opened the door to the hold. Lorenz had recovered consciousness and was lying blinking in the light, his face vacant and sullen. Steele cut the bonds round his ankles and dragged him to his feet.

'What you do with me?'

It was the first time he'd spoken. His accent was thick but his voice was curiously frail and lisping.

'Don't talk, just get into the cockpit,' Steele pushed him forward. 'Marcel, you hold him outside.'

The Browning was still in the locker above the bunk. Steele scooped it out, dropped it into his pocket and joined the others on deck. He unlashed the wooden tiller from its mount beside the hatch and slotted it into the rudder. Then he climbed back to the wheelhouse.

'Right, Don, she's all set.'

Steele took the wheel and Donovan clambered down.

The lights were very close now. Steele gazed through the canopy and spotted the mole, a long wedge of blackness angling out across the bay. He waited until it was only fifty yards ahead of them, then he swung the wheel to port and the launch changed course. Until then they'd been running directly towards the harbour. Now the docks were on their right and they were moving parallel to the shore.

He glanced back. The *Virgen de Africa* had also changed course to avoid the mole. The boatyard was a quarter of a mile in front. Once they were past the mole's seaward end it was simply a matter of turning slightly to starboard again and running in across the bay.

Steele swung round. There was sweat on his face again. He brushed it off and wiped his hands on his jacket. The blunt point of the pier slid by, the *Virgen de Africa* cleared it too, then he gripped the *Lara*'s wheel, spun it full-circle and slammed the throttles open to full power. The launch slewed round and shuddered. For a moment it seemed to hang quivering in a seething whirlpool of phosphorescence. Then the bows rose, the boat surged forward and planed towards a gap in the wall of stone.

'She's yours, Don!'

As he shouted Steele flung the rudder and engine levers over to the cockpit manual control, and dived for the steps. The launch drove under the bridge, there was a splintering crash, the wheelhouse was scythed off at floor level, and glass, twisted metal and fragments of the superstructure rained down into the cockpit.

'Now take her in!'

Steele lifted himself from the deck. On the far side of the mole he could hear the repeated blasts of a siren. He glanced round the side of the cabin. The *Virgen de Africa* was turning but she was too large and too close to the pier to circle on the landward side. Instead she was swinging out to sea.

The engine sound changed as Donovan threw the propellers into reverse and a moment later the launch bumped against a quay.

'Help the bastard up—'

Marcel and Louise were already on shore. Steele propelled Lorenz towards them and they dragged him up from the stern.

'Take care, Don,' Steele smiled quickly in the darkness, 'I'll be back for another run.'

He tapped the American's shoulder again and jumped up onto the quay.

Marcel had vanished and Steele stood for an instant listening.

228

He'd gambled on a guess that Wedderburn wouldn't want to call in the Moroccan police unless he was forced to. Instead he'd depend on his own men and there weren't enough of them to cover the whole waterfront. Wedderburn would be alerting the police now, but in the silence Steele knew the guess had been right. For a few minutes more he had only the surveillance team to deal with.

He reached for the Browning, ripped off the twine binding Lorenz' wrists, twisted him round, and jabbed the muzzle of the gun up under his chin. Lorenz winced with pain and his eyes watered.

'We're going into the town,' Steele said, 'You'll be in front and I'll be right behind. You do whatever I say, walk, run, stop, anything. Because if you don't, I'll cut you down. Understand?'

Lorenz moved his head away from the muzzle and nodded. Then in the distance Steele heard the sound he'd been expecting – the drum of running feet. Wedderburn was still in contact with his men by radio.

Steele glanced to his left. A figure appeared at the end of the quay, silhouetted against the stars. The man saw them, checked and cut back into the shadow of a warehouse. At the same time a voice shouted in English.

Steele hammered the gun against Lorenz' spine. 'Move!'

They crossed the quay together with Louise behind them.

In front was an alley, another wharf, a zigzagging cobbled lane, a spill of light from a teahouse, then darkness once more. Steele hesitated. All he had to go on now was guesswork and instinct. He'd been there just once before with Mary-Beth. There was no memory to draw on because it had been dark then too, and the town still had no shape or pattern in his mind. But he could sense a returning feel for landscape and contours and space, the feel of a fox for its lair, honed and razor-sharp all those years ago on the German heath, and suddenly starting to come back.

'Right at the intersection,' Steele prodded Lorenz in the back again.

He was counting the paces. The building was a hundred yards beyond the *Lara*'s berth and a further two hundred inland from the shore. They were already far enough into the town. Now they had to move east. Only it wasn't just a question of finding the house. There was Lorenz to cover ahead, Louise to help behind

229

and further back the same running feet. In the silence the clatter of their own steps was enough for Wedderburn's men to follow. Each time they stopped Steele could hear the echoes ringing closer.

'Now left—'

It had to be somewhere near them now. Steele pushed Lorenz forward and began to cast round the alleys. In the darkness every block looked the same. The same shape against the sky, the same stench of garbage, charcoal smoke and herbs, the same small night noises rustling and creaking in the stones and woodwork.

Louise was in distress. He could hear her panting and labouring at his back, her shoes slipping and dragging in the impenetrable blackness between the walls. Steele stumbled himself and then suddenly he spotted it. The alley had seemed identical to all the others, but as he recovered his footing he glanced up and saw something familiar in the curve of the façade.

He checked, hurled Lorenz over the cobbles and peered at the doorway.

'Inside—'

They climbed the steps and Steele gazed round. He was right. The littered hall, the ornate winding staircase, the lamps flickering like glow-worms on the upper floors.

'The second landing,' Steele pulled Louise behind him as he guided Lorenz upstairs.

Outside there were footsteps racing down the street and voices calling in English again. Steele fumbled for the key, found it and opened the door.

The apartment looked exactly as it had done before, except now it reeked of disinfectant. He realized Mary-Beth must have had it cleaned, but it wasn't important any longer. Steele glanced at his watch. It was twenty minutes past five. Dawn was little more than half an hour away.

'Lie down.'

Lorenz settled himself awkwardly on the floor. Steele tore the cords from the window-frame, tied the German up again, and looked at Louise.

'Are you all right?'

Her face was streaked with sweat and dust and her chest was heaving, but she nodded.

'Take this,' Steele gave her the Browning, 'if he tries anything, use it. I'll be two or three minutes.'

He'd seen the telephone the evening he came there before. He went down to the hall, pulled out the card, dialled and dropped a dirham coin into the slot as the receiver was lifted.

'*Ben-ah*?'

The voice was the same in Arabic – deep and hoarse and resonant. Steele recognized it as instantly as he'd recognized Wedderburn's.

'Mr Yehuda, this is Callum.'

'What can I do for you, Mr Callum?'

The bell had only sounded once before the telephone was answered. Steele thought of the old man hunched unsleeping on his stool in the darkness.

'I'm in Tangier. I have to get out of the city, out of the straits, very quickly. I've got thirty minutes at most—'

Wedderburn would have alerted the police by now and they'd already be on the streets searching for him. After daylight it would be hopeless.

'I have something I can offer in exchange for your help,' Steele paused, 'a man called Lorenz.'

'He's with you now?'

'Yes.'

'What happened?'

Steele told him. When he finished there was silence for a moment.

Then Yehuda said, 'Where are you?'

Steele read out the address from a card in French and Arabic pinned above the instrument.

'Stay there. I will call you back.'

The line went dead. Steele checked his watch again. There were less than twenty-five minutes now.

He fumbled for a cigarette and lit it, his hand shaking. Suddenly the telephone shrilled.

'There are three men on their way to you, Mr Callum—'

The harsh and imperturbable voice again.

'They will be there almost immediately. Two will stay with Lorenz. The third will take you to the docks—'

'I have a woman with me,' Steele said.

'I had assumed that. You normally do, Mr Callum. It will not be easy as I understand the entire harbour is being patrolled. But

231

I think you will get through. You will be taken to a ship, a cargo boat which sails at dawn. The ship is foreign. Once on board you have immunity. It is bound for Lisbon.'

'They're expecting us?' Steele asked.

'The Captain is a friend,' Yehuda said.

'And Lorenz?'

'He has many questions to answer. He will answer them. Afterwards I think he will be very tired,' Yehuda paused. 'What is the expression you use in English – tired to death?'

'Yes,' Steele hesitated, 'thank you.'

'There is no need for thanks. I spoke before of the natural courtesies that we who belong here owe each other. This is no more than that – no more than I would do for anyone returning with the name Callum.'

Yehuda rang off. Steele stood quite still for an instant. Then he turned and ran upstairs.

The men arrived a minute later. Steele had a final glimpse of Lorenz, whitefaced with terror, as two of them hauled him to his feet. Then he and Louise were outside following the third under an already lightening sky.

'There—'

For fifteen minutes they'd twisted and jinked through a series of tiny alleys. Now the man was kneeling in the shadow of a crane and pointing forwards. Steele crept up beside him. They'd reached the docks. It was almost full daylight and he could see a ship berthed twenty yards ahead across a quay with a gangplank running up to the deck. In the distance on either side there were groups of armed policemen.

The man glanced to left and right. 'Go now,' he whispered.

Steele caught Louise's arm, drew her to his shoulder and they raced out onto the quay. Behind them he heard shouts and the sound of running feet. Then he reached the gangplank and dragged Louise upwards.

A moment afterwards they stumbled onto the deck. Steele stopped and gazed round panting. A flag was hanging above the stern. As he watched it rippled out in the early morning wind. Steele stiffened. Framed by the pale sky was an oblong of scarlet cloth stamped with a black hammer and sickle.

Then he relaxed. 'The Captain is a friend,' Yehuda had said. Steele understood now. It had started with them and it was

232

ending with them. He let go of Louise's hand, went forward and stood on his own at the bows.

The last of the mist had vanished and the whole of the dirty area was spread out before him in the clear luminous light. Callum's kingdom. It had been once, briefly it had become so again. It wouldn't matter that it was finished now. The legend itself would survive. It was too strong and vivid to be lost when Callum disappeared again. Over the past few days it had been made stronger still. Velatti was dead but the transfer had been stopped, the guns had been delivered, faith had been kept.

That was what would be remembered. A victory that wasn't Callum's alone – but his too. Steele lifted his head, felt the crisp morning air on his face and laughed. He'd been wearing Callum's clothes. He didn't need them any longer.

The sun rose, he turned and walked back to Louise as the ship swung out into the straits.

All Futura Books are available at your bookshop or
newsagent, or can be ordered from the following
address:
Futura Books, Cash Sales Department,
P.O. Box 11, Falmouth, Cornwall.

Please send cheque or postal order (no currency), and
allow 30p for postage and packing for the first book
plus 15p for the second book and 12p for each additional
book ordered up to a maximum charge of £1.29 in U.K.

Customers in Eire and B.F.P.O. please allow 30p for
the first book, 15p for the second book plus 12p per
copy for the next 7 books, thereafter 6p per book.

Overseas customers please allow 50p for postage and
packing for the first book and 10p per copy for each
additional book.